CONFESSIONS OF A LEFT BANK DOMINATRIX

GALA FUR

TRANSLATED BY NOËL BURCH

BLUE MOON

BLUE MOON BOOKS
NEW YORK

Confessions of a Left Bank Dominatrix

Sessions was originally published in France as *Séances* by La Musardine in 2000.

Memoirs of a Left Bank Dominatrix was originally published as *Les Soirées de Gala* in France by Ornicar in 1999.

Published by
Blue Moon Books
An Imprint of Avalon Publishing Group Incorporated
245 West 17th Street, 11th floor
New York, NY 10011-5300

First Blue Moon Books edition 2004

ISBN 1-56201-403-X

9 8 7 6 5 4 3 2 1

Printed in the United States of America
Distributed by Publishers Group West

Sessions

Prologue

THIS WAS HOW IT ALL BEGAN. One Fall evening, near the Sacré-Coeur, with little Fanfan perched on stiletto heels, hands in the pockets of her mink coat, striding gracefully up the steps of Montmartre. A few days before, at an exclusive Saint-Germain-des-Prés party, I'd been approached by this pert brunette. Beneath thick bangs, the whites of her eyes sparkled through dark strokes of eye-liner. I was impressed by her cheekiness and quick sensuality. She was myself, minus a few years. But when it came to kinks, my timidity had always held me back. Instead of swinging with a situation when it arose, I'd run away. Then feel frustrated at my own cowardice.

What fascinated me about Fanfan was her cheerful way of publicly flaunting her peculiar tastes. Her provocative manner advertised a vocation of which I knew nothing till then: Fanfan had a taste for the whip.

Presumably she had sniffed out a counterpart in me,

someone to play opposite her. She was taking me up Montmartre to one of her "masters," a widower drawn to domination *à deux* . . . and who was going to give me money.

We crossed a vacant lot filled with cats. The master was to be found in the windowless basement of a nondescript postwar building. He greeted us in gray flannel trousers with a string in lieu of a belt. He was tall and sturdy with a white beard. He led us into the kitchen. Where it was all going to happen. The metal units lining the walls were the kind one sees in hospital kitchens. I pictured them full of children's corpses or dead cats for medical experiments.

"Strip!"

Fanfan kept her shoes on, and her pearl necklace. Between the naked girl and the ogre ogling her, I felt *de trop*. I was so embarrassed that I withdrew to a chair in a corner. *Voyeuse* . . . There was a role to my taste. In front of the sink, Fanfan had struck the pose of the Roman She-Wolf. Rounded by the tension in her bosom, her breasts hung from a torso that belonged to a thirties chorus-girl. She had the tapered legs of a store-window dummy. Ankles, calves, and patent leather shoes seemed molded in one piece. The man leaned back against the sink and gently asked her to lick his feet. The toenails were thick, the color of tarnished ivory. With her hands behind her back, Fanfan sucked his toes one by one. She must have done it often before. From her exclamations of childish greed, one would have thought they were made of candy. Then, at her master's command, she crawled to the corner where she'd left her handbag and solemnly brought me the small flogger in her mouth.

I sat there flailing a naked woman on her hands and knees, upset by the way she moaned in response to my reluctant lashes. And yet I knew the sounds were only punctuation marks in an over-arching beatitude. The master's gaze bothered me. I wanted his approval and yet I was botching the job. I struck her this way and that, on the back, on the buttocks, I wanted to pass for a jerk, it was like being back in school.

"Harder! She won't break! Let yourself go, she loves it!" he urged me on.

There was something indulgent about his voice. Almost loving. My arm felt heavy, but I threw myself into it. I started whipping frantically. I felt like a jockey trying to keep a promise to his trainer, but I also wanted to live up to Fanfan's touching expectations. Her body reeled with each blow, trembling in anticipation of the next. As I watched bliss spreading across her face, the small of my back began to tingle. I didn't want the master to see my excitement and kept a straight face as I flailed away, bolt upright on that chair in my leather raincoat.

Sated with new sensations, my arm aching, I held out the flogger to the man, but he passed his turn with a wave of the hand, like a professional gambler. I went on whipping even harder but I was getting tired and clumsy, lashing out haphazardly. Frustrated by the way the leather thongs flapped about and landed at random, I stood up. Now I could bring the whip down with a steadier beat. My arm could gather more momentum. I found the right rhythm, quick and regular. At last the thongs were snapping in unison. My heart beat faster. My eyes had begun to blur when the master called me to order.

"Not always in the same place!"

High on the buttock on which I'd been concentrating, a purple welt had appeared, dampening my enthusiasm. I gave the whip to the man and he motioned for me to sit. Fanfan exclaimed: "Thank you, mistress!" Sliding her hands over the tiles, she crawled to me with catlike undulations and lay her head on my knees. Her shining lips were like a burst cherry: she wanted a reward, a kiss. I seized her lips, ate them, swallowed her tongue, devoured it whole. Her head swayed, her belly pressed against my boots. I relished the warmth of her tenderized body. In the small of her back, my hand touched "our" marks, a corrugation of plains and burning arroyos. Mouth glued to mine, she climbed onto my knees. The insides of her cheeks were like mother-of-pearl. Seawater trickled down my throat. Cold saliva.

She pulled away and got down on all fours again, facing us. Concentrated, waiting. The master took a kitchen knife from a cupboard and pressed it to her throat. Harshly, he told her to sit up. Get on her knees. With her breasts held high and her hands behind her back, she raised her chin arrogantly. Her gaze was lowered but the tilt of her head seemed to defy him. Her whole body cried out: "Cut me if you dare!"

The tip of the knife traveled across the base of her neck and a bloody line appeared. The master ran his finger over the gash and showed her the blood. Fanfan hunched her shoulders and stared wide-eyed at the red smear. Her whole body recoiled at the sight of its blood.

I was frightened, too, I had gooseflesh under my coat and instinctively turned up the collar to protect my own throat. After all, how did I know where all this was leading, that he wouldn't cut some other part of her, the vagina lips, for example, or the tender skin under the pubic hair? What actually went on in this kitchen during the day? The metal furnishings, the unbreakable dishes . . . An insane asylum? Secret medical research? Had this widower murdered his wife?

Roughly, the ogre blindfolded Fanfan with a scarf. A tuft of hair caught in the knot and she whimpered. He pinched her nipples and studied her reaction. When she made a face, he squeezed harder. After two or three louder squeals, he let go. The game went on and on. Neither seemed to tire. Then the woman began wobbling on her knees; she looked about to collapse. Feverishly, the master seized my hand and guided it to the black tuft. I started to explore the warm slit, but found the man's directiveness inhibiting. Finally his fist opened and my hand was free to explore every nook and cranny. Her sex would have been exactly like mine had it not been for the long, moist clitoris like an aquatic plant, a sea anemone.

I tried to share with my accomplice the wave of desire she'd aroused in me, but the man resented my generosity. He brandished the knife over the slit. I withdrew my hand, fast. There was a ferocious expression on his face as he ran the knife over Fanfan's breast, scratching the skin. I was petrified I might see blood again. Rather than stroke her to alleviate her fear of the knife, I jammed my hands into my pockets. I kept my legs crossed, I was just visiting. I wanted to shout "We're out of here!" Hand in hand we'd go hurtling down the stairways of Montmartre, find refuge on the red moleskin seats of some quiet café.

The master must have sensed my withdrawal. Ordering the woman not to move, he invited me to follow him into the bathroom. While he used the urinal, he congratulated me: "Fanfan was right, you are talented . . . We'll be seeing a lot of one another, I hope. If only she had other friends like you!"

His flattery was cheering.

"Now you're going to pretend to leave, you'll slam the front door to make Fanfan think you're gone."

Softly, for fear that Fanfan might hear, I addressed the man's reflection in the mirror:

"I don't have much time, couldn't I just leave?"

"Leave the poker table in the middle of a game? That's all this is, you know, a game!"

He got me with that appeal to the gambler's ethics, I always was a sucker for the role of plucky adventuress who raises "just to see."

Back in the other room, it was the ogre's voice again: A beginner could not be allowed to witness the cruel punishments to come. He was going to pay me now so I would clear out. I played along. I opened the door, closed it again, tiptoed back to my chair and curled up on it. The fact that Fanfan thought I'd left increased my excitement immensely. I was looking forward to the thrills of voyeurism through a one-way mirror. If things got out of hand, I could always cough.

The master held a burning cigarette close to Fanfan's naked breast. She pulled back, but he held her by the waist. Sobs racked her chest that were a prelude to tears. Under the black bangs, her brow and the wings of her nose were covered with sweat.

He reminded her that under the terms of their verbal contract, she owed him absolute obedience. Did she prefer to be locked in the basement with the meat he'd left there to hang? A piece of fresh game. A hare he'd skinned, dripping blood into a plastic bowl. He'd tie her up and replace the bowl with her face.

The glowing tip of the cigarette was approaching one of her nipples. I felt as if my own breasts were in danger. I wrapped my coat around me and huddled on my chair. Fanfan was standing firm. Her lips scarcely trembled. The cigarette was less than half an inch from the flesh. Suddenly, she screamed her preference for the dead hare's blood. She was prepared to grovel on her belly in the basement dust rather than be burned!

"Pity, master!"

Taken aback by her reaction, he ordered her to suck him. She was to make him come very fast, or he'd burn her anyway. He put on a condom, grabbed her by the hair, and began counting. Fanfan had to hit pay dirt before he reached twenty. Puffing on the cigarette, he imparted the appropriate back-and-forth movement to her head. He counted slowly to sixteen, stopped . . . For a few long, suspended seconds the gobbling mouth panicked, after which he pushed her away.

Placated by his silent orgasm, the master removed Fanfan's blindfold. The scarf left marks on her face. Under streams of mascara, her features were smooth and relaxed. Gradually, she recovered. Amazed to see me. "You're still here, I thought you'd gone!" She laughed good-naturedly at our joke, but complained to the master. She'd been really afraid. Cigarette burns were out! She would never let anyone leave a burn testifying to her special habits: the day would come when she would opt for a different lifestyle.

The nameless man became the absent-minded professor he no doubt was in daily life, kind and good-natured. He fiddled with the flogger, trying to give it back to Fanfan while she was dressing. He would tap her leg with the handle, as if he were afraid she might leave it behind. Here was a man, I suspected, in whom such precautions had become second nature after one of those long middle-class marriages, conducive to a double life and the dissembling that goes with it. A pat on Fanfan's behind, a peck on my cheek, two envelopes slipped into our handbags in place of the words I'd been waiting to hear: the master's impressions of what had just occurred. "Out, ladies! It's closing time!"

The ogre was famished. We made our way to a brasserie on rue Lepic, where an accordionist was playing for an audience of tourists who joined in the chorus. The service was slow. Fanfan's joyful chatter conferred a festive spirit on a meal which would otherwise have been hard to bear. The master confessed he had no idea how to hang game. He did feel capable of skinning a hare though, and asked if we knew any hunters who could provide him with one. He regaled us with stories of mountain outings with academic colleagues, then switched to the subject of his dead companion, drowned in a swimming pool in California where she'd been teaching for the summer session. He'd considered a second marriage with a semanticist, but she set up housekeeping with one of her students. She was a strong-minded woman and he was only excited by submissives. He'd tied her hands and spanked her a little hoping to spark his libido. She hadn't wanted to see him again.

"How crude! With those uncouth manners of yours, how do you expect to find a partner!" Fanfan retorted. The master called me to witness his rustic ways: "It's true, it's true . . . I'm not God's gift to women, but who knows . . . All it takes is a little luck . . . !" I agreed half-heartedly. I had the impression he was propositioning me. Listening to them, I realized his ideal woman was sitting across the table: little Fanfan, dominant in her everyday life, docile in private. But in my new friend's eyes, this man was merely the agency of an occasional punishment.

As I munched my filets of mullet, childhood images came back to haunt me. I remembered another submissive, an insipid, anemic, ten-year-old, a cousin my own age, whom I loved to torture, burying her up to the neck in sawdust. My whipping-girl envied me my unruly bangs, my sharp eyes, my expertise with a bow and arrow, and my grandfather's affection. Every summer I spent three months on the family property. I had all the venom of a lonely child and disgorged it in furtive teasing amidst the work-benches and machines of my grandparents' sawmill.

Fanfan had sensed my dark side, the cruel power within me. The past, the present, Fanfan, my little cousin, all flowed together, diluted by white Burgundy. I felt an immense fondness for no one in particular. I was on the verge of tears, devastated by a storm of emotion. She put her hand on mine: "You're not eating . . ." I felt a gut affection for her. I wanted to show my gratitude for the way she'd given herself to me in the ogre's den. When we left the restaurant, with no ulterior motive, I kissed her full on the mouth.

What I took away from that threesome was the desire to dominate. Henceforth, I had only one thought in mind: to see that woman again with other masters, to gaze on her face while they abused her, to feel how excited her fear could make me when I threatened to lock her out on the balcony stark naked or stick my toothbrush up her cunt and scrub. And we'd pocket our envelopes without so much as a thank-you, since it was always our duo from hell that earned us the man's undying gratitude.

The second time in Montmartre, her master showed me how to target the insides of the thighs and the tops of the breasts, avoiding the super-sensitive mammary glands.

"You have to aim for the middle of the buttocks, otherwise the thongs can slip and hit the belly."

He taught me drumming sequences with a switch or with my bare hand, techniques of intimidation, the use of silence. At the end of the session, I brought Fanfan off as he instructed.

"There, like that, gently . . . Look, each little lip is infibulated . . . Go on, put your head between her legs and lick."

My tongue came up against the two gold rings: Fanfan attached great symbolic meaning to them, but they set my teeth on edge. Those pieces of intimate jewelry gave her a feeling of personal commitment, of noble grandeur.

At the end of the session, the man threw some bills on the kitchen tiles. One by one she picked them up, piously pronouncing the words "Thank you, master" with each, pressing the money to her lips. I was afraid he was going to ask me to do the same. I think I would have slapped his face.

Fanfan and I also went to the movies together. We didn't

do anything out of line during the show, just kissed each other on the mouth when we separated.

Those kisses took me back to the kitchen in Montmartre and the blade at her throat. The memory caused my sex to burn as I watched her retreat down the boulevard towards the Métro station, dignified and disdainful on her high heels. It was too late now.

I was excited by my failure, the impossible possibility, the Freudian slip. Sitting in a café after the show, I would champ at the bit instead of taking her to my place. It was in my power to enjoy unobserved the jubilation of a session between the two of us. But a sexual duet might leave her unsatisfied, I thought, perhaps she'd miss the man, his cock, or his money . . .

Substantial remuneration, I had discovered, was a source of happiness similar to staying in a four-star hotel at someone else's expense. I did not yet understand the pleasure men derive from paying. Before she took herself off to Japan, Fanfan had no trouble convincing me that professional domination would suit me to a T. When I thought of the money involved, I promised to save the price of sex for my old age.

SESSION 1

After little Fanfan, other women approached me without my having to lift a finger. No sooner had one gone her way than another would be ringing my bell. An unplanned succession of hungry docilities. A marathon. Lesbians, bisexuals, submissives, masochists, paying customers or passing playmates, all could sense the dominatrix in me. The fates seemed to conspire to spare me the boredom of conjugal life, and the very idea of domestic cohabitation with a man repelled me anyway, because it just didn't go with girl-to-girl jokes about menstrual periods and tiny cocks.

Bad mother, vamp, Lilith, bitch: By virtue of some magical powers invested in me, I dominated a chosen few. And yet, in spite of myself, I felt somehow distanced from them. I was convinced that a relationship I had not initiated was doomed to be short-lived; it was like moving into a hotel room, always ready to sneak off in the middle of the night. And yet each would bask in my intimacy for months. Sometimes years.

In the weeks that followed Fanfan's departure for Tokyo, I suffered from her absence. Our special friendship was already three years old. I traded my thirties furniture for Zen designs in precious Japanese hardwood.

I dredged up memories of our sexual relations and fantasized about some detail which had struck me. I could feel the texture of her tongue in my mouth, the rough taste of mentholated tobacco. As I lay on cushion-covers "made in Japan"—white storks and pink cherry trees—and imagined I was pinching her breasts, a new playmate appeared out of the blue. Macha rang my doorbell in the middle of the night.

I'd met her in a diplomat's kitchen: a tall, haughty man in his fifties, who entertained fellow racehorse-owners on certain afternoons in his apartment overlooking the Place du Trocadéro. Surrounded by a suite of sycophants, he would exhibit his latest discoveries, female submissives of all sorts, models or athletes, covered with hair or tattooed. All beginners, to be initiated under his auspices. He was a former ambassador and he spent his evenings with his fifth wife, a blonde with no illusions, who kept him company at the races.

A silk jacketed Filipino butler had opened the door. In the kitchen, the diplomat was giving orders to a nurse, making her sit on a stool bristling with nails. He was demanding that the gaunt, naked woman sit more heavily on the seat. He regarded the courage of the Other as a personal exploit of his own.

"Ah, Gala, come and look at this! We'll get there with a little perseverance. You'll see the marks later. Blood is what we want, isn't it Béatrice?"

The woman was crying; her face was contorted by pain and upset me deeply. Between sobs I heard her say that she made us an offering of her pain.

I had already been this dominator's confederate and it was not the first time I'd seen this woman here. Between tours of the rest of the apartment and its dim-lit bedrooms where the martyrs of the day were taken in hand and gentler games were in progress, the nurse in the kitchen was his personal "whipping boy." The ringmaster and his confederate affectedly congratulated one another on the achievements of Béatrice. He was the bogy-man, the lion tamer, I was the bogy-woman, the paid assistant. I fought back my sensitivity, my feelings of pity. I kept telling myself the nurse was a true masochist, otherwise why come back to sit on the nail-studded stool for the umpteenth time: Shedding tears in front of us was what really turned her on. With a heavy heart but a voice that was steady enough, I congratulated her, secretly hoping the diplomat would soon be sated and send her home. When he showed his friends the buttocks pocked with violet holes, he was so proud you'd have thought he'd made them with his teeth. But then he quickly lost interest.

"There's a Swede in the blue bedroom, very statuesque. Come and have a look at her," he said to me in confidential exaltation. Belly-down on an Empire bed a juvenile body lay, long and slender: The hair of a Celtic sylph was fanned out like a peacock's tail on the ultramarine bedspread. A remorseless man with a riding crop was conscientiously flogging the lifeless figure's back. Imagining she was drugged or catatonic, I bent near her face. She opened her eyes and shot me a mischievous glance, winked, and bit her lips to keep from laughing.

"Your turn to whip her a little!"

I took the riding crop and rubbed it, getting the feel of it. I would have to get used to an instrument that was not my own. I began by lightly smacking her on the ankles, calves, and thighs. A little harder on the buttocks. More gently on the small of the back. I measured the distance with my eye and wham! across the shoulder-blades. Swish, swish on the shoulders, the arms. Her face was inscrutable again, but a vague smile floated around her lips. Suddenly, a fluttering eyelid summoned me. I put my ear to her mouth.

"Hhhharder!"

This time, I began at the top, just beneath the nape of the neck. Her shoulders reddened quickly. I crisscrossed her back with little lozenges all the way down the spine. On her backside, I etched an even tighter design. The red welts began flowing together, overlapping. I striped the calves and finished with the soles of her feet. I expected her to beg for mercy. Nothing.

"Good thinking, the soles of the feet," said the diplomat. Girls who pose for magazines never want marks. Let's see what this does."

He began hitting her with the crop. Sharp taps with the stiff middle part. Fanfan had once whipped me on the soles of my feet just to show me what it was like. After the seventh or eighth blow, it had been unbearable. The woman's cheeks were pallid; her eyelids had turned blue and she was no longer smiling. At the fifteenth blow she began to moan. And yet her little yelps didn't quite ring true. She was faking to please the master.

When she came into the living room to say good-bye, she wore a royal blue stewardess uniform that buttoned down the front. Ever the connoisseur of objets d'art, our diplomat exclaimed:

"What lovely legs, slender and shapely!"

Macha, that was her name, scribbled a phone number for me on a scrap of paper. Recently arrived in Paris, this nineteen-year-old Swede was staying *au pair* in the 17th *arrondissement.* Out in the street, I reminded myself how much I hated blondes, crumpled the note, and stuffed it in my pocket.

It was almost midnight when she rang my bell in Saint-Germain-des-Prés, tearful, dripping rainwater from her suitcase onto the red cat that graced my doormat. The family she'd been with had dismissed her suddenly with no explanation. The racehorse owner had given her my address, probably to get her off his hands.

There was an edge to my voice as I showed her around the apartment: "Suitcase in the dressing room, umbrella in the kitchen, shoes under the coat-rack, toilet articles on the bathroom table." The woman was down to a gray velvet G-string, toothbrush in hand, when I remembered the dildoes soaking in the basin.

Bending over to inspect my unusual laundry, she let out peals of childish laughter and fishing a diminutive black rubber dildo from the soapy water, pressed it in the hollow of her hand as if to milk it, then began licking it shamelessly. Between licks, she laughingly stuttered:

"With this little friend, I . . . I . . . won't be c . . . c . . . cold at night . . . don't you . . . you think?"

I took the dildo from her and gently inserted it between her buttocks.

She spent the night on my sofa. The clock radio went off at 9:00 A.M., syrupy sounds from Radio Latina, a bolero or a tango. The blonde radiance of my unexpected guest affected me like a glass of champagne. Bending over my bed, she handed me a cup of tea, then dropped between my legs. With a corner of the sheet, she improvised a servant's head-dress, rolled her eyes at an imaginary audience, laughed and wriggled. Putting her hands together, she dived under the sheets, propped herself on her elbows, and with knowing glances began to lick my crotch. I caught myself regretting that her blue eyes were too pale to reveal her moods. Here was a woman who talked with her body because her eyes had nothing to say. Or so I told myself as her tongue busied itself around and in my sex. The cup of scalding tea I held was an excuse to remain passive. My head lolled on the pillows while I savored my *farniente*, the smokey fragrance of the China tea, the smacking of the greedy tongue.

Despite the excitation that prickled my sex, I looked down at her mermaid skull and suddenly had the reaction of a spoiled child, hankering for what I didn't have: a racy brunette with cat's eyes and a hyena's smile. Ill-disposed to fair hair in general, at war with every azure iris on the planet, I had to resist an impulse to push away the high, smooth forehead of my new soubrette. I shut my eyes. Her presence was instantly reduced to the diabolical sucking of my juices.

An image loomed before me. Jane Russell, belly-down on my bed. Jane, with her vermilion lips, her thrusting breasts and blood red cleavage, a ravishing Mexican femme fatale on the border near Tijuana, her gold bangles tickling my thighs. Through half-closed eyelashes, I saw the dark mass of Ms. Russell's hair flowing over my open legs while my handmaiden's tongue swirled on. The orgasm erupted, a clitoral wave diffracted into a myriad neuralgic vibrations. Cuddled in Macha's arms, I slept till noon.

When the Swede started talking about herself, I realized she stuttered. This, then, was the handicap which day by day, year by year, had modified her body language. She made up for her impediment with mimics and gestures all her own. Nor did her infirmity prevent her doing the rounds of the model agencies in hopes of posing for magazines.

It was a bad time to come from Sweden. Exotic types were the fashion in Paris: Eurasians, Mongolians, Peruvians, Aztecs. A recent remark from a booking agent had been the last straw: the woman wouldn't hire her because of her "big ass."

From an erotic viewpoint, her buttocks were matchless. The shapely curves, the grain of the skin, the full plumpness, were the single obscene feature of an otherwise androgynous body with skinny arms.

That morning, arching up on the bed, she showed her

behind with pride and made fun of the pathetic bum on the woman who'd insulted her the day before. Near the cleft of her buttocks there was a round bump in the velvet G-string. She'd kept the dildo inside her all night.

I dragged all my gear out of the closet. Red silk shoebags sporting famous brand-names contained whips, collars, nipple-clips and clothespins, fur handcuffs, bondage gear made of rubber or leather. I laid out my equipment on the bed. I took a bundle of switches and crops from the umbrella-stand. She could help herself to whatever she wished.

"Whatever you wish, *lila scorpa*[1], I believe in share-and-share-alike . . ."

She came crawling into the living-room on all fours, a cat-o'nine-tails with a braided leather handle dangling from her maw. A farewell gift from Fanfan, its lashes worn from countless sessions. Whipping Macha, I rediscovered the pleasure of dominating my initiator. Beating her whipped up my blood, gave me a sense of fullness. My head felt hot. Once again, I was totally present to myself, to the tangible sensations of life. I was sure her sex was sopping wet but the truth was I didn't desire her, and desire you can't invent. I didn't even like my new friend enough to check out her pleasure by touching her sex. As I realized this, my enthusiasm waned. My arm was getting stiff. I was about ready to stop but she begged me to go on with a glint of madness in her eyes. So I gave her all she wanted. I was inside her desire by now. This moment of total communion was short-lived, however, for a thought came to me as I flogged away: Did the whip have any meaning for her other than gruesome punishment? I slid my fingers between her lips: she was as dry as a sheet of Kleenex.

SESSION 2

WOULD DOMINATING A MAN give me as much pleasure? It was an idea that was gaining ground. I was having tea at the Café de Flore one morning when my eye fell on a want ad: a young serviceman was looking for a phallic woman. I was dying to meet an Air Force officer. On the phone, I was charmed by his sexy voice and arranged a meeting, despite Macha's having wrapped herself around my chair, her bare feet in a pair of my shoes that were too big for her, growling and snorting, the riding crop between her teeth.

With no respect for the privacy of my conversation, she was determined to be beaten. Nudging her mistress's slipper with her chin, she was like a puppy trying to get a rise out of me, such as a demonstration of my expertise at savate. Blithely pursuing my conversation with the lieutenant, I wrenched the instrument from her mouth. I hit her with the handle because I wanted it to hurt, annoyed with myself for responding exactly the way she wanted. The hard leather stalk thudded against her vertebrae. She finally made me lose the thread of my conversation. Three times I repeated the hour of our appointment.

With the phone back on its cradle, I railed at Macha: "You are a pain in the ass!" Her moonlike face was ecstatic; she stuck out her behind. With the stem of the crop, I beat her on the small of the back, then on the skin between buttocks and thighs. She dispensed with the made-to-order squeals I'd heard in the diplomat's bedroom. Body taut as a bow, she uttered not a sound. And I worked off all my frustrations. I got back at the submissive who'd stood me up the day before, when I'd dolled myself up like a queen for him.

I stepped back: the crop flailed her ribs. Having rid myself of my tensions, I gave her one last whollop with the handle smack on the tail bone. I pulled on a coat over my leather blouse with the flounces and left without so much as a glance at her.

For his mid-winter début in the "Personal" columns of the *Nouvel Observateur*, "Alexis"'s Greek-sounding alias rang of the matinee idol. I knew next to nothing about this "Air Force lieutenant, 35, well-built, submissive." But I had a weakness for uniforms and I was curious to know what made him tick. In my reply to his ad, I'd suggested he put his fantasies in writing. I received a few sentences on a sheet of typing paper.

You wear a wasp-waist bustier, a pair of boots and a strap-on

I'm on all fours

a gloved hand squeezes my balls while the rubber tip spreads and distends my anus

you push, all the way, I scream, the buggering lasts a long time

the ass must be forced wide open

I had chosen an atmosphere classy enough to intimidate a serviceman stationed in sleepy, suburban Melun—at least that's what I was counting on. The waiters still wear long white aprons in that elegant Paris café, while downstairs the woman in charge of hygiene and good manners sits between the phone booth and the oak-doored toilets, forever buffing her nails.

Ruddy-faced from dashing through métro passageways, Alexis arrived late. He looked around for a leather blouse with flounces. He was in mufti, sports jacket and jeans. A stocky, flat body, without a trace of vulgarity, attractively juvenile. To draw his attention, I swung a glove. Through the cleft in his face, I glimpsed healthy gums. He had Fernandel's smile.

He took off his jacket and eased himself at last into the ringside seat reserved for him across the table. Thousands of times round the assault course had done away with his flexibility. As he settled into his seat, his head and torso swiveled about in one piece while he gaped at the customers, no doubt expecting to see some TV celebrity. He was like a dog who felt safe in his master's presence, cocking a snoot at the world from a car window.

"Well?"

He gave a start and looked me straight in the eye. From the start, his curiosity was insolent. He wanted to know how old I was, how many submissives I had, did I take the occasional transvestite? His impudence, I said to myself, would certainly get results with the right person—a quick exit preceded, with any luck, by a smack in the face. Deliberately annoying a severe woman, exasperating her in hopes she'll put you in your place. But the bright eyes and childlike countenance revealed only a perverse form of innocence. A facetious look would probably have been hard for him to manage. In a flash, the mystery of the pseudonym was solved. Alexis, *aléxie*, alexia: verbal blindness. In French, Alexis with an *eeeee* like the shriek of a soldier refusing to obey. Being fresh was his way of fighting back.

To evade his trivial questions, I played the scatterbrain socialite, sipping my glass of Chablis and paying no attention to him whatever. Faced with my silence, the serviceman soon dropped his interrogation.

Now he made me an awkward compliment about my hands. He found them intelligent, elegant, skillful, and he gaped at them. Behind the adolescent trained to obedience loomed a cannibalistic desire to swallow the hand that lay curled beside my wineglass, stiffened from the impact of his desire.

He glanced at my boots. To his mind, each and every one of a woman's extremities was an instrument that could penetrate him: the sharp toe of my leather boot, my whole arched foot with the protuberant heel.

Metallic clanking on every side, steel-tipped boots, chains, surgical instruments—actually spoons on porcelain teacups—inflamed my rambling thoughts. I pictured a barracks shower-room full of men with him in the middle, willingly buggered by each in turn. With the "cerebral" type of john, an encounter with another phallus destroys the perverse pleasure of fetishizing. Not with this one, most likely, but I did sense that he needed a woman's presence—If only as mistress of ceremonies or merely as voyeur. I suspected he could come just sitting on my fist, or impaled on the booted foot swinging below the café table.

Next to me on the red leather wall seat was a woman visibly amused by the obvious expectancy of the man across the table. Under her arm she was ostentatiously holding a little tan basset as if it were a feather boa, and she seemed ready to brandish it at any moment for a caress or a bite.

Charmed by the sound of a voice which told him

nothing, Alexis let himself be taken in. I snowed him with a well-tried number that always left the other person hanging in the air. Hide-and-seek, evasive maneuvers.

I told him I was attracted to pert, dark-haired women like Louise Brooks (a name he'd never heard before), that I made an art of touring Europe in driving gloves and a pilot's helmet at the wheel of a leather-lined roadster. I spoke of fetish gear made to order in London by Pigalle, of fittings in her workshop with that mysterious Oriental whose face was like a Persian miniature. All this nonsense wafted Alexis away to the land of the frivolously feminine, a gynæcium usually beyond the reach of his sort of man. Thinking back later, he'd find nothing to pin down, nothing but the memory of a hand and a glove. One hand curled round a glass with an empty glove beside it, the other lying flat on the table, fingers rigid in their rings.

Suddenly, the waiter's white apron came between us, a silver saucer, a slip of paper and a mug of beer dropped onto the table. Recovering his poise, Alexis rested his elbows on the table, and his beardless chin on reddened knuckles. When the waiter had left, I teased him about his chapped hands: "Dish-pan hands, Lieutenant?" My dig took him back to his base in Melun and suddenly he began telling the world at large, the lady with the dog, perhaps, how the Air Force had assigned him to logistics, software, computers, in short nothing very exciting.

"You're ground crew!"

I rammed the insult home with a contemptuous toss of my head. The words snapped like a whip, frightening the lady and her dog.

Alexis lowered his eyes and leaned across the table:

"The ground I crave lies under your boots, Madame."

I opened my lizard bag, took out lipstick and powder-case, and a small package wrapped in crumpled tissue paper. And I pointed, for all to see, towards the stairs leading down to the toilets.

The lady with the little dog on her hip watched the man coming back, kept her eyes glued on him till he reached his seat. He sat down gingerly, like a cowboy trying to play it cool.

"A man's button-hole must be to my taste before I will consent to take him in hand . . ."

His eyes narrowed. I could tell he was afraid of having to walk past those people again, back down those basement stairs to show me his button-hole dilated by the dildo he'd just inserted behind a bolted door. Afraid of being locked up with me in the water-closet with the attendant straining to hear above the rattle of coins in her saucer.

When he opened his eyes, I'd put on my gloves and laid the check in front of him. With my coat over my shoulders, I walked to the exit. He ran after me and gave the revolving door a push. I slipped under his arm and out into the early evening.

My car was double-parked under a street lamp. I invited him to be my guest. And with my lieutenant in the back seat, puzzled but confident, I drove away through the maze of ill-lit streets. The sky and the pavement were exactly the same shade of gray.

I parked in front of a coach-doorway on the rue Jacob. The soldier kneeled on the seat, his chin on the back shelf. He pulled down his trousers and showed me the hole filled by the prosthesis. He handed me a flashlight, a special pilots' model, that had just fallen out of his pocket. Training the beam on the shiny, black protuberance, I inspected the rim of flesh around it: the grain of the plucked buttocks, the freshness of the pink flower. I pressed the tip of the dildo this way and that; I twisted it in my gloved fingers, pushing it slantwise into the greedy orifice. The cleft was hardly darkened. I had a disgusted thought for the buttocks of old men, their cleft colored by sixty years of excrements, waltzing around naked in harnesses at fetish parties, exhibitionists to the bitter end, and I said:

"That's fine."

Pleased to have passed muster, he pulled up his trousers and plumped himself down on the front seat. I took a small Tupperware box out of the glove compartment. At the bottom lay a condom, bathing in a colorless fluid. I slipped it over his cock and rolled it down . . . slowly . . . Alexis bit his lips. He squirmed and wriggled in a futile effort to relieve the fiery sting of the mouthwash. I reached over and flung his door open, motioning him out. He staggered slightly as he walked away on account of the fire burning his cock.

Near the Odéon theater I left the Renault in my underground parking space. From the top of the ramp, I saw him posted on the corner by my building. He had his arms folded and was hopping on the sidewalk to keep warm.

"I would like to give you back your dildo."

With a twist of his hips, he showed me a sheaf of bills slipped into his jeans. I motioned for him to follow me into the building. On the stairs, his steps locked with mine. His physical presence, his yearning desire, made me tingle to the roots of my hair.

Buggery . . . I'd made his fantasy my own. With feverish fingers, I pulled out my collection of dildoes. Soft ones, barbarous ones, vibrating ones and very thin ones for beginners, black, flesh-colored, speckled . . . It was an eight-inch molded plastic strap-on with sequins that caught his fancy.

His arrogant cock defied me through the tails of his shirt. Harnessed and virile, I moved behind him, reached down, and weighed his testicles in my hand: they were large and hung close to the body. At the same time, I gave a thrust of the pelvis and watched my ersatz phallus disappear inside of him. Each blow I dealt him shook my womb. My pubis was irradiated by the texture of his buttocks and the vibrations of the dildo. My fingers tugged convulsively at his balls. I wanted to go further in. He too was insatiable, pulled his buttocks apart with both hands, told me to keep on coming. I was to dig my nails into his flesh if that would help, he wanted me further in: "More . . . there, that's good . . . Oh, yes . . . Mistress . . ."

His sex was dripping down his thighs. I felt for his mouth with the tip of another dildo, flesh-colored and with realistic veins. His pink gums engulfed it. I was fucking him top and bottom. Each time I came into him, excitement thrilled through me like an electric wave. Belly down on a muscular back, my nose buried in hair that smelled of paper and Brylcream, I was galvanized by my own thrusts. His spasms washed against my stomach. The blood rushed to my head. My skull was burning. Between convulsions, he ejaculated under himself. His cock in his hands, he lay on his side on the floor.

My boots framed his haggard face. I looked down at the big exhausted body. His expression was ecstatic and the blue eyes feasting on his madonna were as steady as marbles. Squatting above him, I too got rid of my fluids, urinating into his open mouth.

SESSION 3

THE VIRAGOPHILE HAD GOTTEN my number from a movie director, a hard-bitten masochist whom I'd given a pretty tough time. He was one of those manipulative johns who treat a mistress as a whipping machine; She can put her shoulder out of joint for all they care. When he phoned for another appointment, I sent him to a TV in Montmartre who beat his johns with an iron-tipped cat.

Yet despite such an unpromising recommendation, the man's phone call put me in a good mood. He was a professor of film history and his earnest chitchat revealed more than a touch of Anglo-American feminism. His pet subjects were misogyny in the French cinema and Hollywood's obsession with the murder of the father. His theoretical writings were translated into many languages. "Leopold"—a name that smacked of butlers or grumpy old aristocrats—suggested a quiet bar near the Opéra.

From the depths of my club chair, I saw a pint-size

hippie in his sixties slaloming among the tables. He looked preoccupied as he tramped about, peering at lone women through his bifocals. Golf cap, ponytail, red-brown corduroy jacket and twill Ascot, I watched him looking for me, bouquet to the fore. Unpretentious wildflowers, red, white, and blue: the colors of the Republic, a sign of recognition chosen by a john who'd kept his Communist convictions if not his party card.

I waved to him. He quickened his pace, tripped on a carpet, and only just avoided a pratfall by grabbing at a Chinese vase that swayed dangerously on its pedestal.

He wanted to sit next to me, but I waved him to the chair across the table. I wanted to hear him talk while I got used to his disconcerting features. We resumed our phone conversation on misogyny in the movies, exemplified by the films of François Ozon and especially his latest effort, *Woman of the Sand*, about a tight-assed academic who can't handle the death of her husband, or by *Sue Lost In Manhattan*, another much-touted flick about a woman who can't cope without a man in her life.

Leopold reveled in my cruel repartee. From the mischievous gleam in his eye, I knew he was seeing me as Lilith herself. I felt flattered and took to studying the hunched body in search of a detail that would make this old man more appealing to me . . . And there it was, right before my eyes: his skin . . . The skin on those hands that twirled as he talked, soft and smooth, with no visible veins. Discovering those youthful hands, I imagined him brimful of natural hormones, afflicted with priapism, perhaps, a permanent hard-on.

"You understand, dear Gala, I expect no sexual services. I don't want you thinking I have ulterior motives. Of course, like any starving mongrel, I'll take whatever a woman is prepared to give. But Miss World in flounces is definitely not my ideal. I have my university paycheck and occasional royalties, nothing lavish. The vivid images you will create in a single session can provide me with a year of fantasies. You'll see, I can make a Manga heroine of you . . . That is . . . if you'll let me tape you . . ."

"Come to the point . . ."

"Our mutual friend tells me you are skilled in the martial arts . . ."

"You might say that. I've practiced combat tai-chi, a little kung-fu, a bit of jui-jitsu, but I'm mostly a staunch dilettante. I earned my green belt in karate two years ago but I've made precious little progress since."

On my way to our appointment, the rain had soaked through my boots and I sat tapping my feet discreetly while he conjured up the women athletes he'd known, wrestlers, body-builders, self-defense experts. My personal preference had always gone to solitary martial exercises and I suddenly felt a need for advice from one of those fighting women. I was immensely intimidated by the prospect of taking on a new kind of domination.

Overpowering him in hand-to-hand combat, pinning him helpless to the floor, this was what Leopold expected of me: bare-handed, implacable strength and skill. No more hiding behind the paddle, the crop, or the lash of my tongue. Without my customary weapons, I knew I was going to feel naked . . .

He'd laid a package on an empty chair.

"Open it, it's for you!"

Wrapped in a square of black velvet were a pair of soft kid jazz boots and black elastic tights, made in Japan, with a white stripe down the legs. Our go-between, the director, had given him my measurements. I stroked my fighting footwear-to-be while he showered me with technical details. He wanted a woman to clamp his neck between her thighs in a "scissors hold," cutting off the blood-supply to the brain by squeezing his carotid arteries. When he was about to pass out, he'd slap on the floor.

His tendons were still robust: elbows, knees, shoulders, wrists . . . I could apply my twists and locks as hard as I liked. But I'd have to watch out for his glasses: he needed them to tend to the video and still cameras.

I sat there listening and I said to myself: "Why not? I can play this game if the guy is willing to fight back a little." I recalled the way the movie director who'd given him my number had played whipping post to my mule-driver. Leopold's fervent speech and manners made me doubt he'd be the rag-doll type.

The corners of his mouth were white with spittle from his impassioned expostulations. I handed him a glass of mineral water. He drank compliantly and went on with his explanations.

Mounted above the mat, video cameras would film the scene. Later he would take photos, but these would never leave his possession; no one else, he swore, would ever see them. In passing, I learned from Leopold that Chekhov had had much the same hang-up and that Sacher-Masoch himself loved to wrestle with the muscular maidservants in his employ.

Suddenly, I read panic in his eyes: Had he gone too far? In referring to a writer who indulged in wrestling matches with domestics, was he not implicitly putting me down? Would I change my mind? Would I pick up my gloves and leave? Pretending to ignore him, I peered into my compact mirror, touching up my lipstick.

In an effort to make up for his blunder, his hands twirled again as he told me how Kafka fantasized an encounter with a jui-jitsu-wise millionaire's daughter in *Amerika* . . . Then up he got and stood ready to run for the door should I decide to send him packing. I sat placidly, showing polite interest as I watched him arrange his Ascot.

Reassured by my silence, he put on his cap: "Don't throw away the wrapper!" he said.

As he walked away, I braced the back of my neck against the velvet chair-cover and let myself drift on the hum of conversation around me, floating in a dimension where thought was superfluous.

Returning to earth, I slit the green wrapper around the stems of the anemones. Damp banknotes were stuck to the inside of the paper.

When the time came for our appointment, I parked the Renault on a pedestrian crossing on rue des Petits Carreaux. My fighting gear was in my backpack. A pair of giant scissors over a shopfront signaled the three-story building. The crooked, red-brown stairway smelled of urine, and Leopold's doorbell made a sound like a mechanical bird. Under a mouse-gray workman's coverall, several layers of foam gave him a bulky chest. He wore basketball shoes and padding on his elbows and knees. A boxer's mouthpiece gave him faintly simian lips.

He spluttered a greeting through the plastic in his mouth and showed me into the living room: the furniture had been pushed back and the hard floor-tiles covered with blue mats.

He became absorbed in last-minute preparations. Adjusting the cameras to my height, checking the edges of the frame. Bathed in the light of a single flood, I acted as stand-in for the glamorous virago soon to be making her stellar appearance. I looked out of the garret window at the chimney pots on the ancient buildings: I dreamed of an imaginary combat, aerial Kung-fu on the sloping zinc. My anxiety had vanished and I felt raring to go, eager to pounce upon my prey.

He snapped his fingers and said moodily: "This is the acting area . . ."

He scampered over the matting with a piece of chalk:

"You have this much space to move around in. Past this mark, you're out of shot.

He could see I was perspiring under the glare of his wattage. He apologized for the discomfort, but his bad faith was evident. I asked where I could change and he led me down a maze of low-ceilinged hallways to his bedroom.

On the shelves above his bed were dozens of female figurines beating up on their male counterparts. The faces all had a waxy tan, with arched eyebrows and purple mouths. The male roles were played by Ken or Action-Man in various costumes, arms twisted, legs flying, biting the dust on their Plexiglas stands, vanquished by Spider-Woman or The Huntress, by a lady cop or a Chinese boxing girl, all frozen in acrobatic, martial poses. Having poured myself into my clinging, one-piece suit, I gazed at my image in the mirror. The resemblance was unmistakable. Did he keep his icons dusted? My finger removed a wad of fluff from behind Catwoman's ears. We were in *le Sentier*, the heart of the ladies' garment industry . . . the air was thick with lint . . .

Planted legs apart on the far side of the mat, kisser contorted by the plastic mouthpiece, Leopold was losing patience.

"Places! Camera! Action!"

Two video cameras were staring at me. Further back, a still camera looked down from a tripod. I moved forward with springy steps and began to circle round him, striving to keep within the chalk-marks. I shot out my leg and tried to deck him with a judo sweep to the back of his calf, but he skipped away and laughed: "Ten years on a soccer-field! Right wing-back! You'll have a hard time tripping me, my legs are my strong point! The waist and chest are more vulnerable, or else . . .

I didn't let him finish his sentence; a kind of jubilation swept over me, a sense of liberation, and I treated the chatterbox to a major hip-throw that dumped him flat on his back. An expression of childlike glee came over his face as I pinned him on his side, locked his arm across his throat in a strangle-hold, and pulled up hard on his wrist, crushing his carotid artery.

"Are you going to stop that yammering?" I scolded him.

In his helplessness, there was a blissful smile on his face. I shifted my grip, pinned his forearm under my knee and twisted his palm towards the ceiling, painfully squeezing the bones of his hand. His face went red and his eyes were bloodshot as he wailed:

"Wonderful! More! Pay no attention to the faces I make, just lay it on! Owwww!"

Three-quarters of an hour later, I'd used every trick I knew: startlingly off-handed aikido throws, vicious Muy Thai knee-lifts to the plexus, paralyzing karate chops on the diaphragm, jui-jitsu arm- and leg-locks that rendered him instantly powerless.

At one point, having pinned him under me thus, I spied a short leather thong that just happened to be lying there. It had slip-knots at either end so I used it to tie his left thumb to his right big toe, forcing together the opposing limbs in the middle of his back. I appreciated the cunning of the bondage device: any attempt to pull free would only make the excruciating knots tighter. Leopold wisely lay still. Trussed up like a rodeo steer, he was beaming.

"You made the thong yourself?"

"All it takes is a strip of soft leather. A kunoichi specialty . . . They were the female ninjas . . . They hid the thong in their kimono sash . . . I have other toys you could use!"

Pain puckered the flesh under his chin. He was forcing himself to keep cool in the lady's presence. Flushed with heat, I sat down on the mat. Beads of sweat ran into my eyes. I was sweltering under the floodlight. But Leopold, helpless as a newborn baby, went right on fantasizing, oblivious to my technical knock-out;

"You can lock me up, if you like; come back and untie me later. My next class isn't till nine in the morning."

My only reply was to reach out and undo the punishing thong.

"Is this photo business going to take long?"

"Just one roll of twenty-four, that's all, I promise, a "Best of," in black and white. *En garde*!

I decided I could handle it and agreed to strike the poses again.

He ran to the camera, released the timer, and began counting to ten as he hurried back to take his place. This time I struck in slow motion. With the first blow, one of my rings caught him: he bit his lips and grimaced with pain. *Click.*

"But look, that would have been more effective if . . ." "You could have jammed your elbow under my chin while you gave me that kidney chop . . . If I fought dirty, I might have bitten you."

For the bondage shot, he had to run to the camera and back with the thong already around his thumb. When he dropped to the mat, I had to tie it quickly to his big toe and press my knee into his back. *Click.*

When he stood up, I noticed the hump in his trouser crotch.

"I'm wearing a plastic jock-strap," he told me proudly. "In moments like these, I'm likely to get a hard-on and I'd rather take advantage of it alone. I live by myself now, my wife died last year . . . But she was a black belt . . ."

"I'm afraid I have to go now."

As I changed back into my street-clothes in his bedroom, I thought about this man's distress. The only comfort I could bring to someone as hung-up as this was to get him talking about his fantasies again. My backpack slung over my shoulder, I asked him kindly:

"Show me your toys!"

He opened a cupboard and took out a *shuriken*[2], a *yawara*[3], and a pair of *nunchaku*[4], a weapon with which I was already familiar. I asked him how the fantasy of being beaten had come to him.

One Sunday morning, at the age of seven, Leopold came upon a comic strip in which a busty "battle axe" drops in to give Blondie jui-jitsu lessons: when Dagwood tries to get rid of her, the woman flips him all over the house. Inexplicably aroused by this story, the boy asked his father what "jui-jitsu" was . . . At about the same period, an older girl twisted his arm behind his back to make him tell his little friends to stop throwing rocks. And a few years later an illustrated Sunday supplement feature, in which a woman in a gym suit performed a "circle throw" on an attacker and finished him off with a "judo chop" had been the occasion of little Leo's first self-provoked orgasm.

With a flourish now, he pulled back a white drape revealing hundreds of hand-labeled videotapes: *Lovely But Deadly, Faster Pussy Cat, Kill! Kill!,* and many more.

"You see? It's my hobby that's kept me alive. I collect pictures of women in the martial arts that abound today on specialized Net sites."

He looked ten years younger than the day we met. I sensed he wanted to make me some special present but didn't know how to go about it. His voice faltered as he finally asked:

"Would you let me polish your boots?"

"If it will give you pleasure . . ."

He opened a cupboard and took out a shoeshine box he'd picked up on a trip to Mexico City. His wife used to make him care for her shoes. Bending low over the boots he started buffing the beveled slopes of black leather. When he looked up, I noticed that his left eye was swollen.

A blow from my knee . . . I was worried about his students' reaction the next day, but he proudly exclaimed:

"I came out of the closet the day I gave an interview to *Cinéfreaks*, a magazine that's popular with students. Everybody knows movie-buffs are weird, anyway! I'll be proud of my shiner in class!"

At the door, he kissed my boots and inhaled the smell of leather.

SESSION 4

ON HER WAY TO THE BAKERY, Macha stopped to watch Miss Johnson, the Englishwoman who lived in a maid's room on the fifth floor. Stark naked on the sidewalk, this neighbor of ours was having her morning workout in front of the building's coach-door, with a Walkman plugged into her ears, hardly startling passers-by used to kooks of all kinds hanging around their neighborhood. At nine o'clock in the morning, before the swarms of tourists appear, Saint-Germain-des-Prés still belongs to its inhabitants. Across the street, the salesperson known as Lulu who worked in the boutique Yellow was resting her white breasts on her window balustrade, gazing down at the pedestrians. Macha was nonplussed by the neighborhood's permissiveness. She romped about the apartment in her altogether and never had any complaints from me. One of the advantages of being nearsighted is that I can ignore the stares of the occasional voyeur across the street. But I didn't need glasses to see my Macha, and never tired of watching her jiggle her behind around the living room with the windows wide open.

The manager of a nightclub where we used to drop in for the occasional drink spied on her from his apartment with field-glasses. He was a ruddy-faced Belgian with long, curly locks who spent his afternoons hanging out at the sidewalk cafés on Rue de Buci. He was full of pep, and used to chase after us between the displays of sandwiches and tee-shirts, shouting: "Hey, girls! I'll let you in free, you can have a bottle of bubbly!" Whenever I saw him in the street, I felt like hauling off and slapping him. One day, frothing at the mouth, he grabbed my arm as if he knew me: "If your girlfriend will put on a little strip-show, I'll buy you both pretty undies and a Belgian always keeps his word!"

When I told her the story, Macha was sorry she'd missed a chance to show off her body. She began having an urge to exhibit her derriere to passers-by. A boy she met in a model agency, a model himself whom she'd mentioned to me, high-assed and broad-minded, prominent nose and chunky fingers hinting at the rest, promptly accepted her proposition: in lieu of a drink at a sidewalk café, fellatio in her car. She made love right under my windows and I didn't even know about it.

The next day she was still obsessed with the idea of her buttocks pressed to a car window at 7:00 P.M., with shoppers jamming the sidewalks. She wanted to do it again with me.

Seated behind my steering wheel, I felt weird about performing such an act in my own neighborhood. I'd never told her about the young soldier in the car with the dildo on rue Jacob, just a few steps away. I gave the matter some thought and came up with the Palais des exhibitions, near the porte de Versailles, where the big auto-show was being held.

I parked the Renault so that the headlights shone along the sidewalk. That way, I imagined no one could see us. I'm no exhibitionist. A few passers-by went round the car to avoid the glare of the headlights, and walked past Macha's white behind squashed against the glass. The warmth of her skin caused a mist to form, a frosty halo around her bum.

She leaned forward to lick my sex. I held up my head for a quick look outside at the expressions on people's faces. Occasionally someone did actually stare. But mostly anyone who glimpsed her head between the driver's thighs would just hurry on by. Their discretion came as a relief to me: my tights were already halfway down my thighs. In the shadow of the car, only Macha had a bird's-eye view of my fleece. As excited as a convent girl hiding her fun from the sisters, I watched the people walking out there like a black-and-white movie. Their shadows pulsed to the blinking beat of a neon sign over the graffiti scrawled on a roll-down shop-front shutter, a blue light that gave the flesh pressed against my car window a sickly pall. Macha was conscientiously nibbling at my sex. My pleasure throbbed, mounted, peaked in lapping waves.

A cop on the *boulevard* looked over to where my white Renault was blocking a crosswalk. Planted next to his patrol car with his legs apart, he scratched his cheek. The fact that he would soon be peering into the car sparked my orgasm. "Pull your skirt down Macha, here come the cops!" Ignition on. I roared away.

My permanent guest was ever prepared to put on a show. Whenever I was seeing a submissive, I was haunted by the fear of her barging in unexpectedly. She had no respect for privacy and always assumed her precious person was a bonus. This was sometimes the case, such as the day she found Jeremy kneeling on the kitchen tiles.

I'd met that mysterious character on some Internet site,

Alternative Sex maybe, and been charmed by his refinement over the phone. There was an old-fashioned elegance in the way he spoke, as though he'd practiced reciting "The Kitten Is Dead" with just the right intonations. He made an appointment in the courtyard of the Musée Delacroix to see what I looked like.

On the appointed day, it was raining. I'd decided to wear my violet leather Chinese dress. A taut garter belt held up my smoky gray stockings and stood out in low relief through the thin, clinging leather sheath. The effect was hidden by a black cape but was plainly visible when I raised the hem ever so slightly. He was a small, slender man under a big black umbrella, furtively examining the straps on my high-heeled shoes.

The following week, he dropped into my letter-box a list of shops specializing in working clothes for domestic help. Alexandra, rue du faubourg Saint Honoré, Dutilleul, Rue de Turbigo and of course the basement of La Samaritaine. He had a thing about prestigious brands of linen and especially about coarse sailcloth aprons.

I agreed to act out one of his scripts. We were meant to be in tête-à-tête in the kitchen of a family estate. Our roles were variable. Maid and valet, or else mistress of the house pretending to be on an equal footing with her valet.

Gwendoline, recruited some time back by Minitel and who cleaned my apartment wearing a fuchsia-colored mohair smock and a black wig trimmed with a bowl, had starched and pressed the new aprons. The scent of ironed linen wafted me onto Jeremy's little stage, the world of his childhood, as I read the little scenes he sent me. A manor-house, a mischievous, sadistic countess whom I would be impersonating, a severe Countess De Ségur[5] who treated her spouse like a servant.

Jeremy was on his knees in the kitchen, naked under a dark blue gardener's apron. I was wearing a white apron with a wrap-around bib and those shoes with the straps that had turned him on. I'd taken off all my rings and felt utterly naked under the rough cloth.

I blindfolded him with a napkin. I took a good length of white cotton rope, tied his wrists behind his back in a certain way, keeping two long loose ends in my hands. I pulled. The man lost his balance; his torso hunched forward and he gave little sighs of satisfaction. I rolled up a dish-towel and stuffed it in his mouth.

I dropped to my knees facing him. The hump in the cloth made by his swollen sex rubbed against my apron. Heat passed through the twin layers of thick material like steam. We were extremely close, but only our apron-fronts were touching. Under the blindfold, the delicate skin on his cheeks was stretched taut by the elastic bulk of the dish-towel. His chest smelled of English *eau de cologne*; my grandfather used the same citronella scent. The odors and the moisture of the air in that silent room joined with the man's excitement to make a deep impression on me. I was carried outside of time by the warmth of our mingled breaths, by the ties that linked us. Liberating bondage . . . We entered into a kind of mute erotic communion.

Playing with the ropes, I made the apron-hump come towards me. The man put up a fight; every muscle was tensed against losing his balance again. Then the body went soft and his defenses collapsed. His vulnerability filled me with a sense of power. I could have had a fit just then and killed him. With the tips of my fingers, I pinched his nipples gently, observing the effect of my manipulations in the lascivious way he lolled his head against my breasts. Lightly, slowly, I drew the back of my hand across the hump in his apron. His breathing came faster, shrill and erratic. I twisted his nipples with my nails, digging in hard from time to time. He responded like an automaton, as if I were pushing buttons.

I ran the tip of my tongue over his lips, distended by the gag. At the same time, I pulled firmly on the rope running through the crooks of his elbows. He moaned, strained for my kisses. I turned my face away. He stretched out his neck, seeking my mouth. I pressed my pubis against the bump in the blue material. And then, from the way his knees sagged, I could tell he'd ejaculated inside his apron. In my ropes I held a child who could hardly wait to get out of the house.

So there he was, kneeling quietly in the center of the kitchen, his head on my white apron, when Macha made her entrance unannounced. The man frowned beneath his blindfold. He was worried about this interloper he couldn't see. Her foreign accent, however, reassured him.

"What pretty aprons!" Macha exclaimed.

My friend's fascination with luxury and hyphenated names sharpened her sixth sense. Girls from Vienna or Sweden still fantasize about the court of the kings of France and its lavish lifestyle, which their own nobility envied. Whenever she smelled a family tree, Macha pulled out all the stops. Naked under his apron, Jeremy still looked like an aristocrat and my Swedish rose was under the spell.

She found a black governess's dress with a narrow white collar hanging in my closet, waiting for another master-servant script. A simple headdress topped off the costume. She was a cinch for a remake of *The Diary of a Chambermaid*; she was staggering. But my submissive could see none of this.

After a glance at me for permission, Macha kneeled in front of him. She began by touching him through the rough cloth. The citronella fragrance must have gotten to her too, because soon she was inhaling the nape of his neck like a fresh-cut flower. Macha had once confessed to me being in love with her father, a terribly conventional man with a fleshy mouth that she adored. Across the top of Jeremy's head, she gave me a long little-girl-lost look.

I tied them close together, face to face with their hands in their back, then I blindfolded Macha. I stood holding the two ends of the rope over theirs heads, controlling them like marionettes. Breathing heavily, they sought each other's lips. Their cheeks rubbed together. Holding both reins in one hand I pulled, forcing their elbows towards their shoulder-blades. Shoved off balance, they fell together. I liked this game. I'd let out some slack and then jerk on the reins again. I made my pleasure last; I suddenly wanted to master the art of the puppeteer. I became so involved I lost sight of the session.

"The first to make the other fall gets ten lashes!"

I was taken aback by the sound of my voice. Normally, I never spoke to Jeremy. Our silence created a fragile, delicate magic, like a chance meeting between strangers. An opportunity furtively grasped. My voice startled him too, all the more so as it cracked like a whip. His shoulders stiffened.

I shifted my attention to Macha. I was sure she was going to play fair, wouldn't fall against him deliberately in hopes of a thrashing, because she knew that among other retaliations I wouldn't whip her at all for a long while to come. Each of my puppets countered my efforts to raise the ropes by letting their weight sag. It was almost as if they'd been practicing. Maybe they were just afraid of toppling over. Or else it was a plot. Macha dropped her head on her partner's shoulder and Jeremy's own resistance evaporated. He seized the opportunity to rub his nose against her neck and suck her hair. She butted him viciously on the nose with her forehead. Had she done that on purpose? I punished her with a slash of the crop on the nape of her neck. A look of joy flashed across her face. I'd forgotten it was pain that turned her on more than anything else.

Standing over them, I tugged on both ropes at once. Macha moaned and nibbled her lips. She was clinging to the man's shoulder with her chin. I had the feeling that for once there was actually something sexual about her excitement. I pulled them this way and that. Macha's head was glued to the man's shoulder but suddenly he fell forward with all his weight and dragged her down with him. I let go of the ropes. They collapsed on the floor, entwined in a fetal position. Their mouths met and they began kissing greedily. I was watching the hump in the middle of the fallen man's apron. When it disappeared, I would set them free.

With his eyes open, Jeremy was dazzled by his partner's beauty, carried away by the sight of Macha in that governess' uniform, with the starched collar around her neck, the maid's headdress and the golden ponytail reaching halfway down her back. He couldn't find much else to say beyond "Perfect, absolutely perfect."

After he'd gone, Macha plagued me with questions. Did he have a château near Paris? A town house in le Marais? Was he old nobility? Alas, all I knew about Jeremy was his pseudonym. She was disappointed and went to sleep on the sofa without taking off the headdress. Later, I found out that an audition arranged by her agency hadn't gone well: She'd failed to get the job. Professional setbacks sent her into bouts of depression which she tried to dispel with long afternoon naps and fifteen-hour nights, from which she emerged with canceled eyes.

Naturally, Jeremy's appetite was whetted by such a moment of grace. During the days that followed, he insisted I let him catch Macha in my kitchen, washing the dishes and wearing—"Please, Gala, use your influence!"—a white linen apron with a bib. He wanted to be tied to her, standing naked under his blue apron with the soubrette's behind snuggled against his belly. Annoyed that her one weak point, that bête noire of booking agents, should be the focus of Jeremy's interest in her, Macha took offense. She was repelled by the thought of a man coming on her bum. "Ablution" was her word for that sort of session. There was something of the quick rinse, she thought, in such a covert ejaculation.

SESSION 5

"RUBBER JOHN" was a Dutchman, serious as only a Dutchman can be. Generous, too, according to a dominatrix friend of mine who knew the "scene," was a habitué of fetish parties in London and Amsterdam, and had given him my number. I rang his bell at 11:00 P.M. He welcomed me into a Passy apartment lent him by a friend, spacious and impersonal.

With eighties high-tech furniture on every side, including several Starck armchairs, he stood there molded from head to toe in black rubber. I was impressed. He must have been about six feet six. A weird hood gave him a woman's face with an oval opening for his thin lips. Blue irises shone like agates through two button-holes. The frogman kissed my hand. I turned down the drink he offered. Small talk about things like the weather with a man I didn't know would irremediably ruin the aura of mystery that mattered so much to me.

I had a bag full of rubber gear. A short skirt that zipped up the back, another that had tucks and was long, gothic, and as inviolable as his suit, a corset with red and black garters, a shiny black bustier that laced up the front. There were fishnet stockings, some fine-mesh, some large. Silk stockings. Stockings with seams. Murderous shoes with metal heels that were ideal for trampling. He inclined his head towards my feet. His movements were slowed by his infinitely flexible armor. The faceless man spoke: his French was flawless.

"I love the boots you're wearing," he said. "Perhaps you'd like to keep them on?"

My boots had sharp heels and clung to my legs like gaiters.

"Did you read my last e-mail? The rules of the game?"

"Yes, but actually I'm afraid I'll kill you."

"No one saw you come in. With a little luck, no one is likely to see you leave either. The building belongs to a British insurance company. Foreign executives sleep here between seminars. If I do die, it will be very hard to identify you. They might even think I suffocated myself."

"I can't help imagining the worst!"

"My personal record is two minutes fifteen seconds. I'm asking you to help me shatter that record, as they say on TV. Dominatrices in Germany are very competitive, and in the Netherlands too. I'm expecting as much of you. You have gentle manners and that gives me confidence. You exude a kind of eroticism which is . . . unusual."

While he was speaking, he unpacked my gear. He held each item up in front of him until he understood how it worked, then shook his head. In the end he lay the garter-corset and tight skirt on a coffee table and pulled out of the bag a scarf I'd forgotten was there.

"You could blindfold me with this if you like."

The rubber suit erased his virility. I didn't have the

impression it was a man talking to me. More like an iguana. I felt no embarrassment undressing in front of him. I looked him over and thought that eelskin might be a way of concealing physical flaws. I undid the complicated laces on my tailored suit of ochre silk, then my underwear. Over the skirt I fastened the black and red corset he'd chosen.

"May I help you with your laces?"

I granted his request. Behind my back, his quick, cold gloves performed surgical movements between my shoulder-blades, then down to the small of my back. What was he after? Some kind of complicity between two human beings dressed in latex, a kind of cloned androgyny, the abolition of gender difference? I sat down to pull on my fishnets then began walking slowly across the room.

I had to pull myself together again like the scattered fragments of a mirror. My tight skirt heightened my awareness of my body. I felt sexy. I concentrated, I had to get back into a dominant frame of mind, overcome the mild excitement I was feeling on account of that tall, opaque, silhouette.

While I was walking around the room, Rubber John lay down on the floor with a small cushion on his stomach, a pink silk cushion with a blood-red heart on it. The sound of his breathing slowed and grew faint. He was waiting for me.

I crouched above him and picked up his fetish cushion. I thought to myself he probably took his silk heart with him wherever he went . . . There were pinholes in the rubber opposite his nostrils. I buried them under the wad of feathers and silk and sat on top with my knees pressing against his ears. I tensed the muscles inside my thighs and stared at the second hand on my watch. When a minute had gone by, I jumped up.

"Wonderful!" he exclaimed. "Don't be afraid to press on

the cushion with both hands. I got the impression you weren't bearing down with all your weight. How long was that?"

"Just over a minute . . ."

"Let's try it again, all right?"

I sat on him again. Hard. Forty-five seconds more, while I imagined I was a racing driver taking a curve, eyes glued to my watch-dial. The last straightaway filled me with terror. There was a knot behind my glottis, a stone weighing on my solar plexus. I crossed the finish line and leapt from my seat, mentally waving a checkered flag.

He said nothing for a long time. But his eyelids fluttered. Phew! He was alive. When he finally opened his mouth, he sounded just like a pit-stop mechanic.

"I think we're going to get there, you and me. If there's a problem you'll feel me squirm. I'll move my legs or groan. And you'll bail out, the way you did just now. O.K.?"

His flat tones overcame my apprehension. A team like ours was a shoo-in! I climbed back into the saddle. I braced myself, one hand pressed on the cushion, the other keeping my watch in sight.

I peered at the dial. I felt determined, combative. I took a deep breath and the seconds began ticking by. A comfortable respiration took a quarter of a dial. That was a luxury John couldn't afford just now, I thought mercilessly. Breathe in. Breathe out . . . John, what a name for a john! And then right away I began to worry again. I studied his reactions. Nothing. Maybe he'd passed out. I jumped off and prepared to play dutiful nurse, bringing my mouth close to his. He let out a cavernous laugh:

"I'll bet I'm as red as a lobster under my hood! You were going to give me the kiss of life, weren't you?"

Reassured, I collapsed onto the floor next to the frogman. I was panting like a wounded animal and my breath bounced off the latex and back into my face. I was sure he thought it was very funny, the way I'd jumped off. Come on Gala, get hold of yourself. He's the one flirting with death and you're the one in a panic! I got right back on top.

I felt subtle sensations. His heart beating under my buttocks: reassuring as a grandfather's clock. His breath through the silk, warmed by the feather stuffing. It was a long way to the finish-line, but I felt confident now. After two and a half minutes I released him without haste. He shook his head from side to side and gasped:

"Well? The record?"

"To smithereens! Two minutes and thirty seconds! Now that's enough; you rest."

I settled back in an armchair, I tried to think what came next, but the experience had taken everything out of me. I felt a satiety that numbed my imagination, like after a regatta on a rough sea. I didn't know how to prolong the session. Crawling towards my feet like an oversized pollywog that's lost its pond, Rubber John came to my rescue.

"It's my turn to serve you, Madame."

The tip of his tongue appeared from inside the hood. He licked my rubber dress, slipped his head underneath. But the hole in the latex was too small. His tongue only barely touched my sex. I could hardly feel a thing. A partner's lack of savoir-faire always irked me: ignorant fingers, clumsy penetration, unskilled tongue . . . or one that was too thin, like his. I had a whole set of personal images that came to my rescue in cases like this, an encyclopedia of fantasies I could run through my mind. When I liked one, I would play it back. I sat Macha's comfortable behind on the arm of my chair; she was naked and ready for anything. When I shut my eyes, she really was there. She smiled at me, laughed, caught sight of the man with his head under my skirt and rolled her eyes lasciviously.

A slender, supple body stood out against the dusty drapes, one of my old lovers come to visit. I could call that one up whenever I wished. A tall mulatto with well-toned muscles and eyes that shone with desire. He was holding his limber cock in both hands; it reached his naval and threw a diabolical shadow on the wall. He threatened to use it to bugger the man kneeling before me. Rubber John had no idea there was a horny creature creeping up on him. The lover's mouth hung open as he jacked off vigorously in the rear. His mane snapped like a lasso. His prick brushed the rubber man's back, inching towards the hole in the seat of the suit. Suddenly sea-spray jets of sperm sprinkled the black mass that had run aground at my feet. The image touched off my own explosive orgasm. Rubber John stood up, the top of his head shining.

"Do you wish me to continue, Mistress?"

His voice told me he'd felt my orgasm and even took some pride in it.

"It's late, I must be going."

I changed back into my street clothes, ears humming with the sound of pebbles rolling with the waves. John poured me some whisky. I scarcely wet my lips, for fear of losing touch with the ebb and flow of my sensations. He folded my rubber gear into my bag with loving care. I knew that the effect of novelty would have worn off for me with this single session, whereas a pure fetishist like this Dutchman could be pleasured a hundred times over by a proper dominatrix. Rubber John carried my bag to the elevator.

SESSION 6

WITH THAT SERIOUS LOOK on his face, Patrick was my idea of a cleaning man. Parisian, 55, we exchanged messages via Minitel and then he sent me some handwritten letters. He boasted of his fancy Trocadéro apartment, his taste for theater, opera, and Russian ballet. His references came from a handful of "Omphales" I was likely to know, housewives whose function was to manage the leisure activities of their couple by bringing in a female submissive, a handyman, or a circus performer, unpaid extras meant to remind the husband he could never be submissive enough. Patrick prided himself on having served several of these women who made sporadic appearances on "the Scene." He was a book collector himself and offered to dust my library volume by volume, a few bookshelves sagging under the weight of novels, reference, books and miscellaneous nonfiction.

On the appointed day, I prepared to receive him in a

mouse-gray high-fashion tailored suit and Moroccan slippers. He separated the two pings of the doorbell in such a way that they resounded majestically. I delayed replying while I tried to make up my mind: should I put on heels for the dusting session or combat boots to kick his ass? But I felt lazy and kept my slippers on.

He wore a tie with a hooded parka, and he was carrying a heavy briefcase.

"Ah, Patrick! You could have put your case on the floor!"

A hang-dog smile lit up his face.

"I preferred to carry it waiting for you, Madame . . . Will you allow me to call you "Mistress"? And perhaps you would allow me to kiss your hand as a token of the high esteem in which I hold you . . .

I shoved him into the apartment and slammed the door behind me.

"Go somewhere else if you want to fuss about! Who ever heard of a submissive making a display of himself on the doorstep of a dominatrix?"

"You are so right, Madame. Forgive me. I was completely oblivious, subjugated by your refinement, your style . . . Under your spell, dear Madame . . . Forgive me, Mistress . . ."

He fell to his knees, forehead to the floorboards. I felt like giving him a good kick where it hurts, saying to myself that single-minded men were always egotists, sometimes to the point of losing control.

"All right, that's enough. Stand up. Out with your equipment and down to work."

I gave him one of the aprons Jeremy wore—the one he liked least, out of respect for him.

"You wouldn't have a pair of dirty panties, Madame? I'd like to wear the scent of you . . ."

I threw him the panties I'd worn under my gi at my last

karate class. With humbled face and drooping mouth he gradually got into his role, stripping with funereal gravity, my panties stuffed into his mouth. I was torn between laughter and exasperation at his solemn sluggishness; he looked like a bonze preparing to immolate himself by fire in compliance with some fatal obligation.

Naked, his bag under his arm, he scurried quietly into the bathroom. Through the doorway I could see him bent over, in a world of his own, wrapping a black stocking around his testicles. As he tied the knot, he admired his organ, which he'd called "donkey cock" in a letter, and indeed it was a veritable elephant's trunk with a shrunken tip. Casually, he took a steel dog collar out of his bag. Standing in front of the mirror, he adjusted the pressure of the metal points digging into his neck.

I was lying on the sofa reading a newspaper when he came to me wrapped in Jeremy's white apron, clearing his throat to get my attention. His speech was impeded by the nylon between his incisors as he asked me:

"Will you take a photograph of me some day in this outfit, Mistress?"

"Hey Patrick! Stop fooling around and get to work! The stepladder's in the hall closet!"

Perched on the ladder, he'd begun ostentatiously slapping the books when the doorbell rang: he froze with an aviation manual in his hand, eyes bright with curiosity.

"Perhaps Madame would like me to answer the door."

I looked at his bare buttocks peeking through the gap in the apron.

"No, Patrick, I'll get it."

A friend I hadn't seen in years stood at my door combing his hair.

"Jean-Pierre! What a nice surprise!"

The bony-faced actor, known for his performances of Molière, made a spectacular entrance into my living room.

Puffing on an herbal cigarette, he scratched his right calf furiously.

"What do you know! A man with a bare ass in your apartment!" said he, discovering Patrick on his stepladder, where he had now been joined by the cat.

"Patrick, my cleaning-man."

"Hello, siiiiir," said Patrick ceremoniously, dust-cloth in hand.

"Jean-Pierre Briard, of the comédie française."

"Yes, Madame."

With a look of concentration, the valet returned to dusting my books, the cat between his feet.

"I assume you can tell us which production Jean-Pierre Briard was in this year? You do have a season-ticket to the Comédie française . . . ?"

"Yes, Madame . . . Forgive me, sir . . . in which production did I have the honor of . . . ?"

Jean-Pierre took a little bow, relishing the professional polish of his every gesture.

"*Ruy Blas*, my dear Patrick, I was the villain in *Ruy Blas*."

"Ah, yes sir, I missed the play, but the reviews I read were excellent!"

Fearfully, Patrick wrapped his apron around him and dropped the dustcloth on the cat, who clawed at his legs and scurried away.

"Relax!" the actor went on. "The display of your natural charms will be all the more appetizing, will it not, Gala?" And turning to me: "I have friends who live on Rue de Paradis, the Tomasini brothers, and they have a remarkable manservant, trained in the German school before he went into their father's service in Corsica. After his master's death, he worked in the hotel business until he ran into the sons selling china in the tenth *arrondissement*. He was over sixty, but he offered to work for them, wearing high-heels with his chauffeur's uniform . . . In the brothers' townhouse, he holds forth in Chinese, plate of canapés in one hand, umbrella in the other, sometimes dressed as a bald soprano . . . Under his wig, there's not a hair on his head! His first mistress scalped him! It turned him gay! He must have driven his girlfriend crazy that she should actually pull out his hair! . . . I hope Patrick isn't as insufferable with you! The Tomasinis are straight . . . But now and then, one of them will shag the butler, just for the helluvit . . ."

Sprawled on the sofa, he whispered scatological obscenities into my ear.

"I wouldn't mind going to the toilet to "drop a load" as they say. Do you think your man would eat some?"

On his stepladder, the object of his remark was doing violence to my books and looking worried. I could hear him breathing.

Jean-Pierre stood up, went over to the window, and then began pacing back and forth, brushing up against the stepladder, where the cat, who had surreptitiously joined the visitor's camp, had resumed his observation post, this time on the flunky's toes. The actor pinched one of the cleaning-man's buttocks. He complained about the dust he was raising in the room and slapped him on the calves. Claws bared, the feline changed sides again, hissed at the actor who stood eyeing him scornfully. Reaching out cautiously, Jean-Pierre raised Patrick's apron. The latter froze, a dictionary in one hand.

"Heavens! No hard-on!"

"You're embarrassing him."

My friend pranced out the front door.

"I've finished for today, Madame."

I felt caught out, like a housewife dreaming of being buggered by her nearest and dearest.

"All right, Patrick, you may go home."

“I was very frightened, Madame,” said he with a lovelorn look on his face. “But I want you to know I would have done it if you’d asked me to. It would have been the first time . . .”

“That’s fine, Patrick.”

SESSION 7

IN THE VESTIBULE, Serge held his coat out to me as if I were the cloakroom attendant, a long camel-hair duster, slightly flared behind the calves. He stood there with outstretched arm, the coat hanging in the air.

"There's a rack behind you for your clothes."

He was in his sixties, with a white silk scarf rolled inside his collar and a head of thick black-dyed hair. The coat, the scarf and the dye-job gave him the gawky look of an old-style Mafioso.

He took everything off but his socks. The sight of a man in socks always annoys me. The jaunty way he stood there in the raw, corn-paper fag dangling from his lips, sporting his pot-belly like a medal, suggested he was a habitué of spas or brothels. I felt overdressed in my black Lycra sheath with the slit skirt and my heavy Berber necklace.

"Repugnant" was the word that came to my mind as I growled: "Socks!" Difficult to send him back to Deauville now he was stripped! Our correspondence by fax and phone after our first online contact had forged a link that kept me from throwing him out. Besides, I was curious . . . I could have just said "Sir, I've changed my mind" or "Sorry, you don't live up to my expectations" and shown him the door. I'd done that often enough with men I'd contacted by Minitel for instant encounters—the occasional binge of submissives to keep my mind off things that mattered with wonderful adventures in the clouds.

Macha . . . She was having a nap in my bed . . . Perhaps this would be less depressing if she got involved. Operating in a twosome gives a different perception, and we might have some fun at his expense . . .

The man knew that I lived with a woman. He'd already asked me to have her join us. Over the phone, I fed him a line: On the day he was coming to Paris, I claimed she was likely to be in Deauville for the American film festival. A white lie meant to make him feel frustrated.

"If you like, I can wake up my girlfriend and ask her to play with us, but she wants a lot of money."

The man opened one of those Italian-style leather shoulder bags that men still carry in provincial towns, and took out a wad of bills with a rubber band around it. Prancing into the living room, he laid the bankroll on the table with an elaborate flourish.

"That's settled. Now hurry up, Gala, I have a train in two hours from the Gare Saint Lazare.

Actually, this retired pharmaceutical tycoon had all the spare time in the world. He divided his days between deep-sea fishing and gambling: baccarat and blackjack at the casino, duplicate bridge with his wife and her friends, surfing S&M sites on the Minitel. In short, he was hooked on everything; it probably went with his cigarette-smoking. As a former smoker and professional seducer, I couldn't be too hard on him. I was hooked on kinky relations too, on sex without sex. Besides, he was impotent.

A miniature roulette wheel and a pack of dog-eared cards came out of his shoulder bag. I went into the bedroom to explain the case to Macha who sat leafing through her bible, Baltasar Gracian's *The Courtier*, a seventeenth-century book of etiquette. Her precious jetliner mask lay on the bed. When she took a nap, she isolated herself in a kind of sensorial caisson, with mask and earplugs.

Casino, roulette, Deauville were magic words for my Swedish friend. She was in awe of the jet society. I explained what the john looked like and how his authoritarian manners would have to be squelched.

"We'll take him for a ride, cheat at roulette so he loses every time, send him home covered with welts!"

She laughed cheerfully and I knew it was in the bag. So long as he was here, we might as well have a ball with this wreck of a man.

She slipped into a black tee-shirt mini-dress, put on a black eye-mask trimmed with plumes. If her lover took her for a weekend at the Hôtel Royal, she didn't want this guy recognizing her on the streets of Deauville.

In the living-room, the man hoisted his ass out of his chair in greeting, then dropped back heavily. Naked and unashamed, he was busy putting together his portable roulette wheel. There was a green baize cloth on the table. He glanced briefly at Macha.

"A fine head of Nordic hair . . ."

He spun the drum and went on without looking up:

"I suppose it was Gala who told you to wear that silly mask . . . Well, a submissive must obey her mistress, of course . . . okay, girls, bring on the rakes!"

"That's what Serge calls the crops and floggers, Macha, so fetch some "rakes."

The size of the miniature roulette wheel had come as a disappointment to her. She wrinkled her nose in disgust and pointed at Serge's pot belly while he was stooping to retrieve a chip from the floor. I steered my friend back into the bedroom and took out my two best belts.

"I'd love to be your guinea-pig," she said, "but not in front of him. In here . . . right now . . ."

I wrapped the end of a belt around my hand and whipped her behind through the dress. She looked at me with one eye shut, a code between us which meant "not so hot," and leaned up against the wall. Not wanting Serge to know what was going on, I hit her five or six times at short range, putting a bit more force behind the thin strap. She turned towards me and I kissed her on the mouth, trying to rekindle our complicity with the feel of our tongues. She pursed her lips and sucked my tongue, guzzling my saliva. A flood of desire made me weak in the knees.

"Mozart! I adore Mozart!" shouted the man in the next room.

I pushed her away. I had to regain my professional composure before we both got the giggles. I avoided looking at her as I got the ropes that Serge required out of a chest. During our last phone call, he'd let me know he wanted to tie himself up. I was to supply fifteen or twenty feet of rope and a mooring on the ceiling. He would bring the shackles and snap-hooks.

"*The Magic Flute*?"

"Why not?" Serge conceded. "I like the part where Papageno begs the ladies to take off the padlock they've put on his mouth!"

While he was fastening the ropes to his wrists with leather bracelets, he explained the details of the game. In order to limit the number of strokes, there would be only eighteen spins of the wheel, eighteen spins to keep the whippings bearable. In order to avoid repetitions, I was to keep track of the numbers as they came up by placing chips on the cloth. A repeated number didn't count: in the event, we'd drop the little ball on the spinning wheel again. Red meant the traditional whips and crops, black was for the thin belt that Macha preferred. The number that came up determined the number of strokes. Macha was the croupier, I was the torturess.

That miniature roulette wheel reminded me of the Mickey Club on the beach at Deauville. The blot on the club was him. Tied to a rope hanging from a beam, hands stretched over his head, he looked like a boa constrictor who'd swallowed two footballs that were stuck in different places above his rickety legs, one in front and one behind.

The 2 was his first bet and Macha lay a chip on the corresponding square. She smiled ferociously as she spun the ball: 36. My confederate winked at me. She must have wished very hard for the big number to come up and was savoring her triumph.

"From now on, if my number comes up, I will have oral caresses coming from both you girls." Macha and I looked at each other, unsure whether to laugh or be angry. That tone of his!

I gave him his two strokes but my heart wasn't in it, I used the whip since two was red, but Macha lost her temper, clenching her fists on the green baize:

"You're letting yourself off easy! The wheel decides the number! If you're changing the rules, I'm out of here!"

He muttered "All right, Macha, whatever you say . . ."

9 came up. After one smack of the belt on his fleshy buttocks, our gambler protested:

"That didn't count!"

"No? Why not?"

"The strap hit my stomach. Back away a little and do it again."

I complied but my blood was boiling. Grumpily, he counted the strokes aloud. I added two for good measure.

"That wasn't fair, Gala. The number was nine, I had only

nine strokes coming. And that mask upsets me. Please, Macha, take it off!"

I shot back:

"Is it the little bonus I gave you or my girlfriend's mask that's put you in a bad mood?"

He kept staring at the mask:

"Come on, it's not Halloween, take off your mask, Macha! I want to see what you look like, don't I? . . . You wouldn't have a strawberry mark by any chance?"

She had no idea what he was talking about. Her wiry fingers flicked the ball onto the spinning wheel and centrifugal force threw it into one of the little channels.

"Twenty-three! Black! . . . The flogger," she stammered.

"Oh no, we said black was the belt!"

I came to Macha's rescue.

"Well, the rules have changed, Serge. Now black means whip."

"That's not fair. We decided once and for all which rake was which color . . ."

"Who makes the rules? YOU decided! Are you the dominator now? Throwing your weight around?"

"All right, all right, hit me with any rake you please . . . Since you will go your own sweet way."

I pursed my lips and walloped him once on each of those deflated life-buoys that were his buttocks. The blood-starved skin turned blue. Next, I unleashed my hatred on the small of his back.

"It's too sensitive there, Gala. Lower down, please . . . And further to the left . . ."

Macha kept throwing me exasperated glances. I whipped him twenty-three times, harder and harder, trying to blow off the anger boiling up inside me, then I told him what the rest of the program would be:

"I'm going to blindfold you. You're going to guess

which of us is doing the whipping. If you get it wrong, you get twice as many strokes!"

"Okay! . . . You're on! That's a cute idea!"

He perked up for the first since he came in. While I was tying a scarf over his eyes, Macha made soundless faces at me. I caught a glimpse of her sharp teeth under the feather shell that clung to her nostrils. She twisted her lips, stuck out her tongue mischievously, wriggled her bottom and took an enticingly obscene pose, her thighs pressed to the green baize.

"I love this aria!" said Serge.

I rolled Macha's dress up to her pubis. She almost never wore panties. I uncovered her sex, only half-plucked. The day before, she and her twin sister back in Sweden had had a hair removal session over the phone, each in front of a mirror, one on the left side, the other on the right. I was intoxicated by the contrast between the smooth left lip I was stroking and the untouched blond fur on the right. I trailed my finger slowly along the furrow that separated them, clamped my fingers on the piece of fruit. Forearms flat on the table, head thrown back, Macha fluttered her eyelids. I squeezed harder and she bit her lips.

"Louder the Mozart, girls!"

With one hand I turned up the volume on the remote, with the other I wanked her off. Fast. Her gaze swept the room, the roulette wheel, Serge in profile tied to rope-ends, the scarf still over his eyes. Her sex was dribbling into my hand. The man's presence added to her excitement . . . She would probably prefer he could see us . . . When she's old, she'll have half a dozen poodles to watch her masturbate.

"Hey, when you dykes have finished! If you think you can fool me, you've got another think coming . . . At least you could have done that before you put the blindfold on so I could watch!"

Macha clapped her hand over mine to keep it pressed to

her sex, and spun the man's wheel. The zero came up. She stammered:

"18 . . . red!"

She raised my wet fingers to her mouth. She licked them, staring me in the eyes. Then she picked up the little black belt. I realized she wanted to learn my technique. After a first stroke that was much too gentle, she gave me an imploring look and then struck again. I folded the belt double and guided her arm through the air to convey greater flexibility. She stepped back and practiced a few times. Now the belt fell properly, sharp and light, on Serge's buttocks.

"That was Gala!" he exclaimed.

"You lose," Macha said arrogantly.

"You can do whatever you want anyway, since I can't see."

We took turns calling out fictional numbers, often far removed from those that came up. Five would become 23 or 32. The masochist began complaining about the inordinate length of the whippings. While the little ball spun round the cylinder, my fingers would be burrowing into Macha's sex. Her pelvis thrusting, her dress rolled up around her hips, she spread her thighs before me with a theatrical flourish and mimicked an orgasm.

"Now that's enough Gala! Wait until I'm gone, you two!" growled Serge from behind his scarf.

His buttocks were streaked with purple, the hollows of his thighs covered with scratches. He was never sure who'd whipped him and invariably got it wrong.

"What about finishing me off, girls?" he whimpered after the eighteenth spin. "You're going to leave me in this condition? I can get a hard-on if you like!"

But neither Macha nor I was interested in his genitals.

"I bought what it takes at the pharmacy," he added. "One shot will make any cock stiff for more than two hours. I'll have a hard-on all the way to Deauville, but if it pleases you, no problem. Get the hypo and the little bottle out of my bag."

I was curious:

"What are you going to do with your cock?"

"Nothing special . . . It's for the pleasure of the eyes, the image a woman likes to keep of a man, nothing more."

"A magic potion for his flute!" Macha joked.

She ran to the vestibule cupboard, brought back a feather duster and began tickling his testicles. The man probably thought it was a finger or a tongue. Reassured, he gave a sigh of satisfaction. But his geisha soon got bored. She jammed the duster handle between his buttocks and planted her nails in the dark skin around his nipples. Serge lost his cool.

"OK, girls, that's enough for today! I don't know what you're up to but I'm not missing my train just for the sake of your kicks. Come on, get this silly blindfold off me!

It was Macha who handed him his camel's hair pelisse. In jeans and leather jackets we left the apartment soon after he did. Sitting in a gourmet restaurant Boulevard Saint-Germain, we'd both dismissed him from our thoughts. We didn't mention him. Not one word. There was nothing to be said. There was only oblivion.

SESSION 8

WHO IN THE WORLD COULD HAVE given me that blonde wig? Pulling it over the head of a hung-up little businessman named Louis was like guiding a horse by the mane, I thought. I examined with a critical eye the lips I'd thickened with rouge and cunningly tapered at the corners. Faced with "Mistress"'s candid gaze, Magali's pupils wavered.

"Now let's see the woman in you . . . Walk around!"

A cross-dresser was breaking in a pair of high heel shoes on my living room floor. Very respectable shoes purchased on Boulevard de Clichy "for his wife." These sessions were the only chance Louis ever got to play his alter ego. At the office, he sometimes wore a teddy under his trousers, an elderly woman's ample panties pulled tight as a girdle.

"Don't look down, your feet are doing the walking."

Magali's sun-hat bobbed upward as she straightened her neck. Legs tense, knees stiff, the little outmoded handbag

I'd lent her dangling at the end of a gilded chain. She performed a kind of goose-step I'd taught her, a technique transvestites use to walk without bending their knees. With its rows of yellowed pearls, the secondhand violet dress had a vintage look about it.

After our initial contact on the Minitel, Magali had begun writing me long letters which I devoured in my spare moments: gang-bangs in a girls' boarding school, hip students wearing strap-ons to the playing field, milk-filled dildoes in the dormitory, spatters on the blankets, peals of laughter while Magali is raped over and over again, boarders jumping the wall, a high-heeled shoe in each hand. When I reached puberty in a boarding school, no girl ever dreamt of leaping over the wall to promenade on the Champs-Elysées in high-heeled shoes.

I was bored with giving the same lessons in deportment week after week, so that evening I'd opted for outdoor field work. Magali was to be on my doormat at 9:00 P.M. sharp, in her raincoat. The disaffected toilet on the landing housed her frills and flounces, dresses, rayon negligees, polyester see-through nighties, Scandale girdles and corsets.

I dressed butch for this outing on the ring-road: bomber jacket, tight black leather trousers, and sneakers.

Magali rang my bell and then scampered on tiptoe to the garbage room, where she hid from my neighbors until she heard me honk. None of the tenants must be able to connect that creature in the tan raincoat with the woman who drove my Renault.

"All aboard, Magali!"

Wedged into her seat that way, she looked like a secretary out for an evening on the town. At a stoplight at Place de l'Opéra, by the pale glow of the ceiling light, I examined her face crusted with a mix of foundation cream and powder. The blue eye-shadow was beginning to run. The metallic odor of her apprehension started to bother me. Whiffs of menstruation . . . Under the raincoat, Magali wore a yellow mini-skirt. Steel clips on her nipples stretched the cloth of the senior style bra she wore under a lace blouse.

I left Paris by the Porte de Saint-Ouen and slowed on a stretch of the ring-road taken over by Algerian drag-queens. Huge trailer-trucks with sex-starved drivers slumped in their cabs, four or five prostitutes with gaping cleavage and hip-length boots. Two drag-queens were sharing a sandwich. Another was peeing against the wall of an underpass where cars hurtled past into the darkness. On the north side of the expressway, there were voyeurs in black or gray sedans, shady pick-up artists puffing on cigarettes.

My passenger's hand was on the door-handle. Head held high, she gave the competition the once-over, secure in the protection afforded by the expensive car, flashing seductive glances at the men out of the corner of her eye.

"Those guys fantasize about women with penises like you, Magali."

"Do you think so, Mistress?"

I parked along the walkway and killed the engine.

"Take off your raincoat, you're going to hustle . . ."

Magali did as she was told. She stood motionless a few yards behind the car, shivering in the gusts of wind that swept the boulevard. A truck-driver slid out from behind his wheel and approached the brunette in lace. I saw him in the rear-view mirror questioning her. How much? . . . A man's fantasy: selling himself like a woman, getting praise from his "Mistress" . . . The trucker took a bill from his pocket. Magali turned away and headed for the car just as I started the engine. She ran towards me waving her arms, miniskirt floating in the wind. As soon as I saw the man coming after her, I slammed on the brakes. The truck-driver slowed down. He was hoping she'd twist an ankle, fall on the sidewalk at his mercy. I could hear my submissive beseeching me:

"Madame! Come and talk to him . . . Please . . . Madame!"

When she was within a few strides of the trunk of my car, I stepped on the gas again. The man was running. This time he was right behind her. He put his hand on her bum and tried to shove her off balance; maybe he meant to rape her right there on the asphalt. He held her by the arm and I saw her face screwed with pain. I was amused to watch a man experience such strong female sensations. I laughed to myself behind the steering wheel. When I saw Magali sag and fall on her knees in front of the man, I reversed the car and called to her through the open window:

"Magali! We're out of here!"

The transvestite leapt into the moving car. He was sobbing as I sped down the boulevard.

"Madame, it was too much for me . . . I can't suck somebody just like that . . . no condom!"

"Stop your fussing, Magali! Here, look what I've brought for you to put on after the truck-driver's buggered you."

I held out a sanitary napkin, king-size for nighttime wear, bristling with self-adhesive tabs.

"Put it on right away. I'd rather know you're protected before I turn you loose in the vacant lot where we're going, you might get my seats dirty."

The sanitary napkin worked like candy with a child: Magali stopped crying. She spread her legs and writhed about trying to slide the napkin under her panties. I braked just as she lifted her backside off the seat. She was thrown forward and only her seatbelt kept her from bloodying her forehead on the windshield.

"Madame, aren't you driving a little fast?" she ventured timidly, with her chin on her chest.

"Since when do maids criticize their mistresses?"

"Forgive me, Madame, it was just that . . ."

I made a U-turn. With a twist of the wheel, I parked near a group of drag queens.

"Go and tell your fellow creatures your mistress drives too fast."

"Oh, Madame, mercy! I wouldn't dare! Those are professionals, they're dangerous people . . ."

"You're just dying to be a slut! So go on!"

She was intimidated by the hard edge to my voice. She opened the door, put one foot out to test the water then took the plunge. Swaying her hips, she walked towards the three silent figures who stood watching her. She felt ill at ease in the presence of her fellow creatures, rubbed her arms against her chest. Hands on hips, one gum-chewing drag-queen looked her up and down haughtily. Walking carefully on the edge of the sidewalk, Magali tried to disguise her lack of composure by hailing a truck that drove slowly by. Instantly, the transvestites pounced on her. One had an umbrella and beat her with it. I started the engine in a hurry and stopped opposite them, shouting: "Leave him alone, he's my submissive! It was just a test!"

"Well you better test your slave someplace else! Got that?"

Magali settled into her seat. She said not a word all the way home. On the third floor landing, I whispered sweetly "Good night, Magali" and unlocked the door to my apartment while she ran for the water-closet to change.

SESSION 9

My roommate Macha met Yasmin at a contest where submissive females spread their legs and exhibited themselves in the nude. The diplomat presided over a jury of men who were free to touch and feel the contestants, checking their muscle tone before and after each performance. The women had to fetch little objects that were thrown for them, and undergo various forms of corporal punishment. First prize was a Rolex watch. It was whispered that on the last such soirée, the prize had been a cup won by the Diplomat's Labrador at a dog-show. He'd simply removed the animal's name.

The two women met up again now and then, turning tricks like that. One evening in the apartment we shared, Macha was putting on a pair of flesh-colored stockings for an evening at the diplomat's when Yasmin dropped by to pick her up. In her boots and riding coat, she couldn't have weighed more than a hundred pounds. The snakelike body was humanized by a pair of dark smoldering eyes.

Sitting perched on the edge of the sofa, she lit one of my Cuban cigarillos. Enraptured by my black silk negligee, she began questioning me about B&D.

"Do you think I'd make a good dominatrix?"

"Every submissive woman has a potential for domination. Why not you?"

"I've become such a glutton for pain I don't think I can handle much more of it. I'm counting on you to show me some of your methods. And if you come across a well-disposed guinea pig, bring him around to my place."

Yasmin's avenue Foch apartment looked out over the tops of the trees lining that exclusive thoroughfare. Modernist furniture, computers, etchings, terminals of all sorts were scattered amongst thick embroidered drapes and camel-skin lampshades. Leaving the building at night with a date, she would hide her Moroccan profile under a long blonde wig, for fear of running into her uncle, who lived just a few blocks away.

One evening, while we lolled on cushions by a low table of beaten copper where a couscous was laid out, Yasmin told Macha and me that one of the things she loved about her neighborhood was the prostitutes who prowled up and down the side paths, or stood with their backs to the garden fences.

After dinner, I began to realize how highly strung this woman was. She'd just had a dispute with her Moroccan servant, whom she suspected of stealing a large sum from the pocket of her gray suit. Searching her, she'd found the money in her bra. She locked the bedroom door and knocked the maid's head against the wall until she drew blood.

She insisted on showing us the red smear on the wallpaper and proclaimed with all the arrogance of her twenty-two years: "See what happens to someone who steals from me?"

A few days before Christmas, I received a visit from an American submissive, a dancer in his thirties. Stuart shaved his scalp to conceal a premature bald patch, and his pale head emerged from the collar of his leather coat like the stump of an arm from a sleeve. He handed me a long package of orange paper tied with a brown satin ribbon.

"A riding crop! You could have thought of something more original!"

I decided to take him to Yasmin's in thumb-cuffs. I hid the crop in the back of his coat, taped to the cashmere lining. So accoutered, I walked him across the Pont des Arts, through the Louvre's Cour Carrée, past the glass pyramid, into the Rue Saint-Honoré and on up towards the Faubourg.

The chrome-plated steel cuffs were hidden by a pair of black gloves. In a shop window, we saw a beautiful pair of boots: Stuart cleverly managed to type his credit card code on a tiny keyboard the clerk held out to him. Back in the street, he carried the bag pressed to his stomach with both hands. In a stylist's shop on the Faubourg Saint-Honoré we discovered "stretch leather." The American picked out a violet bustier suited to Yasmin's tiny breasts. I ordered a black catsuit with gussets under the armpits in view of future wrestling matches with my viragophile.

On the Place de la Concorde, Stuart was in trouble: How to hail a taxi with his thumbs cuffed together? But my New Yorker was full of resources. Raising his hands with the dangling packages knocking together, he looked for all the world like a thief caught in the act. But when he whistled, a Peugeot pulled up immediately: "In you go, Gala!"

Stuart was ready for anything. He had no special requirements except for the thrashing he expected to receive from the dominatrices he patronized, one in every capital of Europe. Nor was he the kind of masochist who will foul up deliberately just to get a whipping.

At Avenue Foch, Yasmin complimented me:

"What a pretty slave! You're spoiling me! Let's open a bottle of champagne! The slave can serve it. Glasses, Stuart! . . . in the first cupboard . . . the bucket is on the shelf, and don't forget the ice cubes . . ."

She stroked her new leather bustier, but mostly she was intrigued by the thumb-cuffs I'd just removed. She studied them from all angles.

"You know, darling, they still haven't delivered my Christmas tree! I bought all those trinkets Christians hang on them! If my family ever found out! A devout Moslem having a Christmas tree!"

Toying with the ratchets on the cuffs, she pressed one around her own thumb until it bit into the bone; she laughed, turned the key one way, then the other, then back, until it finally opened. With a conjuror's flourish, Stuart pulled the crop out of his coat. Assuming this was a gift as well, the mistress of the house seized it eagerly: "Oh thank you, that's so sweet!"

She smacked his behind with it.

"Strip! And be quick about it!"

Stark naked, a white napkin over his forearm, Stuart began filling our champagne glasses. He had a chrome-plated ring hanging from each nipple. I told our host how a woman artist had suspended a steel tray on two small chains from those nipples for the opening of her last show. The women thus got their cocktails from a waiter trotting around after his potential mistresses wearing only a thong.

In defiance of the prevailing rules of hygiene in the U.S.A., his parents hadn't had him circumcised, so that a more imposing piece of jewelry peaked out through the folds of skin. From where I stood, it looked over two inches thick. Yasmin pulled on it and watched for the man's reaction, but he just stood there with his chest out and a condescending smile on his face.

Stuart had certainly spotted the mistress of the house for a novice, but his manner failed to intimidate her. There came a rustling of tissue paper as her fingers rifled through the box of Christmas ornaments. She hung red balls from his nipple rings, then wound a string of tiny bulbs around his arms.

We turned off the lights in the room and gazed at the winking spots of color. The pale body with outstretched arms became a floodlit cross. I was back at one of those sea-cliff cemeteries in southern Italy, where light bulbs flash endlessly on and off over the gravestones. Sitting beside me, my friend seemed lost in memories of her own. Suddenly she broke the spell, shooting to her feet like a coiled spring:

"The tree needs more decorations!"

Quickly she turned the lights back on and dug more ornaments out of the box. A silver bell in one hand, a rabbit in the other, she tried to decide where to hang them. I had an idea:

"Get me a pair of nail-scissors."

As soon as my friend had left the room, Stuart implored me:

"No marks please, Mistress, please, remember what I do for a living!"

I cut one end of the wire loop close to the thin colored glass. Yasmin understood immediately and with her nose inches away from her chosen target, dug the hook I had fashioned into Stuart's flesh. Soon the American's silky epidermis was studded with gold stars and candy Santas.

She took snapshots of him from every angle. Proud of

her close-ups of the red balls hanging directly from the skin, she promised to show the prints to Macha.

"No one would believe I'm so cruel, would they Gala?"

The punishment dealt out to her maid crossed my mind as she tugged viciously at the dancer's rings and pulled on his sex: the Christmas tree had a hard-on.

There was only a box of little candles left on the floor. Yasmin was trying to figure out how to put them on. I showed her. Now the human Christmas tree sparkled with myriad lights, burning candles stuck with hot wax to his shoulders and arms.

From her balcony overlooking the avenue, Yasmin whistled through her fingers. She had a code for communicating with the women who worked the sidewalk, shrill whistles mingled with the *youyou* made famous by protesting crowds of women during the Algerian war.

A small troop came up from the street, four or five women in eye-catching boots and transparent PVC. Each one made a wish and hooked a ball on the tree, in the soft skin under an arm, on the chest or inside a thigh. They watched for signs of pain on Stuart's face, but saw only a smile of resignation. He looked like a piece of modern sculpture, and the girls began to look upon him as a quasi-miraculous living statue. One of them asked for absolution. She begged him for a better future, provided there would be plenty of money. A blonde with silicone breasts dubbed him "Saint Rita," patroness of lost causes and prostitutes.

Absolved by the male incarnation of their saint, the girls decided to play with Stuart's body until "he went off his rocker." They tugged on the ornaments. When one fell off, they pinned it back into some sensitive spot with airs of lamentation.

A brown witch built like a man removed the red ball from his cock.

"Fuck me any way you can, I love a cock blessed with

candle wax and purified by fire!" She lifted her skirt and impaled herself, oblivious to the hot wax drippings. The other women sat on the sofa guzzling oriental pastries and watched.

But Yasmin felt restless. She was bored with her tree and decided to show the other women the thieving maid's blood on the bedroom wall. She was acting tough to impress her friends. In the meantime, Stuart had grown weary of playing stallion to the big woman. The mistress of the house had found the riding crop he'd brought and I showed her how to use it.

"When you strike with the tip, you should begin by heating up the skin with little taps."

But she hit him hard across the rings, without any preparation at all. Stepping back, she spread her arms and squinted. The red balls exploded one after the other. It was like a shooting gallery at a fun fair. She didn't miss a single ornament.

After that, Yasmin began talking about little Jesus in the manger, the donkey and the ox, those four-footed witnesses that warmed him with their breath, according to the Bible. The image gave one of the girls an idea: She went to her car and brought back a tape for zoophiles which she invited us all to watch. Each of the women gave her impressions.

"The idea of doing it with a dog doesn't turn me on."

"Dogs are even more disgusting than men!"

"That depends! Some men are worse than dogs!"

Yasmin lay on her back with her friends. A peaceful expression hovered on her face that was new to me. Habitually inclined to anorexia, she wolfed the last gazelle-horns and licked her fingers.

SESSION 10

THERE WAS THIS GERMAN on the Web looking for a woman to torture him, humiliate him. He wanted to be raped with a ham-bone, burned with an electric iron, thrashed with a handful of TV cables. Following a long series of tortures, a stretch of solitary confinement would be most welcome. If I didn't have a cupboard, my wardrobe would do: tied hand and foot with wire, a coat-hanger twisted around his neck. I sent him a photo of myself in a colonial army uniform I'd found in the cellar. Hand on hip, I stood haughty and stern. I imagined him fantasizing before a huge blow-up of the picture: he became a devotee of my Website, finally begging to fall into my clutches for one whole night.

He had a long wait before I deigned to reply. There was a month of silence designed to temper the demands of a guy who still believed the bogy-woman was duty-bound to satisfy the whims of every submissive that came along. After that, his requirements were cut down to size.

It was the first time I'd imagined my living room as a torture chamber. Macha wouldn't be barging in on us; she was at home with her mother in Sweden. Once the appointment was made, I almost regretted giving in to such an extremist. Besides, I had no idea how I was going to go about this, and that bothered me. I lay alone while images of movie torturers flashed by, mad scientists brandishing scalpels and electrodes, brutal officers who set upon lady spies running to their death in damp tunnels.

After we spoke on the phone, I wasn't even sure he'd keep the appointment. He'd complained about the amount I was asking.

I opened the door to him in street-clothes. He stood on my mat in a pearl-gray suit. Several amulets hung from a gold chain around his neck. His faded eyes examined me through rectangular glasses. He cleared his throat and introduced himself: "Herbert . . . from Düsseldorf," holding out a delicate little hand with sharp nails and a big signet ring that he wore like a bandage. I ignored the hand.

The stories my grandparents used to tell came back to me: the German eagle hanging over the fireplace, the family banished to the attic, and I suddenly knew he was going to be the Enemy . . .

I went into my bedroom and shut the door. I needed to get into my role. Out of his presence, I took my head in my hands and emptied my mind. Silently, I put a German accent on the words I would need to speak.

In the mirror, I tucked my bangs under the shiny black visor and brushed brown powder on my cheeks to make them look hollow like Marlene Dietrich's. I sprinkled talc inside a long-sleeved rubber dress tight as a girdle which had snaps up the front but was hard to put on, a short sheath with blue epaulettes welded into the black latex. It was a mock version of the uniform worn by Soviet officers, arch-foes of the Germans during World War Two, enemies of my enemy in the next room . . .

The man stood gazing at a black and white photograph over a chest of drawers in the living room, bare feet on a tiled floor, small feminine feet with high arches. He turned around and was struck dumb by the embodiment of his fantasy before him, replete with boots and a wicked twist of the mouth. I looked him straight in the eye. His lashes fluttered and he looked away, but then slowly his gaze returned and focused on the severe set of my mouth. An expression of passive expectation which I knew only too well had come over his face, with a savage glow deep in his eyes. My German accent had a slight lisp as I went into action. I ordered him to keep his eyes on the floor. A riding crop in my gloved hands, I backed him into the hallway, expostulating in guttural tones:

"You are hiding something from me, admit it *kleine* Herbert!"

He persisted in staring at me and I spat in his face, then slapped him. He tried to wipe the spittle from his cheek and scratched himself with his signet ring. A red drop formed on his cheekbone, which I collected with the tip of my glove. I showed it to him at close range and saw from the way his pupils shrank that he was frightened of his own blood. I put my gloved finger to his mouth:

"Lick."

He kept his lips sealed. It was as if he hadn't heard me. I clamped my other hand under his jaw and squeezed.

"Open your mouth, show me what you're hiding under your tongue.

He obeyed, closing his eyes. His mouth smelled of Turkish tobacco, a sweetly sickening scent. I inspected the orifice with harsh impatience.

"Now undress."

He stood naked in front of me, but had kept his glasses. I jerked them from his nose.

"Turn your pockets out . . . All the pockets . . . Now hand over your clothes!"

He gave me his shirt, then his trousers, and I picked at the seat as if to remove a bit of excrement. I examined the collar, the hems, the lining. I threw his clothes in his face one after the other, and he never so much as flinched. The effect of the drop of blood on my glove had dissipated; his arrogant poise had returned.

But when he was kneeling on the floor in the drafty hallway, with his hands behind his back, and I told him to stick out his ass, he lost his composure again and drew it in instead.

"Arch your back. Put your hands on the floor . . . Yes, like that, on all fours . . . You ought to be able to arch your back like a ballerina . . . Go on, open your asshole . . . Your buttocks are too tight, use your hands to spread them . . . Better than that . . . Now cough . . . Push . . . I said push! Have you lost your hearing?"

And I clapped him on both his ears at once.

He shrieked.

"That hurt!"

I kicked him repeatedly on the buttocks, and he fell flat on his face. I slipped the tip of my boot under his chin, and pulled up till he propped himself on his elbows. I drove the handle of the riding crop into his anus, obliging him to arch his back and open wider. I made him clean the soiled handle with his tongue, then I stuck it down his throat, all the way down till his neck began to go scarlet.

"Raise your arms!"

This time I used the whip-end of the crop on his tender armpits. His eyes had mellowed; they roved up my legs, caressed the tight rubber sheath. I could sense he was on the verge of ecstasy, about to show his gratitude. I slipped behind him and began flogging the soles of his feet. They had thick yellow calluses, wrinkled around the edges. That was where I aimed my blows. One foot, then the other. His toes curled. His chest sagged but he had staying power, I'll say that for him.

"No marks on a shit like you! That would be too easy! You could show them to people and say you'd been tortured. You'd better talk if you want me to stop . . ."

He said the first thing that came into his head. He hadn't done anything wrong—he swore he was innocent. Before he came to see me, he hadn't expected me to hit him so hard. But now I could do as I liked, I could pull out all the stops if I felt like it, he was mine, body and soul . . . His phlegmatic expression was getting on my nerves for real, and I drove the tip of my boot into his stomach again and again . . . The metal tips left red marks that looked like swallows. The guy had managed to get me into a rage.

"Confess!"

He looked at me and gritted his teeth. I told him about my uncles, both timber sawyers, both amputated by bandsaws, one at the elbow, he had a stump with a hook on it, the other lost three fingers on his right hand. Then I held up my own left hand, the Yakusa hand, with the top of the ring-finger missing:

"A lie I told when I was little . . . See what can happen to liars?"

Panting from the slashes that fell on the base of his neck with the regularity of a woodpecker, he begged for mercy. The crop worked its way down the vertebrae as if it had a will of its own. He was ripe.

"Now jerk off!"

His squirrel's paws busied themselves. But his feverish gestures contrasted with the placid look on his face. He was in no hurry, he wanted more punishment. I wanted him out of there. I could have sent him packing with a few well-placed kicks and thrown his gear onto the doormat after him. With one eye on my watch, I told him to hurry.

"Quick, Herbert! There are other people waiting! Go on, hurry up or I'll waste you!"

He came on the tiles and fell forward on both hands. It took him a while to recover his wits. Picking up his clothes scattered about the floor, he gradually returned to normalcy. After a long stay in my bathroom, he tried to shake my hand. I folded my arms:

"Good-bye, *klein* Herbert."

I don't like masochists who manage to get on my nerves, manipulators who deliberately enrage me. I stowed the gear, washed the whip, and wiped away every trace of his visit, rubbing him out of my life as it were.

SESSION 11

A BALLET OF WHITE WINGS soared above the waves of heat rising from plane that sped down the runway at Toussus-le-Noble. The Falcon lifted off, gained altitude, and disappeared to the west. The air vibrated from the optical mirages of the sun. On the overhanging terrace, I kept an eye out for Gregory Mackinnon, due to arrive from Scotland in his private Cessna because one of his racehorses was scheduled to appear at a French track. Dangling one shoe from the tip of a bare foot, I peered up into the sky.

At the far end of the runway, a plane was coming in too high for a proper landing. Three kangaroo bounces on the tarmac, a run between the red and white lights at well over the speed limit, and the aircraft finally lurched to a halt in the parking area. From the rough time he gave his plane, I'd recognized his lordship's style, and there he was stepping out of the cabin in one of those starched and ironed suits of his. He gave a good-bye kiss to an English wife who bought her clothes from Escada, "high fashion in outsizes." She waved to the driver of a waiting taxi.

Sir Gregory began limping in my direction, smiling affably.

"It's not what you think, Gala, I twisted it at tennis, that's all. The wife might get suspicious if I came home half-crippled from one of your dominatrix sisters!"

Gregory knew dozens of mistresses. Just then, I was among the favorites. He'd invited me for twenty-four hours to Angers where one of his mares was running. The prizewinner's name was Squeaking Board—the one that woke up the wife at night and gave you away when you came home late to the castle.

As I buckled up inside the cabin of his pressurized twin-engine job, Gregory was leafing nervously through his maps. He writhed about on his seat, touching knobs and switches on the instrument panel, sitting back to judge the position of the wings on the artificial horizon gauge.

"Are you ready for takeoff, Gala?"

"Ready for takeoff when you are, Gregory!"

"Damn! I forgot to check the fuel!"

He tried to jump out, realized his seat belt was holding him back, released himself, jumped out, and landed on his bad foot. Grimacing with pain, he squinted at a little plastic goblet, inspecting the color of the kerosene taken from the bottom of each tank.

Back in his seat, he muttered a few words into his headset and got permission to taxi onto the runway.

We touched down at Laval, just long enough to see the name on the terminal building, and took off again immediately for Angers. It was ten past twelve, lunchtime in the provinces, and no one had seen the valiant pilot from over the Channel mistaking one airport for another . . . "Thank God!"

The Lion d'Angers racetrack was graced with spacious lawns on which customized trailers offered all sorts of leather accessories with a good horsy smell. Gregory made me a present of a tawny leather switch that matched the lining of the Cessna's cabin.

Jostled at the gate by the other starters, Squeaking Board came in second. Gregory applauded wildly. In the bleachers a blonde with too much suntan turned and admired the fortunate owner.

As I stood in line to collect my winnings, I caught a distant glimpse of Gregory in conversation with the blonde woman whom I now recognized from a feature spread in a B&D magazine: a famous dominatrix from Nantes. We bumped into her again in the hotel dining room. An insipid, frail, submissive carried her handbag.

In the suite of rooms my Scotsman had reserved for us, I had on my riding clothes and was preparing for the domination session I owed my john, but Gregory seemed restless. He helped me on with my boots rather grudgingly, whereas usually triggered his fantasy. I sensed he was looking for an excuse to get away. And indeed, on the flimsiest pretext he left the room.

I shadowed him across the park, beneath century-old oak trees. He went into a hangar where a few ancient planes were kept, poignant museum pieces for anyone interested in aviation. He went to a pre-war Bréguet mail plane and climbed in the cockpit. Through the window, I could make out the blonde locks of the woman from Nantes. I'm a Peeping Tom by nature. I crept closer and pressed my nose to the worn plastic. She was holding his head back with one hand. From Gregory's groans, I gathered she was working on his breasts. Then her hands disappeared from view altogether and I heard a lapping sound: probably pulling him off with some jelly. Gregory shouted:

"No, not now! My friend is waiting for me in my room."

I tiptoed quickly away just as the Bréguet door was being unlatched. Back at the hotel, in an upstairs hallway, I ran into the jockey who'd ridden "Squeaking Board," a dark-haired little man in his early twenties with long eyelashes. We were both wearing jodhpurs and boots . . . I'd been fantasizing about the virility of jockeys ever since I first heard Gregory's repertory of stories about the countesses and other budding amazons who try them on for size after the races at Longchamp. So I came on to him:

"I guess we're both on the same floor. I wonder if the rooms are all alike?"

"You can come and look at mine, if you wish!" he answered. "We can compare!"

In his room, he turned out the lights and felt for me in the dark. He grasped the hand I was holding out for fear of bumping into the furniture and guided it to his sex. I wondered what use a club like that could be to a woman. I insisted he turn on the lights so I could inspect the thing; with my own eyes. The penis had rings of flesh and spots, it was monstrous.

"Got a riding crop up here?"

"Of course! What a question! There, on the TV . . . What do you want with it?"

"I want to hear a whip cracking in the night."

"Not too hard, Madame, the owner or the breeder might hear us . . ."

He pulled his jodhpurs halfway down his thighs and bent over the back of a chair. I smacked him lightly. Every two or three strokes, I would put my hand between his legs and stroke his cock from underneath. It was the first time I'd ever caressed a man shorter than I was. I would have felt like a pedophile had it not been for the size of the organ. Finally I sensed he was nicely ripe.

"Pull yourself off!"

He must have been used to women being put off by his cock. He took it in both hands, moved them back and forth a couple of times and immediately shot his load. He stood rubbing his buttocks and looking annoyed. I felt I ought to console him.

"You'll weigh in a few grams lighter tomorrow; it could make a difference . . ."

The next morning, Gregory made no secret of his ill humor. After the hors d'œuvres in the airplane, he'd counted on pursuing his education in the comfort of our suite. But he had spent the night alone: I slept on the sofa in the lounge. In the dining room, his strained smile told the world that nothing had taken place between us, nothing good at any rate. The woman from Nantes, breakfasting with her submissive, shot him a glance full of promise. At another table with a colleague of his, my jockey smiled at me behind his lordship's back. We exchanged gazes loaded with meaning.

Seated in the Cessna, I waited until Gregory had reached the altitude assigned by the control tower. Then I ordered him to turn on the automatic pilot.

"Now Gala, you know those damned things aren't reliable!"

I switched it on myself. Then I caught him unexpectedly by the wrists, brought out a pair of cuffs and manacled his hands together behind his seat. I put a blindfold over his eyes.

"There! . . . You see, we are going to have a little fun this weekend, after all!"

I unbuttoned his shirt and bared his nipples, bruised by the Nantes woman's nails. I pinched one after the other, unhurriedly. I squeezed them with my fingers, kneading the swollen parts. He screamed:

"Get these cuffs off of me, I want to fly my plane myself!"

I took a ball-gag out of my bag. I had to pinch his nose till he opened his mouth; then I pushed the rubber ball past his teeth and buckled the strap behind his neck. I opened his fly and slowly drew the nail of my index finger over the tender skin. He squealed but I knew his weakness. I took the tawny crop he had given me out of its case and patted the tip of his sex with it. The anxiety of not being at the controls spoiled his pleasure. He rolled his head this way and that, hoping I would set him free. I quelled him with a slap and took over the controls. I pushed the stick forward and went into a dive. I pulled up the nose: the plane bucked and stalled. I did a couple of loops in the clear blue sky and felt him squirm. I took nearly as much pleasure from his anxiety as from flying the plane myself. I'd gotten my license in the U.S. ten years before, and was amazed at how quickly it all came back.

I freed him shortly before we landed and knew my disgrace was imminent. When the plane came to rest in front of the terminal, Gregory handed me an envelope with his gaze averted. Disdaining his gift from Angers, I ditched it on the floor of the cabin beside my seat. It blended in perfectly with the tawny leather, until the next woman found it.

SESSION 12

"YOU'RE NOT TOO ANGRY with me for taking her away from you?"

On his third-floor landing, Macha's lover was taunting me. A wrinkled linen shirt stuck out of his trousers. A draft of air ruffled the baby-blond hair which was growing thinner on account of his daily jogging, or so Macha said. Pupils contracted by the adrenaline he was generating, he stood tense as a torero in the doorway of his bachelor pad.

I shook his hand.

"I've come as a neighbor, you might say. I live just on the other side of Saint-Sulpice church."

He had insisted with Macha bringing me to watch him in action. Was he hoping to make "the woman in me" jealous? Or contract an alliance with the dominatrix? Macha must certainly have told him about how we met at the diplomat's, about the bogy-man and the bogy-woman; he would want to rise to the challenge.

"Macha never stops praising you. I just want to understand: a woman with another woman when neither is really a lesbian, that can only be some form of affection . . . If you want my opinion, what our friend needs is an iron hand."

Within a matter of weeks, she'd gotten the key to his flat, a holiday in Rome, and a credit card. He was enchanted by her docility and good looks, and gave her whatever she asked for. And she struck while the iron was hot, before one of them lost interest.

The man had an exaggerated opinion of our relationship, investing it with the same emotional charge that he himself was experiencing. Expecting me to fight tooth and nail. He couldn't imagine the relief I felt whenever my girlfriend could appease her violent thirst at some other fount. By nurturing her deathly masochism in my place, he was giving me a breather.

The black and white checkered tiles set off Macha's lean figure nicely. A lone pawn on a chessboard, standing with her legs held apart by a spreader bar; she looked like a dancer doing the splits. Arms outstretched, eyes down, she was posing. Her head hung weightless. She had muscular legs like Helmut Newton's models, and the stretching of her limbs made the breasts androgynously flat. The tension caused a nervous rigidity in the groin. Her hip joint was like the wing of an albino bat.

It flashed through my mind that constrained thus to immobility, she might just be meditating. Could she endure being left that way all night? I had my doubts . . . Once again I was convinced that she relied on the gaze of the Other to derive pleasure from such an ordeal.

She smiled at me. Whenever a third party was present, the original complicity between us returned. Deep inside, she was laughing at him, a ridiculous man greedy for power over a woman. At him and all the others . . . I could read her thoughts. She strove for the best possible pose. Standing beside me, Arnaud's stance was that of an artist admiring his work. But the telephone rang in the next room and the master slipped away. I went up to Macha, pinched her nipples with my nails and murmured:

"He hasn't found out yet how much you love clips?"

"You're always telling me to keep something for next time," she stuttered mockingly.

Visibly pleased with herself, she went on: "I've been here for three or four hours and it hasn't even occurred to me to make a list in my head of all the clothes I want to buy. I'm happy! It's obvious, isn't it?"

"All the more reason to leave list-making to men. The collector's mania! Remember that American in the bar at Fouquet's who recited baseball statistics, the one we trampled on later in the men's room? And what about those English boys who go out trainspotting, collecting the numbers on locomotives! Don't create a man's mind for yourself!"

Arnaud returned and as he detached his submissive, he began bragging about his equipment. Toys-for-the-boys that went into a locked chest. Screws, nuts, bars, rings, a whole Meccano set for lonely mavericks.

Macha rubbed her sore ankles. She opened her mouth to tell me something, but an icy glance from her master froze the words on her lips. His tone was harsh as he spoke:

"Now, Macha, you're going to show your friend the positions I've taught you. And you're going to perform them in the order I give you."

I knew those positions already: Macha practiced them in the living-room when I was trying to write. There were ten in all. When she offered herself on her knees, I'd stop writing to correct the tilt of her head, the arch of her back.

"Number three!"

The order cracked like a whip. Standing face to the wall, arms spread, calves taut, head hanging, tongue out, Macha was stretching her members so hard that she trembled. I recognized the "Grand frontal panorama."

"You see, it's number three that turns me on most when I have time to come here."

"A lovely tableau vivant!"

"I have my business calls to make, I have to talk to my stockbroker. I can't stand it when she sniffles because I haven't looked at her lately . . . Number seven Macha!"

This was the most acrobatic pose, a "bridge" like we used to do at summer camp. Macha wrapped her wiry fingers around the heels of her shoes, threw her head back.

I sat on one corner of Arnaud's desk and lit up. My friend had told me Arnaud couldn't bear cigarette smoke. He was tapping her on the tongue with the tip of his crop. He hadn't sniffed the smoke yet. He couldn't find fault with her pose and it irked him. Then he caught sight of the lighted cigarette and the regular beat of my foot against the desk. He read my thoughts: I wasn't being paid by the hour . . . This was a courtesy call . . . I'm sure you understand, dear Arnaud . . .

Slipping off the desk and preparing to leave, I sensed the man was at a loss.

"I want to tell you I approve of Macha's choice. You're an attractive man. And you seem quite capable. If you were expecting a hen-fight, you're out of luck. I put her into your hands."

Trying to take control again, he said to Macha:

"Well, can't hang around here all day, love. Got to be going."

But before he went whistling out the door, he kissed the back of my hand with a deliberately distracted air:

"Thank you for your visit; so happy to have met the dominatrix who provides shelter for our little Macha."

He left and our co-owned submissive calmly dressed.

"Well, what do you think of him?"

What can you say to a girl in love?

"Hard, cold, snobbish, spoiled, arrogant."

Deep inside, Macha was over the moon: with all those defects, she'd found a master who really was a cut above the others, the kind only rich kids can afford.

"And what takes the cake is he can't even get a hard-on!" she exclaimed.

Arnaud de Cambrai, an impotent man with his entire family tree behind him. I knew now why he was so keen to keep a girl tied up; it must have felt reassuring.

"How wonderful for a man like him to be loved for what he is . . ."

"Actually, you know, it's his mouth that turns me on. He has my father's mouth."

"Everything passes through the mouth, Macha: words, food . . . seduction. A lover is often hooked on the mouth of the beloved."

It was Macha's dream to marry a French aristocrat like Arnaud. A rich one from a good family.

SESSION 13

BASILE, A.K.A. THE VIKING, sports a thin moustache which hangs down on either side of his chin, an ash-blond mop which must collect bits of food with every forkful. His hair is too long for the executive position he claims to hold. He has my uncle's dark eyes, with those shadows that look like kohl but are natural, Kabyle eyes are often like that. He was a cross between Viking and Arab, just like that uncle of mine, born of an unknown father and who claimed to be half Celt. Basile surfs on the fetishist sites and makes weekly appointments with me.

Sometimes I won't hear from him for a while. Then he'll pop up again with a story about how his plane was struck by lightning over Bora bora, a huge blue flash which the natives took for a sign from the sky. Stranded for days on an ice-floe. Does he make up these adventures to set himself apart from my other submissives? Or maybe some tourist agency does send him to the South Pacific or Peru.

I can imagine him as a tour guide, herding a collection of retired druggists, brow bared to the sun for the benefit of his manly tan.

What does he carry in his luggage during these peregrinations? A woman's stocking? Basile suffers from obstructive sleep apnea (OSA) and sleeps strapped into an apparatus that keeps him alive. Did he use it in the Galapagos? His expeditions are peppered with accidents of every kind. He has a closet full of crutches, canes, braces, surgical collars, and whatnot. Lying naked at my feet, the man endures the only pain he can enjoy: the weight of my stiletto heels.

4:00 P.M. The Viking would soon be here and I felt nonplussed somehow. Wearing a wasp-waist made of amber brocade under a tailored suit of coal-black leather, I stood in front of the mirror, concentrating. I had on smoky stockings with seams, low-cut lambskin stilettos that never left the apartment. I adjusted my round-collared spencer and slit skirt.

I tried to change the frail appearance of my face. Straining to put on a severe look, I was suddenly afraid I'd get bored in mid-session. An apprehension born of my haughty solitude, I'd become a woman who rarely gave more than her toes to venerate, for fear of descending from her pedestal. At the umpteenth performance of the same old play, even knowing the stage is her life and she could never leave it, the actress might throw a fit of hysterics minutes before curtain-time. Playing the same role for the same man can begin to wear.

An eager ring of the doorbell swept away my apprehension. For this man, I'd devoted special care to my private parts and hair removal. The fact is I've never been bored with him. I like him.

The Viking wore a pair of funny crêpe-soled shoes. After a brief chat standing in the living room, I left him to shed his businessman's paraphernalia, tie, watch, cell-phone, headset, and Palm Pilot. My departure meant he was to go into the bathroom, which acted as an airlock where he could divest himself of daily living. Basile needed an isolation booth. It took him a good fifteen minutes to shed his mask, flush away all sorts of mental pollution, scrub himself inside out to be sure to please me.

I had decided he would find me perched on a barstool. He knelt naked at my feet. In keeping with our ritual, he began to lick the shoe I held out for him. He could manipulate my foot without twisting it. Holding it in one hand, eyes always down, he cleaned it carefully with his tongue. The heel, the sides. The strap around my ankle. I wanted to see the leather shine with saliva. I allowed him plenty of time. His moustache tickled me through my stocking.

"Take off my shoe."

I gave him permission to lick my foot through the sheer nylon. But the other foot, still in its shoe, drove him away with a vicious thrust to the chest, while the one he tried to kiss eluded him. He would have to suffer my metal-tipped stiletto if he wanted to go on. The spike made round red marks on his chest. After about ten minutes, he implored a favor: "Madame, if you would just take off one of your stockings, just one . . . just for a moment, please . . ."

I was in two minds. To do as he asked would have been to defer to him, to come down from my pedestal.

"Massage my foot!"

The dilemma he sensed in me clearly gave him pleasure: he had a hard-on.

"Press the soles with both thumbs."

A massage on the pressure points in the hollow of the soles of my feet relaxed me. Now he began squeezing my feet as if to crush the bones. The intensity of his massage had made me go soft. I was choking back a yawn just as he looked up. To keep him guessing, I granted his request to remove a stocking when he no longer was expecting it.

He rolled the nylon between his dexterous thumbs, limbered up his big piano-mover's fingers twisting the filmy veil around my leg. Then he slid it down ever so gently as though removing that second skin might hurt me. Next, he ran his tongue between my toes, the wet hosiery clinging to his lips, again and again with happy little sighs.

I was bored watching the ripples of nylon under his lips. So I smashed the sole of my bare foot against his nose. This was the part he liked best. Toes and ankles arched in a tense, threatening way, as though my foot could become a dildo:

"Do you think you could take it up the ass?"

"I will do my best, Madame . . . I belong to you body and soul . . . I will do anything you wish, Madame, anything at all."

In an hour's time, he would be back in the great social farce, playing clever Dick to his officemates . . . Or else holding forth at the entrance to the Louvre, waving a little agency flag over his head.

I jabbed my heel into his face until his cock once more resembled a soft bent stovepipe. Then I pushed my foot into his mouth, very slowly. His cheeks puffed out, one after the other. He might have been playing the harmonica. Exciting sensations began to run up my leg, electrifying my groin, gradually spreading to my back and shoulders.

Little by little, his mouth was swallowing me. My big toe brushed his glottis. I tried to conceal my pleasure.

"You're so clumsy! Watch out you don't hurt me with your teeth!"

He was like a vampire transfixed by a wooden stake. He took in even more of the appendage, but overreached himself and began to choke. I thought of diving without an aqualung, I thought of his taste for extreme sports and withdrew my foot.

I came down from my perch. Sitting on the sofa, I was more accessible, but felt more vulnerable, too. I drew him to me and gave him my breasts to suck. He did so with a kind of deference but no enthusiasm. Tits, breast-feeding, that wasn't his thing. But elsewhere he was more enterprising, his big hands went around my waist and tried to squeeze the breath out of me. Any other submissive would have got his face slapped for coming on that way. I felt for the tender skin on the backs of his hands . . . and two twisting pinches brought a shriek of pain and instant deliverance.

What interested him were the deep parts . . . what interested us, I should say. I grabbed a handful of hair and led his face to my crotch. He ran his moist tongue over every millimeter of exposed flesh between stockings and panties. My royal scepter hung negligently from one hand, a riding crop that was now little more than a pathetic symbol of power. In fact, if this went on much longer, I might suddenly feel so ashamed I'd use it to punish him in earnest for having let myself go like this . . .

Basile's forehead was now resting against my vulva. He was capable of a lighter touch if one was called for and now he deliberately nuzzled his way through my defenses. His nose was soon scrounging around inside and I still made no objection. Nothing. The dominatrix was taking no calls. I just kept tapping him lightly on the back, while waves of desire threw my sex against his mouth.

I became so fascinated by the sight of my uncle's dark eyes looking out over the top of my tuft that I no longer saw where the crop fell. I was hitting him as a matter of principle, like a baby shaking its rattle because someone is watching. Thrown off balance by the thrusting face, the Great Dominatrix stumbled backward. He'd been wanking me off with his chin and nose! He'd broken the rules.

"Since when do you look mistresses in the eye?" I

deliberately used the plural, to remind him he was just another john paying for the services of the dominas on the "scene." But he went on looking. I rained lashes helter-skelter on his back. I was taking revenge for my spell of weakness as a desired woman. I gave him a sharp cut on the fat tip of one love-handle and he finally shut his eyes.

Now I could curl up in my own personal pleasure. I was savoring my every sensation when his arms lifted me from the sofa. I started whipping harder: his bull's neck, his face, his chest. My crop glanced off the forearm he put up to protect himself.

His hungry eyes were glued to my face. His goal was the surrender of my dominant role; he wanted me to let go. The changes that pleasure had brought to my face had an electrifying effect on the man. His tongue became suddenly knowledgeable, as if he'd read some sex manual on cunnilingus. Actually, I believed he was trying out techniques utterly new to him, anticipating my expectations through some telepathic fluid. He blew on my sex, backed off teasingly, studied it between his thumb and forefinger. He shot me a quick look to make sure I was paying careful attention to everything that went on. While his hands squeezed my waist, his tongue wormed its way inside. He took a big breath, pushed his nose in, brought his moustache into play, that ridiculous brush of his which he maneuvered among the folds of flesh like a tiny silk scarf. His massive shoulders were turning red from my nails. I always like the pink trails that appear on his fair skin when I claw him. When I first met him, he'd been perfectly straight: "I'm a married man; no marks, please." We were in limbo, where scream and echo meet. I was the echo of his scream. Or the other way around . . . I couldn't remember . . . He was watching for my orgasm like a harbor pilot eager to bring it safely to port. He was expecting me to push his head away as I sometimes did, or on the contrary, keep him there by the hair. But I came like an octopus clinging to his face. He drank my juices and then, since I made no effort to oppose him, a rag of flesh languishing on the arm of the sofa, he went on licking in reparation.

The first orgasm was, if I may say so, a "core item." The Viking now was running the tip of his tongue over the whole clitoral zone below the pubis. His hand was pressing on the mons veneris. His tongue patted the mucous membranes, drew butterfly wings around my lips. He was operating in conquered territory, I was irradiated through and through. A second orgasm engulfed me and I turned to jelly right before his greedy eyes. Nothing ethereal, quite the contrary. My heart was knocking against my tailbone, thumping the backs of my knees clamped around his neck.

The apartment was silent. The Miles Davis record had ended long ago. A few engines roared by in the street below. I lay the crop across his mouth. He was no longer allowed to approach me.

I took off my rings and my watch. I wanted to play midwife . . . in reverse. I wanted to see his asshole swallow my fist. I pulled on a surgical glove that emphasized the slenderness of my hand. Eight inches of it, from nails to wrist. It wasn't too difficult to get the open hand inside and then make a fist. But the trick was to curl one's fingers around the thumb first.

"Just four fingers . . . One more effort, Basile . . . Go on Viking, push your buttocks towards me . . . You're the one who has to do it . . . bugger yourself all on your own . . . Do it for me!"

On all fours in front of the sofa, he lay his head on the hardwood floor. In this position, he opened up by pulling his buttocks apart. His anus looked like the neck of a decanter. I went in further still. Sexually, there is nothing less exciting than to rummage about in someone's entrails, but mentally it soon becomes a kind of madness. All my strength was concentrated in my wrist. Thanks to the slowness of his movements to and fro, I was gaining ground. My five fingers had vanished into the grotto. The root of the thumb still wouldn't go in. I ran my finger around the rim, massaged his prostate in passing. Basile groaned. When my thumb folded into my palm finally vanished inside him, all his organs began trembling simultaneously around my fingers. He came on the hardwood parquet.

Then he lay on his back and slept for a few minutes. The sound of my heels near his face brought him awake.

He splattered the bathroom walls, left two soaking wet bath-towels and a cake of soap in a pool of water near the bathtub. As he left, he thanked me with evasive eyes.

EPILOGUE

I WAS RECOVERING from a night of champagne drinking when I found a message from Macha on the answering machine. Some weird story about credit cards which her stutter made incomprehensible.

It was around 3:00 P.M. when I arrived at the central police station in the eighth *arrondissement* where she was under arrest. A young police officer was toying with the flogger found in her bag. She sat behind the bars of a big cage looking pale and wearing a blue dress that buttoned up the front, the kind you can take off without spoiling your hairdo. On a desk lay a pile of bags from all her favorite shops. The officer sat me down across from a typewriter and began tapping on the desk in an offhand way with a car-key.

"Does this young woman live with you?"

"When she's in France, yes . . . I put her up."

"Does she have a profession?"

"She's a model, and it's not an easy way to earn a living!"

"But it does have its advantages. Look here!"

He opened a drawer filled with credit cards.

"How do you explain a foreigner having that many accounts with French banks?"

"Can we discuss this in private?"

On the other side of an office door, he pointed to a moleskin chair. And so I had to explain that Macha took many lovers.

"A nymphomaniac?"

"You might say that."

"She needs a whip to get her going, your girlfriend?"

"Other people like television cables. A little whip like that is pretty harmless."

"But one thing leads to another!"

"Now don't go mixing everything up! There are no drugs involved, there's nothing illegal about any of it. Let her go, I'll vouch for her."

That morning, Macha had awoken in the home of a little master who'd bought her in a slave sale at the Misfits Club, on Rue Crussole. It was still early, something like 10:00 A.M. Rather than wake me up with the noise the front door made, she went for a little shopping spree on Faubourg Saint-Honoré. It was in Gramani's that she confused the pin-numbers of two of her various credit cards. There was the one she had from Arnaud, the diplomat's *Carte Bleue*, Eddie's *Carte d'Or* and others which she carried together in her handbag. She was so upset by this early morning failure of memory that she dropped her wallet and the half-dozen cards fell out. Convinced they had a thief on their hands, the management called the police.

In spite of all my pleading, Macha flew back to Sweden

three days later. She believed she had lost face, and never wanted to see her masters again. It was the very day she left, returning home from the airport, that I found a pert little redhead named Lea waiting at my apartment door. Macha had given her the address. Her breasts stood out like eggs under the white tee-shirt. I tugged at the V-neckline to check what I'd guessed at behind the cloth: a chrome-plated ring piercing her right breast, joined to the nipple on either side by the emerald-green tail of a snake tattoo. I rolled up her shirt, took hold of the ring, and led her to the center of my living room.

Memoirs of a Left Bank Dominatrix

I

I LOVE FAR-EASTERN COOKING, the bright red lanterns of Chinese restaurants and on that particular evening the scarlet hue of Sylvain's high-tops as we dined together on Brompton Road, London. Sitting opposite me, the young man stretched his oversized legs under the table and watched me search for Chinese words to discuss our order with a waitress in lamé leggings. I'm seventeen inches shorter and ten years older than Sylvain. We're both from Burgundy; we both have thick dark hair. I wear mine in a Louise Brooks bob, which emphasizes my delicate features, and sometimes, in private, I give my friend's crew-cut a good pull. There is a tacit pact between us, a complicity of old cohorts. Wherever we are, the curiosity in our eyes makes us twins. During the fifteen years our *amitié amoureuse* has lasted, he has never shown an ounce of jealousy.

It was Ascension Day weekend and my faithful friend

had offered to come with me to London while I collected commissions from "my" gamblers in a casino there. Long before the Asian financial crisis, I'd put together a "portfolio" of punters, wealthy Malaysians, mostly of Chinese descent. I still managed to keep a few in tow. Like a commodities broker counseling clients, I shepherded my flock from one casino to another, Madrid or Monte Carlo, negotiating with the managers gifts to serve as bait: a taste of winter sports, for example, with all the equipment and warm clothes lent them for the day and a helicopter to fly them up and back. They also had access to the top call girl networks. When my gamblers' losses were heavy enough, the casino would hand me a sizable tip.

"I've ordered jellyfish " I announced to Sylvain.

"Cold?" he asked, stroking the hair on his chest through the opening in his shirt. At a nearby table, I noticed a husky Englishwoman dining alone, with a plump Doberman at her feet. She was impressing the waitress with guttural Chinese.

"No, *flambées!* Have you seen that creature? I'd swear she's got a wig on under that hat . . . And stop touching your chest like that to prove how manly you are."

Sylvain was properly mortified and laid his hands on either side of his plate. I still had my eyes on the Englishwoman speaking impeccable Cantonese to the waitress. As she backed away from the table, still giggling, she bumped into the kitchen door. I called out to the woman:

"Ni shuo hanyu ma?" (Do you speak Chinese?) *"Shuo! Hong Kong de hua, Quantonghua, greasy spoon de hua!"* (I speak Hong Kong dialect, greasy spoon lingo!) "*Je parle aussi le français à mes amis"* she added in a friendly voice.

Turning up the brim of her hat, she rose to her feet; her dog followed suit and began to sing.

"This is Beauty and I'm the Beast," the Englishwoman

said. “May I sit with you? Cathy just *adores* spareribs. I come all the way across London to eat in my favorite restaurant! And Cathy gets a run through Hyde Park before we go home. Beauty is called Cathy and I’m Hazel.”

“Delighted. We live in Paris.”

Hazel sat next to Sylvain. The overweight dog made a pathetic attempt to leap onto her mistress’s lap, and fell on the floor with a bump.

Hazel looked at Sylvain through half-closed eyes. “In spite of appearances,” she said in English, “you are a woman stuck in a man’s body. I can always spot a woman in male guise. *Bas les masques!* I’m a girl born in a boy’s body. I like you two. You’re on foot, aren’t you? Let me take you for a spin through the lungs of London!”

“With you, we’d even take the bus,” Sylvain exclaimed enthusiastically, electrified by these unexpected revelations, excited by the prospects of his new double gender. Hazel was devouring strips of jellyfish, plucked from our plates with her fingers, and the sucking noises shook Sylvain out of his reverie. When he held his plate out to me, his expressive face seemed touched by the grace of the offering: His whole being thanked me for serving him. Expecting the same gratitude, Hazel handed him a pair of chopsticks. Receiving only a pinched smile in return, she launched into French:

“In China, jellyfish are the food of fisherman, of *pêcheurs* . . . I, too, am a *pécheur* . . . a sinner! One of the many words in your language with multiple meanings, Madame! But in China, it’s just your poor fisherman and his meager catch. Come away from here and let us sin together! Normally, I would now vomit on the table as proof I’ve eaten well; I like to “repeat” the meal, as it were. Tonight, however, I shall spare you.”

Catching a whiff of the garbage bins behind a restaurant, Cathy dragged us into a back alley as muddy as any in

Canton Guangzhou. Hazel was suitably modest when I complimented her on her fluency in Chinese and French. Her Chinese dated from her childhood in Hong Kong, where her colonial army father was stationed. As for her French, she was originally from Ireland, whose language in its golden past had contained many French words and which had even had French queens: Marmalade comes from "Marie malade"; when Mary Stuart was ill, she'd had a craving for candied oranges. Hazel had always dreamt of being Marie-Antoinette, the deposed outcast, and so she raised one arm and shouted for all to hear "Vive la Fra-an-an-z!" Sylvain did the same, and then we all screamed in unison "Vive la Fra-an-an-z!" making fierce faces like patriots on the barricades. Inadvertently, Hazel pressed the doorbell on a private house: distant chimes struck the first notes of the Marseillaise. A man and a woman, presumably the householders, leaned out of an open window. Sylvain bellowed for their benefit "Vive la Fra-an-an-z." Hazel and I joined in. Overhead, the woman was trying to shut the window. Her husband seemed reluctant, but she won out in the end. Standing behind the glass like a schoolboy in Coventry, the man raised his fist and shouted: "Viv' la Fran-an-an-tze!" The woman shooed away the rebel, pressed her face to the window, and motioned for us to decamp. Hazel gave her the finger: "Hang her from a lamp-post!" For our ears, she grumbled: "Ought to bring back the guillotine for people like that!"

As we rode through Hyde Park in Hazel's Jaguar coupé, it began to drizzle. Sylvain was folded up on the back seat next to Cathy, the "Doberwoman," bravely enduring her fetid breath on his face. The driver had laid her hat on my lap, so I tried it on.

"Too big for you, but I have more. Believe it or not, every time someone dies, I buy a new hat for the funeral. It's not like a wedding; you can't really compete with the heroine of the day, a corpse isn't jealous. Look how depressing Hyde Park is in the rain!"

She braked near a clump of trees. Cathy leaped out and raced for the bushes like a pig grubbing for truffles. Taking advantage of the dog's absence, Hazel pushed her seat back, pulled up her skirt, and straightened her stockings.

"I met Anna under those trees. I'll tell you about that business while Cathy attends to hers.

"I'm out walking my dog one evening and I stop to pull up my stockings when this pot-bellied little man walks by and looks me over. He especially admires my ample bosom. So I say to him: "Five grand for breasts like these!" The man belches, comes closer, and says with a Scottish accent and a worried voice: "Not hormones, I hope?" all the while feeling them very carefully. As one colonial subject to another, we fall to talking. Now it turns out that this bus driver, who's just stopped for a pee in the park, has been dreaming for years of having breasts like mine. And in the end, he spills all his fantasies right there under the oaks; it's wonderfully crude and natural-like. I insist he take out his cock then and there. I examine it and weigh it in my hand, then I lend him my high heels. After he's done a few turns on the frozen turf, I promise him an appointment with a surgeon friend of mine for a complete sex-change.

"All the poor bloke had ever seen in his life was the number twelve bus route! His transformation took three months until the final operation. The results were disastrous. I think Anna should have stayed a man. I'll introduce you to her, but alas! it's too late to see the difference between 'before' and 'after.'

"On her first day out, I sent her to the supermarket with a three-page shopping list and a pound note in her pocket. Already, Anna began to complain: 'A measly pound?' she said. 'That won't even buy a pair of rubber gloves!' Well, then I had to explain how a woman has be able to support her starving children on less than that, and even find a pittance for that drunken husband of hers! She wound up at the police station! Booked her for shoplifting, they did. When she got out on bail, I agreed to let her have a little pocket money if she'd be hostess for my johns: I'm a dominatrix by profession."

"A *dominatrix*?"

"The same as you, Madame . . . I was watching your behavior with your friend Sylvain: we belong to the same race.

"Later, I taught Anna to bake cookies that seem stale when they come out of the oven. They're for my most masochistic johns. And on the day of the Mistress's soup, it's her job to prepare it.

"And now you'll eat the Mistress's soup!!" she chortled for Sylvain's benefit, beating time with her hand. With ogrelike tones we repeated after her: "And now . . . you will eat . . . the Mistress's cookies!!" and had a good laugh.

"Anna admitted she'd agreed to the operation to be like me, but actually I've never crossed the Rubicon. I'd rather see it inflicted on others and keep my male attributes. Well, day after day, I inspected her new sex, that withered scrap of flesh, ugh! One day, I promised her twenty quid if she'd sit on a man's face. The john's teeth were chattering; he'd already tasted my cakes and my soup and he was terrified I was going to stuff his mouth full of more disgusting food. Well, when the session was over, he complained he'd never seen anything so revolting as Anna's cunt. The monster went back to her seat in the vestibule, waiting for the next client, with the twenty pound note in her bra. The bus company finally took her on again, and now she drives in a skirt. All right, I think the dog's finished, I'll take you to my digs."

"Cathy! Let's go, Beauty!"

Cathy came lumbering out of the dark, jumped into the car, and wiped her paws on Sylvain, who fought unsuccessfully to save his white shirt.

In a basement flat near Buckingham Palace (not only were they neighbors, but the Queen used Hazel's perfume, too), Anna was reclining in a dentist's chair. She'd gone to sleep over an open bottle of nail polish and the brush had stained her teeth. I took Sylvain aside:

"This one's on drugs, no?"

Hazel overheard me: " Of course, she is! Every day she pinches enough from my bag to buy her dose. See what happens when you can't identify with the role you want to play?"

Hazel cleaned Anna's teeth with polish-remover.

"She's the only person I know who's willing to take care of my dog. So we keep her here in spite of everything, don't we little Anna?"

"Hussssh!" sighed the creature.

"Give her a fag . . . You'll see, she can smoke in her sleep."

"You are a mistress of provocation!" Sylvain exclaimed, inserting a lighted cigarette between the sleeping Anna's lips. The smoke billowed out through her nose. Picking up a box of dry dog food, Hazel pointed us towards a door hidden behind a thick drape. In the living room, sofas covered with army blankets were arranged in a semi-circle around an electric log-fire. On the wall, there were ordnance maps.

"Do either of you play backgammon?"

In the course of the evening, Hazel beat Sylvain several times. That "daughter" and "granddaughter" of army officers had a whole range of tactics; she would let her opponent capture as many as fifteen pieces and then without warning take over the game.

Around 4:00 A.M., we laid Anna on the floor with her thumb in her mouth so she wouldn't swallow her tongue. Hazel covered her with a wool plaid.

It was decided that Sylvain would also spend the night on the floor by the sofa where Hazel bedded me down. I stroked the boy's neck and he fell asleep murmuring "Vive la France."

The next day he was prancing joyfully about the kitchen, because Anna had just offered to take him to work with her. The prospect of traveling the length of the No. 12 bus route filled him with delight.

"Don't you dare go out of London!"

"The Number Twelve goes out of London?" asked my friend.

"It certainly does not, and there'll be no detours! My bus-driving friend bloody well knows what I'm on about, doesn't she?"

As soon as they'd left, Hazel showed me her torture chamber. The costumes used for "cabaret"—as Hazel called domination games—hung from spikes. Some of these were telescopic, with hooks on the end, and could be pulled out from the wall. I imagined a half-dozen businessmen hanging by the coat-collars, the shorter spikes pressing into their backs. The dungeon's *pièce de résistance* stood opposite the bed where the mistress relaxed after working hours: a guillotine. I fingered it with respect.

"It's a copy, made in England: French antiques cost a leg and an arm!" she said, poo-pooing my deference. "No people on the planet love ill-treatment more than the British, especially if they've been to public school," she explained, putting on a gold-braided army jacket. "If I'd lived in the eighteenth century, I'd have belonged to the Hellfire Club, whose members included the Prince of

Wales, the Lord Mayor of London, the Earl of Sandwich, and the Earl of Bute, who was Prime Minister for a while. Horribly sadistic criminal orgies went on there. As a matter of fact, Lord Sandwich's sexual appetites lost Hawaii for England. But Queen Victoria put paid to those savage goings-on," she went on campily, waving a Union Jack which she then proceeded to wrap around her blonde locks like a turban. "In public schools, which is what we call private schools for the rich, the headmasters and older boys still beat the young ones with belts. The kids acquire a taste for that sort of thing and when they grow up they pay professionals to cane them, because they don't dare discuss their little foibles with their wives."

Hazel's maid, a Scottish transsexual with pale eyes and drooping lids, who took appointments on the telephone, ushered in the first customer of the day. He sat leafing through magazines in the waiting room. When Hazel mentioned an assistant, I heard him object, no doubt because he thought it was Anna.

Hazel made him crawl into the bedroom and kneel before me. I found the sight of that red-faced, pot-bellied man repellant, but it was too late. I couldn't go back on my agreement with Hazel and didn't want to lose face by beating a retreat, as I was sorely tempted to do. I struck a contemptuous pose and ordered him to lick the high-heeled shoes of his French mistress, over from the continent specially to test his docility. Once the submissive had his head down so I couldn't see his face, he upset me less. He took my heel deep into his mouth, contorting his arms to keep the shoe in his hands. He sucked the leather protuberance until a cramp developed in my leg. I trod on his fists with a brutality which surprised me.

"Hands flat on the floor, not bunched up like stumps! Show a little gracefulness, you bloody tea-drinking, whisky-drinking, sherry-drinking porridge-eater!"

"I sometimes drink wine, champagne or cognac, Mistress," he whispered insolently.

"And what about your Mistress's soup, do you get that down without a whimper? Do you?"

"From your hand, madame, I will drink anything with pleasure."

My kneeling guinea pig wiggled the shiny seat of his trousers in a gesture of exhibitionistic contentment. On a shelf, I spied a bottle of "Night-Nurse," a combination cough syrup and sleeping-potion, poured half of it into a bowl of vodka, and held it out to the balding skull:

"Drink up, vermin! Down the hatch!"

His eyes glued on my shoes, he lapped up the potion and then sat gulping over the bowl like a surfeited dog.

"Now dance for me. Remember you're here to make me laugh and excite me, if you think you can manage it, do you understand?"

"Yes, Mistress."

He began bobbing on his knees, his shoulders and elbows beat time to the rear, his belly joggled out in front.

"You look like a duck out of the Arabian Nights! If the princesses saw you, they'd have your head off! Do something else, fool!"

The man tried to look coy, stood up, and went into a gogo act, writhing to the strains of imaginary music, sticking out his ass at me, awkwardly undoing his trousers. Fly unzipped, his eyes upturned, tongue protruding from his lips, he faced me stroking himself languidly until his tongue began to twitch nervously, half-paralyzed by what he'd drunk. He collapsed onto the carpet where he continued to masturbate.

"Am I to your taste, Madame? Will you hire me for your Moulin Rouge?" Hazel suddenly made her appearance, a long skirt floating around her boots, and pointed ring-laden fingers at the john: "Hang him from a lamppost!" She helped the man to his feet and we got him dressed. At the door, he looked about for his umbrella to lean on; the mistress of the house gave him a cane: A john with rheumatism had forgotten it the day before. When he was gone, she exclaimed: "With these Englishmen, cabaret is often *le carnaval des animaux!*"

The next day, the No. 12 bus, with Sylvain driving in Anna's stead, took me to the casino where my Chinese gamblers had been betting heavily in recent days. After several runs in the driver's seat, my friend claimed to know the city by heart. I trembled at the thought of the personnel seeing their delegate for Southeast Asia arriving in such a rig, but at the casino door there were only jaundiced Pakistanis.

When I returned to the bus with the commissions on my Malaysians' losses in my bag, two old ladies were sitting on the plush seats. As Sylvain was dropping them off in Trafalgar Square, he caught his hand in the cab-door. I treated him with a shot of scotch and bandaged the bruise with a Woolworth's stocking.

II

"Are you Masolatex?"

"Call me Guillaume! I just love your code-name: Belledomino . . . so cryptic! Only at a woman's feet can a man forget the pointlessness of life, you know that, don't you? Is it all right to ask your first name? The one you care to give me, of course . . ."

"Gala."

It was after that session in Hazel's dungeon that I'd begun using this name with the men I contacted on the Minitel[1], because it cracked like a whip and because it had belonged to Dali's wife. That little lady in black had seen through me from the start and used to kick me under the table at the informal dinner-parties the painter gave at the Hôtel Meurice. Gala Dali's gratuitous animosity still amuses me today. I had just turned twenty when I deposited in the artist's gift-urn—a bidet in the center of the living room—an armless doll which he proceeded to carry around all evening. It was actually a boy baby in drag, a miniature version of the doll my mother had given me when I was a little girl and which she'd disguised with a wig when I complained it was a boy, causing what was to prove a permanent gender confusion in my mind. In 1989, I borrowed Madame Dali's first name to dominate men in search of a phallic woman.

At the other end of the phone, Masolatex laid his cards on the table: He was so dissatisfied with professional mistresses that he was beginning to feel like an anthropologist researching the subject. His dream was true romance with an intellectual, sensual domina. On those Minitel sites, where the only rule was instant punishment and pleasure, there was something refreshing about his quest. I was touched. It was as if I'd discovered a litter of newborn kittens in my living room, or a young bullfighter in pink stockings and gold jacket asleep on my couch. Such bursts of sentimentality are the Achilles' heel of many a dominatrix, as if it was our lot to sooth the anxieties of yapping puppies.

Masolatex told me how he loved to dress up, and carried on about his PVC, rubber, and latex gear, collected over the years.

"Not many Frenchmen are fetishists, but I am . . . sort of. I hope you won't mind, dear Gala?"

I suppressed a chuckle at his oh-so-familiar clothing obsessions and stated my usual price for a first encounter with a "patient": 1,500 francs.

"That's tops for Paris, you know . . ." He wanted to prove he knew his way around the scene. "Any equipment?"

"A bullwhip, a riding-crop . . . and ten razor-sharp fingernails."

I told him to come to me the following Thursday.

My apartment house is a stone's throw from the Odéon theater. The seventeenth century built its walls thick and its ceilings high. Yet the summer heat was oppressive that evening in the two-room apartment where I ply my trade. After an especially good rendition of my "poor-out-of-work-me" number to my mother over the phone, I slipped a pale green moiré waspy trimmed with black lace over my hips and glued on false lashes, with a touch of kohl to emphasize the mystery of my brown eyes. I pulled on a lambskin suit, with a skirt that laced over the buttocks, panties that laced up the sides, and a short jacket with metal studs. Balanced on my six-inch heels in front of the full-length living-room mirror, I threw back my shoulders and stroked my firm breasts.

At five minutes to the hour, I wiped my armpits dry.

Masolatex had scarcely entered my living room when he declared his mad passion for latex, "that second skin" . . . Yet he hated having to put talc in the gloves, stockings, and corsets to get them on, hated the contortions required to get them off. I should follow his advice and take only PVC on my travels, so much lighter and easier to put on. He conjured up the magic glitter of that shiny plastic, like a Paris sidewalk after the rain.

The big bag he'd brought was brim-full of black gear cut to fit his six-foot frame. In two bounds, my cat sprang inside. Guillaume began carefully laying out his gear on a high table, with the little busybody sniffing each garment in turn.

As Guillaume gave me the history of each item, his feverish eye and a wealth of detail revealed the true collector. His eloquence, his noble bearing, and his tailored English clothes (matted wool suits for best, Swiss cotton shirts for everyday), these were Guillaume's hallmarks. At forty, he could look ten years younger if he paused before a mirror to smooth away the furrows of irritation and fatigue. With childish candor, he added that a co-worker at his office always said "he needed to look his best even to answer the phone." As a marketing consultant, Guillaume cultivated his image.

My eyes always give me away, especially when a quirk of personality, a special charm or defect attracts me to someone. I'm something of a fetishist myself, but like most women, my priorities go to certain body parts—the slim hands of an intellectual or the rough, callused palms of a cabinet-maker, high cheekbones, a dimpled chin, a fleshy mouth, a wide forehead or "love-handles." I've been known to follow a man on the grands boulevards for blocks, unable to tear my eyes away from the roundness of a pair of buttocks under tight trousers.

Always attracted to shiny things, I was like a magpie transfixed by Guillaume's performance: he had the easy grace of an educated adolescent. His affected chatter reminded me of Anthony Perkins as a door-to-door vacuum-cleaner salesman. His demonstration was meant to be seductive, but failed to arouse me. As he held out this or that piece of gear for my inspection, he looked like a store-window dummy come to life, a pixie from a fairy tale book.

And yet somehow that conjuring act of his, pulling yoked waspies and zippered garter-belts out of a bag, suddenly became quite magical to my wondering eyes.

The inventory ended with a thick gladiator's corset: low-cut, wasp-waisted, molded in black plastic that shone like Vietnamese lacquer. A famous mistress had designed it specially for him. He told me the price. It was this strict breastplate that I ordered him to put on, together with rubber gloves and stockings.

Stripped naked, the tip of his tongue protruding from the corner of his mouth, Guillaume rolled the tops of the stockings between thumb and forefinger with childlike concentration, inserted his toes into the elastic sheath. He had a slender, athletic build, matted hair on his chest, but frail shoulders for his height. Halfway between the eyes and the coal-black hair, two diagonal furrows over the right eyebrow belied the innocent smile, revealed a diabolical side to his personality.

Once on his knees, the youthful smile vanished. He stopped chattering, ready to obey. I slipped a PVC collar around his neck, fastened twin shackles to it, strapped leather cuffs on his wrists, pulled his hands up past his shoulder-blades and tied them to the choker.

Behind Guillaume's submissiveness, I could sense some deep hurt. His whole being cried out for violent punishment. Often enough, when a man's at the end of his tether, been controlling himself, repressing himself too long, he needs to be scolded, humiliated, beaten by a woman. In a flash of tenderness, it occurred to me that a marketing consultant is like the horse whose job is to excite the others before the race but is never allowed to jump the fences! Looking up with a bitter pout, Guillaume saw me as a combination schoolmistress and winning post. I decided to give him a reason for that hangdog look. My riding crop came down hard on his scrawny buttocks. As my arm rose and fell to a steady beat, he stared off into some astral void. I was catching the spirit of his mystical ecstasy, starting to feel aroused. Alas! However hard I struck, that foretaste was all I could achieve. I had a glimpse of intense, buoyant pleasures to come, but getting there would take a much stronger commitment than a mere willingness to accommodate another person's desire. I went on with the whipping, but my heart wasn't in it and eventually my arm grew tired.

"Lick my feet!"

He plunged. His experienced tongue burrowed skillfully around my toes. Damp with sweat, my sheer smoke stockings clung pleasantly to my skin . . . A wave of electric pleasure thrilled down the nape of my neck at last. I gave him his instructions in my most hypnotic tones: His mouth moved slowly up my leg to the tender inside of my thigh. But at the top of the stocking, his quickness grew fearful, his instrument went dry.

"Work up more saliva!"

Forehead dripping with sweat, he pumped his tongue inside his mouth and went down again. At the hem of my miniskirt, he paused and swallowed hard. Now I was excited too; my flesh and my sex were becoming moist. I unfastened a shoulder-strap, thrust a nipple at him. His tongue darted out and lapped at the bare flesh: "Lick it! Suck it!" His tongue traveled lightly over the skin—"Go on, lick it!" My voice was suddenly hoarse with excitement.

I withdrew to my pedestal again, a comic-book domina, scolding him for sloshing his tongue around my nipple like a limp dishrag. On that flimsy pretext, I dug my sharp nails into his shoulder tendons, thrilling with pleasure as I punished him for his clumsy haste. I began pinching his swollen nipples between my nails, completely in tune with his pain, echoing it instinctively in my ecstasy.

But under his garter-belt, Guillaume's sex hung obstinately limp. "This guy must play with himself," I thought. "When a real life mistress comes along, he can't handle it." I was surprised to find myself making excuses for Guillaume's impotence, or rather for my own failure to arouse him. After all, he'd come in search of the Absolute, not anything so transient, so trivial as an orgasm or ejaculation.

The sight of his martyred nipples sent a tingle of excitement through my belly. I dug my nails deep into the tender skin beneath the shiny collar. His tongue explored my navel, moved downward . . .

With his nose buried in my pubic hair, he suddenly announced he'd thought of plucking his chest.

"Keep your manly attributes; I have no use for effeminate men."

The sound of my own voice broke the spell. The furniture leapt into view. The music was suddenly much louder: The Thelonious Monk Quintet was playing full-blast, the whole combo was in my living-room. What was I doing there, with this handsome young man in a corset, kneeling at my feet, dripping sweat on my parquet floor? Suddenly weary of my role, annoyed at the lack of any tangible homage, I announced that the session was over.

"Already!" He sighed, pulling himself up onto his high heels. Muscle fatigue made him move like a disjointed puppet. The two diagonal furrows had vanished from his forehead and his face seemed much younger. He rubbed his sore knees like a schoolboy and held out his forearms for me to hear the sloshing inside the rubber sleeves:

"I think there's even more sweat in the stockings!"

He dressed with the same dexterity he had shown putting on his rubber gear.

As the last mesmeric wisps trailed away, a cramp in my arch from the extra-high heels brought me down to earth again. I took his money and dismissed him.

III

Guillaume must have been about my fifteenth client. When he had gone, I felt annoyed with myself, with this Barbie doll mistress who was falling for a john, this hard-boiled chick suddenly ready to sit on a bloated cock! And I was the gal who always hung up the phone when anyone mentioned *la finition manuelle*, who made some of her regulars strap their cocks between their legs before they came to see her!

A lot of French dominatrixes are actually hookers with a specialty, and they fuck their submissives. I feel closer to the ones who see themselves as compassionate nurses, charitable souls who occasionally take pity on tiny tots starved for caresses, who don't always have the heart to send away a john burdened with a swollen protuberance.

Once a male dominator I know told me about a brothel in the Rue Saint-Denis where the madam used to let him have his pick of some fifteen docile girls whom he was free to use as he pleased, fucking them in the most humiliating positions, front or back, according to his mood. In Berlin, where such places still thrive, a hostess recently offered the same friend women who could be dominant or submissive, whichever the customer fancied. I envied such women that all-round versatility, that wonderful capacity to enjoy pain as much as pleasure, even if their apathy was merely a disguise for bulimia or sheer despair. The first person who ever called me "Mistress" was just such a woman, "la petite Fanfan."

It was the dead of winter and there was a party of actors and writers in some movie director's apartment. A guest had just spilled her fruit cup on the floor when Fanfan made her entrance. She squatted down at once and began to clean the carpet, displaying her full breasts and the tops of her thighs. No one could ignore her: she was naked under a black mink coat which emphasized the pallor of her skin. She might have been mistaken for a Japanese, and has in fact since become one, in the Itabashi district of Tokyo. Aware of our lascivious gazes, she writhed gracefully at our feet, rubbing a damp sponge back and forth over the stain. Then she disappeared into the master bedroom to deposit her big orange bag and scarf on the bed with the coats and hats. Still wearing the mink, she returned and began chatting with the guests, her cheerful, expressive little phiz bobbing from group to group, daintily swilling champagne. She would ask perfect strangers to fill her empty glass and thank them with dazzling warmth and affection. Her cleavage was plainly visible above the two buttons of the coat. Everyone stared, expecting to see her naked at any moment.

It was late, 3:00 A.M. or thereabouts when the woman went to get her things. She had eyed me several times before, but now she walked straight at me and asked me to come with her.

We were alone in the bedroom. She reached into her bag by the bed: "Look what I bring to parties!" She took out a riding crop, got down on all fours, and put it in her mouth like a dog with a stick. I didn't turn a hair. She began gently butting up against my legs. I took the instrument and laid it on the bed, trying to play it cool. But I couldn't resist those imploring eyes and she did get a couple of resounding thwacks on the buttocks that protruded from beneath the mink, before I dropped the crop back into the orange bag.

The following week, I found myself dominating Fanfan with one of her "masters." Afterwards, she made him pay us both for our time. In those days, she worked for the Ministry of Education. She has since moved to Japan and settled down with a retired samurai, giving up debauchery for calligraphy, ikebana, the art of the fan, and other exercises in perfection.

I often still see Fanfan in my daydreams, rolling her eyes in ecstasy, her bodice smeared with sperm, showing up at my place in the middle of the night, besmirched by the partner-swappers in some nightclub where a master had taken her to lend her to other men. I remember once coming out of a high-class club near Paris where she'd taken me: I can still see the high fence, the security guards, her slender white hands splayed out on the windows of the limousine driving us home, and the devoted lips of our caretakers who bestowed passing kisses on fingers still sticky from a heavy night.

Compared with Fanfan's, mine was a modest sexual appetite. I exercised it on the male playthings of an entourage that was 100 percent sensuous and sexual, since my entire existence was steeped in eroticism, even the most innocent actions: I would often catch myself misreading certain words in the newspaper . . . In the company of those gentle, malleable men, I was rediscovering the games of my childhood.

As a little girl, I spent all my vacations at our family home in the austere Burgundy forest. From June to September, the days ticked by monotonously, in and around the noisy sawmill owned by doting grandparents. To make up for the dearth of real playmates, imaginary ones came to life and played opposite me—James Dean, among others, laughed heartily at my pranks. When I was overcome with boredom, I'd go all the way to the nearest highway, ready to jump into the first car that stopped. Squatting on the grassy embankment, I watched and listened, making plans for distant escapades inspired by the red-leather volumes of Jules Verne in my grandparents' attic. But when a car finally did appear on the horizon, I would make no attempt to thumb a ride: I was learning to live with my fantasies.

Escorted by their parents, my first victims came to spend Sundays at "The Saw," as the lumber-mill was called in the family. After ten o'clock mass in the village church—a half-hour of torture, kneeling on a rough wooden bench—I got my arsenal ready. I counted the colored suction-cup arrows, limbered up the air-rifle, re-strung the hazelwood bow my grandfather had made for me and sharpened my wooden arrows, which could, I had been warned, put out someone's eye.

I planted a rubber suction cup on the first arrival's forehead.

I was the oldest member of the little troop, and was regarded as the most authentically Burgundian, considering the amount of time I spent at "The Saw." Consequently, I had a proprietary relationship to the lumber-piles where we played hide-and-seek, the secret passageways between house and workshops, the band-saws and chainsaws of which my cousins were in awe. The winner at hide-and-seek was rewarded with a specimen from my menagerie: one of those shiny purple wood ticks

I kept in perforated coughdrop boxes. When he or she got back to the city, the bug was immediately confiscated for fear it would multiply. After lunch, under the lean-to shed, I used to bury my little cousin Clémence up to her neck in the sawdust. Warning her to shut her eyes, I blew gently on the fine powder, soiling those curly blonde locks which made me so jealous, me with my thick braids and stiff brown bangs.

Clémence's older brother, Leo, loved to climb on the garden swing, a board that hung by two ropes from the cherry tree. It was my job to push. "Higher?" I'd shout. When I saw he was getting dizzy, I pushed even harder until the swing went full circle. The following Sunday, Leo would want me to swing him again. "But this time, don't make me loop the loop," he begged. In vain.

Thirty years later, Luigi, a candidate for my ironing board, was on his way to Saint-Germain-des-Prés, looking forward to the little tortures he could expect from the mischievous lady who'd sent for him. I had contacted Luigi via the Minitel, after a long line of submissives offering their services had filed through my apartment and failed my tests. Much vigilance and a talent for reading between the lines are needed to avoid the jokers whose concern is not to relieve their future mistress of bothersome chores, but themselves of their existential angst and episodic urge for punishment.

My want-ads always spell out the chores that are set aside for the "household help," the ones that chip nail-polish or take up precious time better spent chatting with friends, for example. Eavesdropping on Madame's phone conversations with other potential mistresses is in fact an added bonus for the cleaning man on the job.

Observing my first recruit, a high-level executive named

Patrick, who comes straight from the office to polish my shoes and silverware, I realized there were people kinkier than me. After only one housecleaning session, Patrick made his first request: holding a pair of Madame's panties in his mouth while he worked would be a marvelous incentive! Unless, of course, his mistress would be willing to tie an old stocking with a run in it around his sex. If I hadn't complied, he probably would have raided my dirty laundry bag. I suspected him of folding my pink and blue panties into a breast-pocket hanky and sniffing the coveted fetish during office meetings.

To celebrate his ten years in my service, I let him invite me and a few of my women friends to dinner at his apartment, while his wife and children were skiing at Val d'Isère. The meal was a catered affair, stylishly served in the study-cum-dining room by the host himself, barefoot in a business suit. He served us coffee in the living room, after which we took turns whipping him. One of the three friends with me was a beautiful masochist; as it turned out, she was especially anxious to use the strap on the maitre D's back. Her cheeks became flushed with pleasure as she raised purple welts on Patrick's naturally bluish skin.

When his wife got back from her holiday, she complained about the crumbs under the dining room table: The rascal had forgotten to do the vacuuming.

My very first want-ad had brought an avalanche of replies to my Minitel "post-box": thirty men already saw themselves ringing my doorbell, naked under their little aprons. None of the applicants were over forty, suggesting that older men had other fantasies—or didn't relish bending down to dust the baseboards or polish the floor-tiles.

Pseudonyms provided precious hints. How long would *Violoniste* or *Talons Aiguilles* stick to their dusting? My preference went to names like *The Servant, Domestique, Bon élève, Lacquais, Soubrette, Mercenaire,* or *Kenboy.*

One applicant even sent me references, including a handwritten letter from an American lady whom he had served for seven years. Impressed by his straightforwardness and by the testimonial, I granted *Humblevalet* a two-hour test. He was a sportswriter by profession, he told me.

Sadly, on the appointed day, the man standing in the doorway was grossly overweight!

I sat on the couch and watched him work, counting the drops of sweat that fell on my silk blouses, cursing the "kind heart" that kept me from throwing him bodily out the door.

After that experience, I crossed off *Bouche-cendrier* and *Bon chien*. I was not about to take up smoking just to watch a human ashtray chewing on a few butt-ends, nor would I hand out lumps of sugar every fifteen minutes to a two-legged bowwow just to see him sit up and beg.

If an applicant wrote "I want to be at the mercy of a severe, authoritarian woman, naked in her apartment" or "let me be your cleaning boy" (the way Elvis sang "let me be your Teddy bear"), I doubted he would get as far as plugging in the vacuum. Enthusiastic offers like "Madame, I will clean your house all night if that is your pleasure," or "I do dusting in depth" didn't augur very well either, though sometimes I was tempted to meet one of these men who had made me laugh. And of course, the clever-dicks counted on arousing our curiosity so as to throw themselves at some Mistress's feet, like *Pattemouille*[2], a smart young doctor who came to my apartment one day and offered to be my toilet, my toilet paper, and a drying-rack for my panties. He swore up and down that if I would just let him kneel by my air conditioner, he'd never let my lingerie fly away, he'd hang on to it with his teeth if he had to! But *Pattemouille* was a cop-out: when it came to paying for the air-conditioner, he disappeared.

"What do you know how to do?" This is a sure-fire

turn-off for phone-applicants who declare "I love humiliations and above all little dog-whips" or for bondage-lovers offering to mop my floor with their tongues. My ideal would be a cleaning boy I could send for at any hour of the day or night, when I spill a can of tea-leaves on the carpet, for example. On average, one applicant in ten has a mobile phone. But at home, he'll turn it off, casting aside the digital leash and putting on his slippers to sit down to a beef stew the little woman has lovingly cooked for him. In his own house, he wouldn't be seen dead wearing the white apron he loves to sport for me. Chances are, his spouse has never jammed a fork under his nose to make him wash his breakfast bowl.

Punishment-wise, I never spare the rod or the whip, but only after the place is spotless and the cleaning products put away. Any ill-treatments during working hours might leave some chores unfinished, when the subject "accidentally" relieved himself with a twist of the wrist: "I didn't do it on purpose, madame."

Concealed behind all those applications, I soon realized I was dealing with exhibitionists, desperately in need of a stern woman's gaze and the mocking sarcasm, real or imagined, of her beautiful friends. To be allowed to crouch under the table at the end of a leash when Sophie came to dinner was an enticement I used with Patrick among others, or the privilege of being a human hassock at tea-time while old girlfriends reminisced about their school-days, joyfully whacking a naked bottom whenever the hassock sagged. The day that reward was finally granted, my friends got into the spirit of it, far outdoing their hostess's unpredictable cruelties, giving the naughty hassock full benefit of their pristine anger.

Fetishists can provide a whole range of servants' uniforms. Some will want to wear a maid's apron or a governess's dress; others are dying to rent a footman's livery or a bellboy's uniform. A black-skinned Guadeloupean like Filou might want to wear an African slave's grass skirt to submit to a cruel white colonist. Ultimately, I learned that a tailored woman's suit and beehive wig were not a sign that my future domestic was gay but rather that he had always dreamed of being a woman. With his costume on, he could step into his dream-world through housework, under the watchful eye of the good/bad mother.

Ironing is the cleaning boy's Achilles' heel. I weeded out volunteers who claimed that after the two or three lessons madame would be kind enough to provide, they'd feel capable of starching my most intricately pleated wasp-waist corsets. Playing Pygmalion would net me at best some scorched lace and an attack of nerves.

On the other hand, when I land a genuine talent for ironing, it doesn't matter if he has a mobile phone or not. A pile of clean laundry awaits him on the ironing board every week. If no one's home when he rings the bell because his mistress has extended her weekend in Rome, he has only himself to blame, since he couldn't be reached.

Luigi got his job because of his ironing talents and his gentle, cultivated, wonderfully phonogenic voice. When I explained to him about the embroidered sheets left me by my grandmother, I was touched by his enthusiasm.

Tall, with soft black locks and almost no hair on his tanned body, Luigi did the ironing in scanty apparel, stockings and a garter-belt for example, which showed off to advantage his long athletic legs. Luigi's greatest regret was that he couldn't accommodate a dildo: His hemorrhoids deprived him of that little pleasure, as typically male as his unfortunate affliction.

That evening, Luigi wore only the violet rubber briefs he'd cut out of a beach ball. His clothes lay in a pile on the sofa while he applied himself to his task. When iron and board had been stowed away, he dropped to his knees and, striking various dancer's poses, began kissing my feet. Bemused at the sight of that slender, graceful body, I thought for a moment I was dealing with Guillaume.

I led the Italian into my darkened bedroom. I grabbed a handful of his hair, and forced his tall frame towards the carpet. Seated on the bed, caressing the forehead I held trapped between my knees, I tugged at the sensitive hairs around the temples. With the skin stretched tight over his cheekbones, he looked like a cat.

No sooner had the tip of his tongue touched my stockinged leg than a horse's cock popped out of the violet briefs. I spread my legs and then my vulva, all the while watching his long hands, the left kneading the bedspread, the right massaging the spongy member with an elegant motion of the wrist.

In the living room, a jovial male voice suddenly erupted from my answering machine.

" . . . Just drove up in front of your building . . . I'll park at the corner and wait . . . see you in a minute."

I felt guilty about the forgotten appointment and momentarily upset. But the bad feeling soon went away: I only had to picture the man down there drumming on his steering wheel and how his jaw would drop if he could see the mighty dominatrix—whom he took for a lesbian—in this very vulnerable position. The cropped hedge of my pubis was half inside my worshipper's greedy mouth. Wedged against the decorative remains of the violet beach ball, my feet trampled the flopping penis which stuck out like an elephant's trunk. Luigi's tongue was getting more and more inquisitive and as it burrowed like a tiny cock; my toes clenched and unclenched spasmodically. Propped on my elbows, I was having a hard time staying in command, as my role demanded. If I weren't such a voyeur, I'd have let myself lie back and enjoy it, like any housewife in heat.

Again, the distant ring of the telephone . . . The tape-machine began to whir: "I'm alone in my car and I'm bored!"

Luigi's tongue simultaneously pressed and fluttered. Then his nose took over, wandering over the surface of my vulva. His diabolical mouth began sucking up the juices it had caused to flow. In a last attempt to keep control, I tried to think of something else, I remembered my hatred when he took me to a soccer game, my contempt for the way he cheered his fellow countrymen at the Stade de France.

But I couldn't prevent my buttocks from slipping over the silk bedspread till they were nestling in his palms. Spread-eagled before him, my abdominals straining like sails in the wind, I thought to myself there was nothing like a good fuck between two business appointments. Surrendering to my pleasure, I collapsed like a rag of flesh.

IV

AT THE END OF THE STREET, behind the wheel of his steel blue Espace, my *député* sat leafing through a newspaper. He smiled benignly at me in the distance.

Luigi strode buoyantly away in the opposite direction, the sleeves of his flowered shirt floating around his thin arms.

I lifted my leg into the high car and gave the driver a glimpse of my stocking-tops. But his lewd provincial smile vanished when I asked for payment in advance. Scolding Roland that way for his peek up my skirt turned me on a little and was risk-free: No matter how hard a time I gave him, his good mood always came back soon enough. He was a bon vivant in his early fifties, with a childish temperament that smacked of old cautionary tales for children. His suit was black; there was nothing else fetishistic about the way he was dressed. I decided it was useless to tick him off about that for the umpteenth time.

• • •

From the nightclub mezzanine, I could hear mostly women's voices coming from the bar. The sponsors of the fetish party were offering free champagne to unescorted females; most of them had come in groups sporting leather or PVC underwear from the sponsors' shop near les Halles. Perched on high barstools, champagne glasses in hand, some were making fun of a man in a brunette wig, sweating under an angora dress. A treacherous Barbarella stroked the TV's sleeves, while another rubbed her cheek against the sweater stretched tight over falsies like cannon balls.

In tribute to Masolatex, often in my thoughts those days, I wore a black rubber mini-dress, open all the way down the back.

I looked over the balcony rail onto the lower floor. The bevy of booted beauties were dancing among themselves, buttocks encased in flesh-colored or smoked nylon. I saw strict satin waspies, leather corsets, futuristic leotards with the breasts cut out . . . Though the invitation had also suggested lace, there was none to be seen.

In the center of the dance floor, a young Asian woman wearing a blindfold and nothing else was squatting in a tiny cage. Despite the "Don't touch!" sign, men were dodging past the couples of dancing women to stroke her breasts through the iron bars. I assumed these crude types were habitués of the club's partner-swapping nights. At the mere sight of nudity, they automatically behaved like your garden variety asshole.

At the top of the stairs another living statue posed, a redhead in a transparent toga and ochre Roman sandals. Her wrists were tied together and she held a lighted candle close to her bosom. She shivered at the touch of my rubber dress as I brushed past her. Roland borrowed a bit of her lipstick, relying perhaps on the imprint across his mouth to attract the attention of women.

A young teaser accosted me on the stairs, her face half-hidden by a cascade of curly hair, which she drew open and shut like a curtain. With a strong American accent, she bluntly informed me she was "switch," i.e. dominant at times, submissive at others, and offered to go along with any games that would turn me on. But it had to be now she wheedled, before her submissive urge went away. Though my get-up was noncommittal and there were no handcuffs or whips hanging from my belt, she had sensed the dominatrix in me.

"You know me better than I know myself, Mademoiselle . . . ?"

"Jane . . . with a short 'a,' *à l'anglaise*."

The woman was making a big mistake, setting her cap for me. Since capitulating on my silk bedspread, my urge to dominate had subsided. Seeing me backed up against the red velvet drapes on the stairs by this tall, overexcited child, Roland was happy to part with his chaperone and play the field. I was about to push the intrusive woman away when she suddenly fell at my feet, almost as if she'd fainted, blocking the stairs with her long legs. Her golden locks reminded me of the beautiful braids of my very first slave, little cousin Clémence, and I stood staring down into her eyes, petrified by that childhood memory. Clasping my legs, the American admitted she wasn't as humble as a submissive ought to be; she had a fractious turn of mind and liked to provoke people. In short, she was at opposite poles from the gentle docility of my sweet little cousin and I was hardly listening to a word she said. She mistook my silence for a sign of complicity and began licking my shoes and the tops of my feet. I looked her over with cool detachment. High-laced hip-boots, somewhat the worse for wear, emphasized the curves of her perfect legs. On the back of her T-shirt was a photo of Wendy O, the Plasmatics vocalist, on all fours in a bikini. To find out whether I was attracted or repelled by this female body, I tried to feel her flesh, but my fingers came up against a fishnet leotard. I was starting to tear at the elastic netting with my sharp nails when I received unexpected help from a blonde in a visor cap. Intrigued by the shenanigans of the two jack-knifed bodies blocking the stairs, she'd decided to stay and give me a hand. "Nothing like this ever happens in La Rochelle," she said, sticking her fingers into the American's open mouth. My own gloved fingers linked with hers, exploring the woman's tongue and the insides of her burning cheeks. Our victim soon pulled away, however. "I'll get my equipment," Jane declared in a girlish tone and vanished towards the cloakroom.

I felt faintly relieved to be a free agent again. Jane was one of those vampire creatures who feed on others, like some "patients" of mine I do my best to avoid when I discover the emptiness inside them. The woman from La Rochelle pointed out her husband to me, a handsome traveling salesman type, kneeling on the floor behind a bench, in the process of being tied up. The ropes had already turned him into a ship's figurehead, all trunk and no arms. He nodded hello to me from afar. My friend the *député* sat waiting his turn nearby. He introduced me to the woman executing the artful bondage. Faye was in her late twenties; she had eyes like a hawk and dark brown hair rolled into a tight bun with a chopstick through it. Roland had only just met her, but he'd been questioning her about how it felt to be in bondage, and she'd promised to do him next.

Faye had a proprietary relationship to the space she occupied. When Jane finally reappeared, it turned out that the two women knew each other.

Slung over Jane's shoulder was a black plastic canister. She removed the cap with a flourish and got down on one knee, holding the canister like a quiver of arrows. The proximity of her Aryan locks again brought to mind my little cousin, in our grandparents' sawmill, but this was an emancipated Clémence, deft and enterprising. My burst of nostalgia was swept away by what came out of the tube: a short whip, various canes, crops, and fiberglass switches. A few *élégantes* stopped for a closer look at the material.

Jane took off her T-shirt. Her nipples stuck out through the rips in the black fishnet top. Rumpling her hair in a way calculated to excite the women around us, she crawled towards me on hands and knees, determined I should whip her.

My answer fell like the guillotine: "I've changed my mind." Immediately, my accomplice from La Rochelle volunteered to replace me.

She began trotting after Jane who pretended to run away, twisting and turning to escape the swishing. It was like some bestial dance, much admired by the onlookers.

I sat down on a hassock to enjoy the show next to a biker in a one-piece black leather suit. This young woman had a male slave on a leash, held negligently with one finger, as if he were some tiny pedigreed mutt. Kneeling stiff and straight by his Mistress's helmet, the submissive had his head shaven and his wrists tied in front of him. He was in his mid-thirties. His noble bearing, and the sober elegance of his rubber catsuit with the buttocks cut out, added a touch of decadence to the young woman's natural poise. She told me she belonged to the entourage of Mistress Lady Gerda, known for her gender bending, who presided over a stable of submissives. A few specimens had been brought along to the party. Following the woman's gaze, I discovered a blonde in riding habit, dominating simultaneously two younger women. At a wink from Lady Gerda, the biker hastily turned her slave over to me and vanished. I struck up a conversation in French with Gunther, whose native tongue was German. He claimed he could be anything I wanted: sex object, whipping-boy, or attentive escort. After fifteen years of conscientious professional acting, he could always guess what others needed of him;

a few words from any woman, and he could sense what would give her pleasure. He slipped into the skin of the ideal Other like a hand into a glove. Relishing the difficulties caused by the handcuffs, he managed to extract a calling card from his breast pocket. He even succeeded in scribbling on the back a date and the name of the castle near Cologne where a big party was to be held at the end of the fall season. "Together, we could have an unforgettable experience," he proclaimed with Germanic solemnity. Yet there was something mystical about him, an unexpected depth which moved me. I put away his card, blew out a candle on the table beside me and slipped the hot tip between the cheeks of Gunther's behind. With half-closed eyes, he concentrated on opening his body. When the candle had vanished inside the orifice, I ordered him to keep it in him as long as possible.

A few feet away, Faye had woven a macramé with complicated knots around my friend the *député*'s neck. With one hand tied above his forehead as if shielding his eyes from the sun, Roland seemed lost in the desert. A flute of champagne hung from the cords for Faye to sip when needed, but already she was untying her victim, no doubt anxious to ensnare another.

Sitting on the floor with her legs spread, Jane was propped up on her elbows like a gymnast on an exercise horse, her breasts thrust forward. She threw back her head and writhed under the strokes of the cane on her breasts. When there was an even pattern of welts across her torso, she offered the insides of her thighs. The woman from La Rochelle began to tire. Several of Jane's girlfriends seized the slumped body, kneading and nibbling.

A young dandy with ponytail and lace-trimmed shirt sat down on the floor with his back to the mirror. The group of women laid Jane face down, with her belly on the man's knees, and he began gently stroking her buttocks. Taking a black necktie out of his pocket, he blindfolded her. The submissive was now meant to guess who was whipping her. She got it wrong each time. Everyone laughed, Jane included. Soon the game changed to a love-bite contest.

A sudden burst of inappropriate applause spoiled the mood. The partner-swapping habitués were giving free rein to their enthusiasm.

It took only a few minutes to empty the premises. Roland said a furtive goodbye: I suspected him of having taken part in the ovation. The young lesbian took Gunther's leash again and pulled him towards the door. But he hung back, shouting for all to hear that in Germany such a faux pas would have been unthinkable. Faye called me to help her untie her last victim. I was busy undoing the knots she pointed to as best I could, when she confessed it was really me she'd have liked to practice her bondage on, preferably in private. The idea had been in her mind all evening. "Just so you'll understand what it's like . . . from one dominatrix to another." Jane had been taking in every word and now she invited us back to her place, or rather to her aunt's apartment overlooking the Place du Trocadéro. I was hesitant. But then I was surprised to see Gunther's elegant silhouette towering behind the American. He begged us to let him join our party, promising to serve us in every way. With the camera he'd just fetched from the cloakroom, he offered to immortalize our fun. I saw from the intense look in his eyes that he had long been looking forward to something like this. Because he had been the catalyst, and because I thought he could fan the flames inside me, I decided to humor this woman I did not know and offer him a moment of felicity, in memory of my cousin Clémence, buried to the neck in sawdust.

The aunt's bedroom contained an imposing canopy bed

with white muslin curtains. Was it strenuous fun and games that had made the mattress sag to the floor and twisted the wrought-iron uprights? Or had some fairy godmother cast a spell over that princely four-poster?

With a strip torn from the sheer curtains, Faye quickly gagged Jane to prevent her from telling us the history of the bed, and generally forestall any temptation the American might have had to upstage her. A speechless night lay in store for the chatterbox.

While I removed my clothes, Faye took an artist's stance, hands on cheeks and a look of intense concentration on her face, examining my body and the surrounding space. She wasn't sure yet how she wanted me to pose on the carpet Gunther had laid at the foot of the bed. She didn't see me as a piece of cloth to be thrown on the floor for a study of random drapery effects; rather as a ghost to be delicately captured in lotus position, a reference to the memories of India I had evoked on the way over in her car. Black tulle under my buttocks would serve as a ground. Round golden cushions would help me keep my balance.

She took her cords out of her backpack, long skeins in hues that reminded me of Indian saris. Finally, she tied a scarf over my eyes.

A few days later, on the photos taken by Gunther, I discovered the colors and designs that Faye had used. Over my throat, she'd woven a sea-green Aztec trapezoid. A black cord went around my neck and under my armpits.

With her fingers, Faye carefully preceded each cord with a delicate massage of the sensitive spots she'd learned to locate. Her damp mouth brushed over my skin, creating a sensual complicity which lasted till dawn. My hands were moist from apprehension at undressing in front of strangers. Faye stroked my palms for a long while, then went on weaving her web around my breasts. She moved to my feet, tying the toes to my neck with several yards of cord. I could let myself go; I was in Faye's hands, and then in . . . no hands at all, nothing . . . My yoga position was flagging, I started to float. One last thought crossed my mind: the figure 750 . . . Faye had brought that many feet of cord with her . . . For a long time I felt I was leaning to the right. Driven by a ridiculous urge for symmetry, I tried to straighten up and started toppling the other way. My head fell back, and I was instantly reminded of the limits of weightlessness, as the cord bit into my neck. The sharp pain burned my soul more than my body, and brought with it a strange vertigo which I resisted desperately for fear of disappearing altogether.

Minutes or hours later, I began to feel cold and realized Faye was no longer in the room. Alarmed by my shouts, she returned. In a muffled voice, I threatened to go out into the street just as I was if she abandoned me again. She gave me a sip of hot mint tea and covered me with black tulle, leaving only my hands on my knees exposed. Soon the hands began to float away; I no longer had control over them, they had a life of their own. I slipped into a dream: I was a beggar in India, and if I failed to hold my hands out properly, I would be rejected by my fellow untouchables. Gradually my inner landscape was clouded over with softer and softer colors and I became incapable of thought. For a long time I was somewhere far away.

Laughter and whispering close at hand brought me back to Faye. She was stroking my shoulders with her fingertips. Only after Jane and Gunther had removed the cords and blindfold did I venture to see again and for a moment I knew I had the rolled-up eyeballs of a voodoo sorcerer emerging from a trance.

V

I INVITED GUILLAUME to dine at the home of a woman artist who had taken a series of handsome photographs of Masolatex in his fetish gear a few years before, and whom we each knew separately. Wearing white linen, he met me on the Boulevard Beaumarchais, kissed me and immediately began complaining about a canker sore. I cut short his whining before he could test my maternal streak by showing me the inside of his mouth to be comforted.

Madame C. shared her apartment with hundreds of elephants, carved, cast, or woven. Our common friend was amused by the unusual timidity we both displayed and wondered why she'd never thought to introduce us. After the first bottle of Bordeaux, I recovered my vivacity and passed it on to Guillaume, who quickly became the life and soul of the party. I was delighted by the talents of an orator who could quote by heart from Goethe, Apollinaire, Artaud, Radiguet, and Bataille. But while thus discovering our affinities, I was dismayed by the naive blue-stocking admiration rising within me. This would not do, I chortled inwardly, deciding then and there to stop seeing myself as a victim of Guillaume's charm. And to stop envying him that quest for the infinite which I myself had now experienced thanks to Faye's knots.

Leaving the building after dinner, Guillaume proudly revealed that his nipples had been hurting all evening because of the clamps he was wearing. Throughout the meal, there had been severe bouts of pain which it had taken his utmost efforts to hide. In the future, if I would allow—or rather, order—him to wear them night and day as a mark of ownership, I would be with him always, and the delightful pain would give meaning to his life. He would even go with me to a tattoo studio if I wished, to brand him permanently with "my" mark.

I took him to my old Volvo. I felt more comfortable in the overheated convertible with its odor of tawny leather. I opened his shirt to expose the dark curly hair on his chest and stroked his pectorals, working towards the swollen nipples in their clamps. My fingers scraped over the two little fishing weights that hung there. Guillaume's throat tensed. The pain was contagious; it shot through the tips of my own breasts. We were both breathing hard. I asked him if he wanted to come home with me. He looked through the windshield at the roofs above the Boulevard:

"I'm afraid I can't this evening . . . The fact is I've only got three hundred francs on me."

I bit my lip and started the car with a jerk. I drove to Saint-Sulpice without looking at him once. The marvelous communion, the desire to share his pain had burst like an impossible dream. I'd wanted to banish money from our budding affair. Now it had reared its head again; the original pact had caught up with me, and I felt hurt. I felt like a whore. In a fit of paranoia, I even suspected he was trying to haggle over the price. As I drove down the ramp, I experienced the sad resignation a mother must feel when she catches her child cheating. I was trapped, my domination had reached its limit. My voice trembled with muted anger:

"Keep your money to buy flowers!"

"For you?"

"Or for you . . ."

"I'm home so seldom, I wouldn't enjoy them! I'll get some for you though, since you seem to like them. But of course I'd much rather buy you fetish clothing! Leather, rubber, or PVC, whichever you like."

He spent the night without charge in his Mistress's bed, his ankles bound with leather straps. We'd hardly settled down when my cat Rocard, jealous of this male who presumed to lie on his bed, began chewing at his rival's toes. I told my prisoner he was not to let the tiny bells on the leather straps tinkle and we spent an excited moment petting. But at the end of one long, moist kiss, I threw back the sheet and discovered the fiasco. He cried out passionately: "I love you, I want to travel with you, I'll follow you anywhere if you'll let me, because I belong to you forever!" And pressing up against me, he fled into sleep.

I slipped silently out of bed for a shower. Could this handsome young man with the passive penis be a repressed gay? It wasn't uncommon for men I'd dominated and dressed in drag at their request to go on sleeping with women rather than give in to their deepest urge. Still less pleasant to contemplate was impotency; the idea sent shivers down my spine. I decided then and there not to get sentimental over someone with *that* failing. I tolerate all the defects of nature in my "patients," but not in my bed-partners! If Guillaume was suffering from early male menopause, that was his problem.

When I slid in beside him again, he grasped my cooled hand through the sheet: "I missed you." The next moment,

I was asleep. Dozens of gladiators knelt to kiss my feet, broad-chested, cocks erect.

The following morning, armed with his most childlike smile, he told me that in his dream I had come out of a tropical sea encased in a striped diving suit, and come running towards him across the sand.

My sexual frustration had not made me feel less close to him; quite the contrary. My body had become eroticized precisely because his was left dangling. But there was also that dream of an ideal love he thought he'd found; his boyish enthusiasm had actually converted me. Once again I had entered unawares into the desire of the Other. As relaxed and happy as if it had been a night of passionate fucking, I brought him a cup of tea and turned him loose.

"Ah, you buy your tea at Mariage Frères, so do I. But I never find the time to drink it; I have such a hard time getting up in the morning, I lie in bed till the last possible minute. But from now on, I'll brew one of your favorite teas for you."

He went tripping about the living room. "All those adventure books! You've traveled a lot . . . Where did you find those dangerous looking pig-stickers over the sofa?"

I revealed my secret penchant for fighting knives, and promised to tell him the stories attached to some of those weapons, crafted by hunters of Asia or the Amazon. In a confiding mood, I even told him how I filched hundreds of art objects from the archeological sites where I worked and sold them to collectors: daggers, statuettes, ritual bowls . . . I sketched a thumbnail portrait of the globetrotter I used to be, told him of the assignments given me by bold men I admired. Smuggler, journalist, archeologist, gambler or spy, now the muse of those soldiers of fortune, now their equal. I've lived almost everywhere except Australia, Scandinavia and Germany, all nations where men are heavy beer-drinkers, one of the rare vices I abhor. Yet I do admit to a perverse weakness for genuine American rodeo-riders, despite their fondness for Coors and Budweiser. (At least they don't pee in public!) And I'd been fascinated by the clown's deft movements as he roped the calf's legs, a novillero of sorts, whose slight physique no doubt kept him from riding the impressive horned beasts featured in the show.

"You are an adventuress!"

"Mostly retired, now . . . I explore the wilds of the Internet!"

He moved his ankles and the bells tinkled.

"Oh fairy mistress, are these bells a way of keeping tabs on your submissive, or merely a pretext for whippings?"

I scolded him for harping on his obsessions.

"I was just trying to hold your interest: I can't win you any other way."

VI

I'VE WORN MANY DIFFERENT "hats" in the course of my existence; journalism, which I learned on the staff of a major Paris weekly, is one of my favorites and though freelancing pays less and less each year, I was always happy to devote a day to researching an article I'd been commissioned to write. I had given up writing for popular journals on economics or sociology, as well as for women's magazines, all of which seem to have become uniformly hollow and boring. But the erotic press, that familiar territory, is still capable of affording small satisfactions. One such specialized magazine had just commissioned a piece on dungeons. I'd been hoping to visit the Tour de Vichy, a genuine medieval setting for the private parties given by the couple who owned it. Unfortunately, the magazine in question couldn't afford to send me to that exclusive spa. I had to make do with the dungeonettes of Paris, on the strength of recommendations from a handful of proselytizing submissives.

Erika's establishment was in Montmartre. I entered through the concierge's *loge*, which served as a kind of airlock. One simply rang a bell and walked into what looked very much like a travel agency: on a wrought-iron rack were fliers vaunting the authentic look of the medieval décor. Behind the ordinary door leading to the dungeon hung a massive antique from a prison in Nice. The walls of all four rooms were covered with vinyl wallpaper meant to look like bare stones. Though unaware I was a colleague, the ruddy-faced mistress and her kind-hearted receptionist hugged me like old friends and introduced me to some johns at the bar, whose conversation reminded me of a betting shop. The boss-lady assured me that all the iron and wood objects I saw were made by her faithful slaves: the shackles, the Saint Andrew's cross, and the crude buggering-chairs, with pink tongues sticking up through the seats. Erika told me her story: She was a former hooker who'd converted to a specialty where johns weren't too particular about the lady's age. I felt a bit dizzy going down the spiral iron steps, so narrow I was afraid my feet would slip. At the bottom, the sight of the only utensil, an enamel slop bucket, turned my stomach completely. The inferno that came out of Erika's imagination resembled the woman herself. And yet, when it came time for me to go, there was a moment of real affection between us.

Not far from Erika's was another ground-floor setup. Behind a whited-out shop window, an old lady sat answering telephones at a big table bearing a display of videocassettes and posters of a beautiful blonde dominatrix in riding habit. The receptionist made me a present of a see-through plastic key-ring with a condom inside, stamped with the establishment's Internet logo. Then she showed me to the top of the stairs leading down to the dungeon proper.

A small room was set aside for the preliminary interview.

The house mistress, a talking head on a video monitor, was reeling off tips to neophytes. The audience of one, an expressionless man in a suit, sat waiting on a stool, opposite a vacant cane armchair. Next door was a large locker room, where customers could leave their possessions safely in cupboards and scrub down before they took the plunge.

At the bottom of the steps, a large vaulted cellar with real stone walls occupied the entire basement of the former shop. On a raised dais flanked with burning torches stood a throne worthy of former President Mobutu. Mistress Lady Gerda, decked out in fetish gear reminiscent of Barnum and Bailey, emerged from a punishment cell under the stairs. I recognized her from the party where I'd met Faye. She gave me a warm welcome and showed me the rivulets of black wax on the back of the slave she had just been torturing. His head encased in a gas mask, the man was proud to be locked up in that closet, a privilege that would last until the following day.

Gerda offered me a guided tour. Beneath the vaulted brick ceiling, the various instruments had been carefully spaced apart, since Gerda often hosted several johns at once. I imagined the weird sight of a dozen slaves undergoing torture simultaneously, tied to the charley horses or the racks, locked into the stocks, strapped to the splendid multi-speed electric rotating cross, sucked dry by the milking machine, seated on the buggering chair powered by a washing machine motor. Made of polished wood with rubber trimmings, waxed and polished and very handsome, these accessories were all designed and constructed by members of her stable. Speculums, whips, and jars of cream were laid out suggestively, at the Mistress's disposal, on strategically placed shelves.

To answer my questions, the lady ascended her throne. I scrupulously noted down her advice to readers on floorcoverings. For water-sports, she advised a rubber carpet which could be wiped clean with a sponge. She was telling me about her personal weakness for golden showers when the interview was interrupted by a young slave in high-tops, wearing a backpack, who simply walked into the dungeon. Paying no attention to me, he went straight to the edge of the platform, knelt, and kissed the tips of Gerda's boots. Every evening, this impoverished young man dropped in to pay homage to his idol. Saving up his pennies, he managed to pay for two sessions a year, at the student rate Gerda accorded him.

Near Réaumur Sébastopol métro station, I asked the women working the street in front of a run-down building what floor Mistress Maria was on. They pointed to a window where a tiny light told potential johns she was open for business. I had made an appointment through the intermediary of a well-known transvestite who, though a family man, now lived as a woman and acquitted himself of his ministerial consultations in writing only. Claudia, as he called himself, had been feminized and trained by Maria twenty years earlier.

I entered a dungeon that couldn't have been more than ten feet by ten. Dark-haired and plump in her early sixties, Maria greeted me in PVC hip-boots, with handcuffs, a whip, and other accessories hanging from a leatherette belt. She complained that business was slow and I sympathized: Anyone who did such socially useful work should be entitled to a small state pension.

Her red and black dungeonette was thoroughly equipped: from the charley horse on pulleys to the stretching rack, nothing was missing except for a bed, and I suspected there was one folded out of sight behind a panel in the red lacquered ceiling. In the shower bath, a bespectacled, bearded slave in bondage was squatting naked in a tiny cage three feet high. His job was to answer the phone, cockily providing details about the equipment and lies about Maria's age and measurements.

There was another dungeon just around the corner that I was going to have to skip. It was kept by the notorious Fatti, presently "vacationing on her royalties," or so a hooker told me when I went to Madeleine's in the Rue Blondel for a bite to eat. Once every hooker's mother-confessor, sweet Madeleine has now retired to Thailand. Her periwinkle blue eyes brimming with kindness, she'd been a Mother Teresa with a shaved head, cooking all the meals herself in her confidential restaurant for women only.

I got Mistress Saphira's address and phone number from a specialized magazine. Her male secretary had given me a hard time on the telephone but I'd managed to wangle an appointment. He kept me waiting a long time on the sidewalk, asking me repeatedly over the entry-phone to be patient.

Located near the bois de Vincennes, on one of the *boulevards des maréchaux* that encircle Paris, Saphira had set aside one ground floor room for her hobby. The air-conditioner blew ice cold air onto blank, white-tiled walls. A steel cage on a butcher's hook could be hoisted to the ceiling on pulleys. This dungeon chilled me nearly as much as its proprietress: For the first time in my life, I felt ill at ease in S&M surroundings. Except for a buggering-stool, the only place I could see to sit was on the blood-red floor-tiles which the plump Saphira claimed were more hygienic than porous rubber. A former registered nurse, she reeled off in authoritarian tones the rules of hygiene she observed, swabbing the floor with ammonia, carefully disinfecting all the instruments, etc. On my way out, she showed me her own personal instrument of torture: a treadmill on which she worked out assiduously between customers, hoping to lose some weight.

I concluded my tour in the 17th *arrondissement*, gazing at a whole series of shackles hung in a circle around a punishment barrel in which a pretty submissive was half-asleep. In an alcove, there was a towering four-poster bed worthy of Sleeping Beauty herself, designed and executed by the master-craftsman who owned the establishment: a canopy of four-by-fours made it possible, with wires and pulleys, to spread-eagle a slave in mid-air.

Back home, the idea of having a system for putting someone in suspension bondage began to attract me. My sharp nails, slave irons, and whips suddenly seemed inadequate. I bought ropes, clasp hooks, and shackles at La Samaritaine, and called in the master-craftsman to help. He installed a removable pulley and assured me that several two-hundred pounders could dance at the ends of my ropes and never break them.

Around midnight, a guinea-pig called *Epicure* showed up on the Internet, curious to try out my setup. In his parents' art gallery near the Louvre, specialized in Greek and Roman antiques, this cultivated thirty-nine year-old spent his nights surfing on S&M sites. We crossed paths on "Alternative Sex." I ordered him to come over at once. His long digressions, replete with cleverly relevant quotes from the classics of love, had failed to arouse my suspicions.

He was a small, mischievous man, olive-skinned and hairy under the wool suit he wore despite the hot July weather. The hair on his head was so stiff it looked like a top-hat and made him seem inches taller. His bright eyes contained a hint of cold shrewdness that should also have been a warning.

"You don't seem half so perverse as the lady on the Internet!" was his opening shot. While I decided to see how the dictionary defined the word "perverse," he lay down at my feet and started licking my high-heeled slippers.

"This is a first! Believe it or not, I've never licked a shoe before!"

The huge tongue moved up my stockings. Having such a small man at my feet called to mind the Spanish princesses who achieved a permanent state of arousal by keeping dwarves hidden under their hoop-skirts for the purpose. I tried to keep from laughing while I read aloud from the dictionary:

"'The natural perversity which makes man forever homicidal and suicidal, assassin and executioner.' Charles Baudelaire."

The top-hat of hair was already under my skirt, like a chimney sweep's bristly brush, when *Epicure* suddenly withdrew the tongue that had begun to take me back to the Court of Spain, sat up with an angry look, and started hectoring me:

"You wear stockings that stay up by themselves, *you*? How can you possibly make the most of a moment like this—or any other moment of your existence, for that matter—without the delightful, gossamer, fairy touch of a garter-belt!"

We made an appointment the next day to pick out a pair of stockings and a garter-belt to suit both our tastes. When he had gone, I shrugged my shoulders fatalistically, unhooked my pulley, and put away the ropes he had so pointedly ignored.

In front of Les Nuits d'Élodie, I found *Epicure* with his hands clasped behind his back, misting up the plate-glass window as he peered down at the display of lingerie. I thought he must have put elevator soles in his shoes, because he seemed taller than the night before. Inside the shop, I soon realized he was known to the saleswoman, and I took him aside:

"I see you're a good customer here, I thought you said this was going to be a 'first'?"

"Now be patient, dear . . . I promise you'll have your 'first'! I wouldn't want to lose you," he purred, inspecting the lace panties in a pile on the counter.

I picked out some pairs of smoky gray Dior stockings. Epicure handed me a pair of jade-green panties and matching garter-belt. His bad faith became apparent when he refused to buy me the bra that went with them!

"That will be for our next visit, dear friend, I sense that our relationship will soon develop into an *amour-tié.*"

He handed his credit card to the saleswoman, whose face wore a knowing smirk.

"*Amour-tié*, what's that?" I asked.

"A mixture of love and friendship, *amour* and *amitié*, since love per se is reserved for my wife."

"The bras and corsages too?"

"Not at all! I'll buy you dozens, dear Gala! We're almost neighbors, I amuse you no end, and from now on you will find it almost impossible to do without me!"

In the street, he handed me a tiny shopping bag with Les Nuits d'Élodie printed on it. I thanked him with a thin smile. We'd walked a few yards side by side when suddenly he pushed me into a doorway. I was taken by surprise and before I could defend myself, he'd whipped a pair of handcuffs out of his pocket and fastened the bag to my wrist. He watched me tugging in vain at the cuffs, loudly poking fun at the mistress handcuffed to her garter-belt in broad daylight, informing me with a superior air that green was the color reserved for prostitutes' undies in ancient Rome. A few passers-by turned to look, then hurried on their way down the avenue Paul Doumer. At the corner he left me. After angrily tearing up the bag, I stuffed the lingerie into my pocketbook and pushed the handcuffs up under the sleeve of my blouse.

As soon as I got home, I turned on the computer. I had trouble with the keyboard. A message from Epicure was waiting for me. "To open the handcuffs, say 'Epicure' and press the little button at the back."

The handcuffs were a toy. My ego hurt more than my wrist. I hurried to the antique gallery.

"What's the matter, my dear, don't you like your presents any more?" he murmured, drawing me out of earshot of his assistants.

I picked up a small purple glass vase that looked like a hand-grenade, read the price tag aloud in a flat voice: "Rome, third century A.D., eighteen thousand francs" and let go. The grenade exploded on the marble floor, spraying the room with purple shrapnel.

"It cost me six francs fifty" he exclaimed gleefully, while an employee with broom and dustpan hastily cleared away the Roman remains.

After that, I decided to brush up on my martial arts. Epicure was harmless but I had felt physically humiliated and a john can sometimes get out of hand. I remember that pint-sized airline pilot (or so he claimed) who didn't think I was doing right by him and tried to get rough. I grabbed him by the hair and pulled him down into a couple of kick-boxer's knee-lifts to the rib-cage. He was groggy and a little scared, I think. I got him in a kung fu armlock and out the door. It's not often my martial arts training comes in handy, but it has always been a great comfort to me to know that if push comes to shove, I can handle almost any situation one on one. And the strenuous exercise is essential to my equilibrium.

VII

I CATERED TO A FEW SUBMISSIVES, reworked two pieces of erotica for a women's anthology. But soon, against my better judgement and in spite of his inadequacies, I found myself coming back to Guillaume. It was a hot July evening when he ushered me into his small, split-level bachelor's apartment. He was wearing a tight black rubber dress with long sleeves. The furniture was cold, modern, and minimal, with the exception of a mind-blowing Empire desk.

There was a red bat on the dickey of his dress and he complained to me about the woman who made his fetish clothes: she never listened! The bat shape spoiled the classical simplicity of the design. Because of his height, Guillaume had to have all his fetish gear custom-made, which was not always an advantage, it appeared.

The sooty eyebrows and dark bobbed wig notwithstanding, he was as bashful and awkward as a country lass.

Stiff-necked and self-conscious, he turned slowly on his high heels, showing me how his head only just cleared the living-room doorway. But his towering height—six feet eleven with heels and wig—was making me feel uncomfortable, and the sensation only increased when he sat down, crossed his legs, and stared at me. This hybrid creature had become the dominatrix and I the cowed novice. I took off my chiffon scarf and wound it around the severe wig. The touch of color took away that sacred aura. To dispel the austere mood, I tried small talk, and Guillaume loosened up. He became a salesgirl, picking out a buttercup corset from his rubber collection; then he was a wardrobe lady, lacing me into it. The matching skirt was a patchwork of black and cream lozenges, held together by big shiny eyelets.

The wall-mirror framed the delicate features of a pair of sci-fi heroines: We might have been sisters. I ran my finger lightly around the reflection of the red vampire bat. Irritated by this reminder of his *couturière* and her regrettable initiative, my big sister withdrew her image.

Between mouthfuls of smoked salmon, he poured us vodka and downed several glasses himself, bottoms up. When he'd had his fill, he stood behind my chair and wrapped his long arms around my throat. Through the smooth rubbery top, his palms gently squeezed my breasts. I shivered with excitement. Suddenly I wanted him. Against the back of my neck, I could feel his sex starting to swell under the skin-tight dress, as if in response to my expectation. The huge body extricated itself from the bat-winged sheath and dragged me to the floor, where his height and heels were a handicap. He butted me clumsily, while his cock, pressed against my leg, swelled and shrank by turns. He helped me off with my skirt, then left me to struggle with the corset laces while he pulled a condom over his prick. When he lay on top of me, I could hardy breathe; it was like skin-diving without an aqualung. My mouth found a nipple and I gnawed on it until he came, with a loud wailing shout. Cautiously peeling off the condom, he took a Kleenex and turned his sex into a doll, declaring brightly this was something British and American prostitutes did. I took off his wig and sadly stroked his hair, but he evaded my touch again and chuckled triumphantly: "Reassured now? That time we had dinner at Madame C.'s, you caught me without my rubber gear! Bare flesh feels weird to me! I hadn't touched a naked woman in ten years."

I found a vague pretext to get away before bedtime.

VIII

BACK HOME, I felt tired, frustrated, and depressed.

Once again, Rocard was chasing shadows on the bedroom wallpaper. My cat had long ago lost all interest in actual human beings. It was their shadows he would lay in wait for, staring at the wall as soon as he heard the front door open—my shadow especially, printed in his memory ever since he opened his eyes in the broom closet. Now and again, in response to urgent mewing, I would open the louvered door to the cubbyhole where he was born.

Rocard had discovered the shadows on the wall at about the same time I was having the revelation of the virtual world. Since 1989 on the Minitel and more recently via the Internet, I had spent a good deal of my time meeting men for domination sessions. The *messageries roses* offered a wonderful reserve of little soldiers, all S&M devotees, all ready to obey me. There were engineers, teachers, lawyers, journalists, architects, photographers, writers, airline pilots, art-dealers, bank-managers, consultants of every kind, postmen and masseurs. Experience had taught me to eliminate the first two categories: professors and engineers are excruciatingly passive, as dull as a stale lecture. What all those little soldiers really wanted was to be surprised. I wrote little stories for them, knowing they would read them over and over for their solitary pleasure. Computer-users got them on floppy disks as a souvenir of the session, like the cassettes of relaxing music they sell you at the end of an alpha meditation retreat.

IN A GARDEN (Spring fantasy)

I am an unruly plant and my Mistress will speak harshly to me. She will cover my eyes with a sheet of white plastic, like the pears in the Luxembourg Gardens. To keep me growing straight, I will be tied to a stake in the ground with slender cords wound tightly around my arms just above the elbows.

My Mistress will be naked under her dark blue gardener's smock, whose shape and color I can just make out through the plastic blindfold. She will be carrying tools, and the blades of her pruning shears will glint close to my carotid, prepared to shed my sap if do not bend at once, supple as a reed and delicate as a flower, to lick my Creator's feet.

ALPINE AMAZON (Summer fantasy)

—At the beginning of the hike, stuff some cocoons into the suitor's mouth to see if he will spit out butterflies on the mountaintop.

—Seal his mouth with pine pitch so he won't waste his breath in useless chatter on the climb.

—To protect him from blotchy red horsefly bites, flick his bare legs with a branch of larch (soft needles) or a bunch of thistles.

—On the mountaintop, send him to pick Edelweiss: there will be no excuse for returning empty-handed.

I soon learned to detect in a phone-voice the latent sensuality which had quickly become my chief criterion. When a newcomer to the little box (I tried to avoid habitués) showed a modicum of courtesy and poetry, I tempted him with the offer of a domination session. When submissives phoned, vocal inflexions told me instantly which ones would not keep their appointment: procrastinators, practical jokers, bored Telecom workers, or dominators amused at the idea of standing a Mistress up. I was also suspicious of applicants who failed to ask about the terms of our encounter. The worst of all were a fringe of *provocateurs* who overwhelmed you with the sordid details of their penchant for "black pearls" and "golden showers," or else they would claim to be drinking in my every word on their knees. Then there were the repressed types who whispered into the mouthpiece. I would shout back: "Louder, please! You're not in church!" or else hang up on them. By the end of the conversation, one caller in two would be incapable of repeating the address and floor number he had presumably just written down. Or else he would repeat each instruction as if he were hard of hearing. Fantasizers, nothing more . . .

Three would-be submissives in four were generally eliminated by my subsidiary question: "Can you afford these games?" Bye-bye windbags, quibblers, and fakes. The money I took for a first encounter made it easier for me to avoid getting involved . . . or, in the long run, being embittered by experiences that were often just depressing. Sometimes the play-partner became a lover and money went out of the relationship. Otherwise, he sank into oblivion, with money hastening the process.

From earliest years, my world-view has been fashioned by a sense of derision. Already at school, I made fun of my teachers, those nuns of the order of the Assumption, trained to see evil in the most innocent attitudes of the little boarders in pleated navy blue skirts. Sitting on a comrade's knees was interpreted as the first step towards lesbianism. At fifteen, I wore a tiny golden die on a chain around my neck; when a nun insisted I remove that symbol of vice, I told her it was a cubist crucifix. That was the year of my ultimate provocation: I smuggled into chapel copies of De Sade's *Justine or the Philosophy in the Boudoir*. They replaced our prayer-books at morning mass for several days, concealed inside the leather dust-covers. However, one of the little lambs guffawed aloud at a particularly lusty passage and soon the books were piling up at the foot of the altar. The guilty party had perforce to confess her sin. Deprived henceforth of morning mass, I could lie in bed when the others were in chapel and caress myself to my heart's content till I came, giving free rein to an imagination which already explored paths quite different from those of the banned marquis. In contrast to that author, whose detached perversity I discovered at a tender age, my own sensibility was a source of constant suffering. Never have I learned to muzzle it, nor even always to control it. Not that I haven't always tried to keep others at a distance to avoid feeling their hurts and clashes like a soul in torment . . .

I began to regard as a privilege the solitude that went with my situation as part-time dominatrix. I belonged to no club or union, paid no dues of any kind.

Yet now and then the solitude was heavy to bear and I would go looking for distractions.

On the Internet, for example.

A delivery boy from the Multi-Function-Suit company brought me the Love-suit ordered via the Web. I unpacked it with mild excitement. and held it in front of the mirror. The top had the exaggerated lift of a Wonderbra; the long glossy shorts looked like a bicycle racer's. All in all, it bore a closer resemblance to a Lycra leotard than to the rubber diving suit of Guillaume's dream. I had devoted much consideration to the order-screen on the site operated by "Multi-Function-Suit, GmbH." In the end I'd clicked on "PVC"—cheaper than "latex," "electric blue," and chosen the dimensions of two interchangeable dildos that fitted onto an axial screw in the crotch: 10 x 6 cm for the smaller one and 12 x 8 for the larger, sizes I thought would ensure comfortable seating at my computer desk.

Anxious to try out my new toy, I worked through the step-by-step instructions on the CD-ROM that came with the kit, finally lubricating the smaller dildo and screwing it into place. With my knees apart, I pulled the suit up over my legs, and as I sat down to my computer, the round tip slid inside me. The fleshlike resiliency felt good at once. Inside the breast-cups, on the other hand, I was not so pleased with the touch of cold metal on my globes. I knew from the instructions, however, that the sensations I was about to experience would come through those electrodes. To attract some virtual partner, I drew a face and body for myself. In the end, my synthetic image was a compromise between two of the models provided, Tank Girl and Barb Wire.

On the Web site, a host of men, also in possession of a Love-suit, were looking for a playmate, but there was no way of knowing the age or sex of those faraway fantasizers. I watched the pen-names roll by in reverse alphabetical order. Zoë (tv), Zero, Yogi, Yoshi, Xerix, Wendy (tv) . . . ah, Vercingétorix! A stalwart macho for sure! The virtual face on the screen was a cross between Gérard Depardieu and Charlton Heston. Vercingétorix was Gabonese; he lived in the suburbs of Franceville and was twenty-five. I decided a tête-à-tête was in order.

I sent him a mild jolt of greetings, a gentle tingle to the testicles. His synthesized voice came through: "Hello, Paris lady! Go on, go on! It feels so good! " I clicked repeatedly on "soft" and little Vercingétorix, standing center-frame, blew me kisses.

But when his turn came to take control, he gave my breasts a vicious pinch and ordered my virtual replica to her knees, threatening to click on "sadistic" if she failed to obey. My creature-image complied as fast as my mouse could move, but more shocks coursed through my bosom. I drew in my chest and pulled at the breast-cups, but couldn't keep from crying out with pain.

Tank Girl was on her back now, hopefully arousing my opponent's pity and giving me time to mount a counter-attack: I clicked on the nipple-clips of his suit and sent a "severe" jolt to his penis. On the screen, Vercingétorix lurched towards his sexy lover, weaving this way and that, finally collapsing at her feet and begging for mercy . . . Victory was mine, thought I. Downing weapons, I decided to sue for peace. My mouse began to cast about in search of a sexy pose for my virtual silhouette that would mollify this bushman. But oh, the coward! He took advantage of the momentary respite to unleash a series of violent shocks to my vulva. Over the voice-link, my synthetic organ told him he was no Vercingétorix at all but a nasty Attila! He apologized at once: He sometimes got his Asterix characters all mixed up! Still, Vercingétorix-Attila went on mistaking me for the target monster in some video game and returned to the attack. My vanity was my downfall. I'd been trying to improve the appearance of my heroine, when a severe burning in the gut bent me in two.

I struck back with a click on "severe," another on "sadistic," and then decided to break the link. Physically exhausted by all those shocks to my private parts, I sent the kit back to Germany before the expiration of the eight-day free trial period.

IX

BEFORE I GOT HOOKED on cyberspace, my lovers were young artists, poets, and Blacks, gentle males all, who never crimped my style. During the cold months, they were happy enough to wait for my postcards, while I relieved my sedentary Paris existence by wintering in the tropics, paying my way with such intrepid missions as antique smuggling, industrial espionage, and shadowing suspects . . . A patiently assembled network of international connections fed my hunger for thrills and scary adventures. Returning to Europe in the spring, I proceeded to fill any vacancies in my catalogue of lovers.

One morning, on the way to my tai-chi class, I was approached near the Luxembourg Gardens by a small, dark-haired youngster in his early twenties on a pink and yellow bicycle. I was suddenly reminded of the tender pleasures I'd been neglecting since I'd sold my soul to the Minitel. I was walking alongside the tall iron fence when the young man pedaled past me, swerved, and blocked my path. Beneath the curly hair and clownish eyebrows, something careworn about his face made him look older than his years.

"The first time I saw your eyes, I held on to your car and let you tow me to your garage. Did you find the poem I left under your wiper?"

"Stolen, no doubt. Your name?"

"Luc."

He showed me cans of spraypaint in his backpack: "You won't mind if I mark your way . . ."

Later, going home, I saw the fluorescent bicycle leaning against a wall on the Rue de l'Odéon. The boy had sprayed the words "DREAM OR REALITY" in English on the sidewalk, and was adding floral patterns in tones to match his bike. I crossed to the other side of the street, but he called out to me:

"It's for you! I'm writing on the sidewalk where you pass each day: I'm writing under your footsteps!"

Every morning, Luc waited for me by the Luxembourg fence, and finally one day I rewarded his dogged wooing by taking him home. Three days later, he left for his military service.

On his first furlough, I stopped seeing Guillaume altogether. More and more, I thought of Masolatex as a delicate bird to be viewed through binoculars. In between the rare evenings I granted him, all my powers were assigned to my telephone voice, the ideal medium for a fetishist, anyway. At the end of July, in spite of Guillaume's pleading, I went on vacation with the young man.

In an ancient red-brick Tuscany villa owned by a Neapolitan painter, and whose only comfort lay in its huge dimensions, my knight-errant drew countless buckets of water from the well and heated them for my ablutions. He would then wash me with the awkwardness of a child, and dry my dripping body with his lips.

It wasn't that I missed the Minitel, but country life soon began to pall. Luc couldn't work out why his goddess had become so remote, though actually he needed that distance to better worship me, and reveled in a mood of romantic melancholy. One night I awoke to find him gazing down at me: "I've got all my life to watch you sleep!" he whispered.

In the forty-room maze of the Valesi de Borromeo, the foundations of which went back to the early Christian era, I tried to live in the Italian style, cooking with olive oil, observing the long midday pause with a nap in a darkened bedroom, or curled up with a book in the shade of the tall courtyard grass, with Luc nestling close. It dawned on me that I missed Guillaume: From afar, his affected chatter seemed a more attractive way of wooing a woman than the mute, stolid attentions of Luc. The only thing in my young companion's favor, I realized, was his innocence; I was determined that some of it should rub off on me and I pressed up against him. When we fucked, I tried to revive the springlike energy of our beginnings, when he'd been a young dolphin bucking the gulf-stream. My remoteness, however, had unsettled him to the point where he doubted the sincerity of my pleasure, and his efforts flagged. A last-minute orgasm was my only compensation: it felt something like climbing onto a bandwagon.

On market day, I slipped away to the pay-phone in the village bar, *Il Muro pendente*, and summoned Guillaume to join me on the French Riviera.

On the appointed day, I took myself to the station, with Luc at my heels. Tactfully, he decided to jump off the slowing train before it entered the station at Nice. When it came time for us to part, he took me on his knees and stroked my hair with one finger. I hugged him close. He looked into my eyes and solemnly advised me to take good care of myself, since he wouldn't be there to look after me.

I watched him scampering over the ties, vaulting a fence, and felt a twinge of nostalgia as I closed the album of childhood snapshots.

Alone at the end of the platform, Guillaume looked like a fashion plate, as usual. And yet I hardly recognized him: the heat, the vibrations of the train, and Luc's disappearance had scrambled my senses. Guillaume had booked us into a white farmhouse in Haute Provence, a treasure from the Michelin guide: each room had a terrace with an unimpeded, panoramic view. In the evenings, the pine hills were fogged over like a steaming sea.

Across the valley, forest fires soon lit up our nights on the terrace. Watching them at my side, Guillaume wore only a black leather harness reminiscent of a Chippendale show, which squeezed his balls and swelled his cock. Occasionally, sex took place by day, with no other *trajes de luz* than the sun beating down on our tanned flesh.

"Can you smell the sun on my skin?"

He sniffed at my thighs like a puppy: "Wait . . . Mmmmm . . . Well, if you say so . . ."

His taste and smell were under-developed, his hands unskilled, as if he'd never bothered to get to know another body. The attractions I held for Guillaume faded again after the second night. The heat was such that he had had to resign himself to behaving like an ordinary lover, so I had to take matters in hand. I ordered him to cram all my toes into his mouth without touching them with his teeth. His lingual and digital dexterity increased a hundredfold when he had orders to obey. Next, I blindfolded him and tied his hands behind his back: He had to offer himself like a woman. I nipped him with my teeth in the sensitive hollows of the shoulder blades, and he was forced to let himself go. I hovered over his surrendered body, harvesting sensuality, gazing out at the horizon aglow with burning pine.

Everything which Guillaume ultimately intellectualized would first transit through his gaze. With his arm around my shoulders, he would stare complacently at the couple we formed in the corridor mirror, and I would stand purring at his side, sharing in the self-delusion of lovers. After dinner, he would stretch out beside me and become absorbed in the kaleidoscopic movie of desire, fear, and even death that flashed across the back of my eyes.

"You've drawn me into the spiral of love I've yearned for all my life!" he exclaimed one evening. But then he went on to admit how much he had suffered from his recent discovery of the green-eyed monster. He'd been accustomed to women breaking off all other relations from the moment he entered—or re-entered!—their lives.

He was furious to learn that I'd been in Tuscany with my twenty-year-old lover, not far from Sienna where he had gone with his former dominatrix, the talkative Sylvie-Anne from Normandy, who'd smothered him with a violent passion and given him pleasures he'd never known.

By dint of time and effort, Guillaume finally managed to satisfy me once a day. I would swoon from hyperventilation. When I came to, the infernal concert of grasshoppers was biting into my eardrums like a thousand chainsaws. We would remain entwined for minutes on end, hearts beating in tandem. Time had stopped, fusion was achieved.

One night on the terrace, we were lying in our deckchairs looking out for shooting stars when he asked me to tell him a "machete story." He'd been fantasizing about my little collection of fighting knives, imagining all sorts of bloody legends behind each one.

"The knife you like best, with the broad sawtooth blade,

was given to me crossing the Burmese mountains in April, by a student from a Shan tribe who was acting as my guide and soon became my lover. We spent almost a month together, sleeping in little straw huts among the Meos, Akkhas, and Lisus. After a long trek through flowering poppy-fields, I was about to leave the region when he gave me that knife as a token of his love. It was the only thing he owned. Flying home to France with a Persian Gulf airline, I stupidly checked his gift in a suitcase, instead of handing it to one of the crew. A few hours later, we had to leave the plane in Bahrain, and I had to identify the weapon in a plastic bag with a tag on it, dangling from the fingers of a customs official. Other passengers were complaining of the delay and giving me nasty looks. The police decided my fate: I would be detained until the following day. They asked me a lot of questions, then made me apply for a visa to go into town for the night. I was treated to a room in a four-star hotel, and I hid the weapon under a sofa cushion. The management must have known about my case because scarcely had I checked out when they found the knife. The police caught up with me as I was climbing the gangway . . . to give me back my property.

Two or three years later, at a dinner party in Paris, an Italian who had been a passenger on that jet warned the other guests against me. I was a dangerous terrorist, he said, "arrested in Bahrain for hijacking a Gulf Air jet!"

I had scarcely finished the tale of my misadventure, when Guillaume bundled me into the bedroom and fucked me to a T.

The next night, we had already turned out the lights to sleep when he asked me for another knife story.

I told him how the thinnest of my blades was a present from an Indian I met near the little town of Iquitos in Amazonas:

"The young *curador* (a kind of witch-doctor) who

owned that knife, raised a few chickens in a camp near a branch of the Amazon, where we'd hung our hammocks and mosquito-netting for the night. I was accompanying a German bird-catcher around Latin America, and we had to wait for the village mechanic to fashion a spare part for the engine that powered our dugout canoe. Two nights running, I slept with this Indian. He must have noticed the aggressiveness behind my passionate fucking and on the last morning, while I was bathing in the nude, he came and squatted on the river bank. Handing me a knife, he told me to hold it in my mouth while I swam until I could no longer keep my teeth clenched. The idea, he said, was to cast out the violence inside me. When I finally did let go of the weapon, he dived to retrieve it from the river-bottom . . . and gave it to me as a present, advising me to use it for that purpose whenever I felt the need."

My back was turned to Guillaume and I could feel his penis swelling against my buttocks as I talked. At the end of my tale, he fucked me gently under the sheet.

On the third day, because he insisted, but also because his fetishism seemed to be giving ground to more innocent pleasures, I told him another of my adventures:

"I was traveling in Utah when I met a young American who carried under his belt a huge Mormon switchblade, the famous "Buck Knife." During the tourist season, he shot the rapids with holiday-makers in inflatable boats. That summer, he was leading our expedition down the Green River when we capsized. Half a dozen of us were stranded on the bank, waiting to be rescued, when I responded to his overtures and let him fuck me in a sandy hollow at the base of a cliff. Except for my bikini bottom, all my clothes had disappeared with the boat and despite our campfire, I spent the night shivering in his arms. When a party of Swiss had taken us down to Powell Lake in their big rubber boats, our guide invited me to visit him in the cave where he was to spend the winter, on nearby Mount Desolation.

"Come Christmastime, I set out from New York to bivouac in the Rocky Mountains. The nearest town to my destination was Moab. My guide had arranged with the tourist agency he worked for during the summer to fly me out from there by helicopter.

"The campsite was marked with a red sheet spread out on the snow. I was thrilled by the stillness and the immaculate whiteness of everything. I was to spend five days with that boy before the helicopter came back for me. At night, we wrapped ourselves in furs and lay down by the food stores in the crudely converted cave. My hermit turned out to be as rugged as any primitive hunter. One morning I watched him kill a deer with a single arrow, butcher it with his knife, and roast it over an open fire in the cave mouth.

"When the spring thaw came, he sent me his Buck Knife via UPS as a souvenir."

All through this new saga, Guillaume had been masturbating. I was amazed to see how excited he could get as he listened to these tales of castrating instruments. Paradoxically enough, each of my knife stories had taken his mind off his fears of sexual failure.

X

I SPENT A FEW RESTFUL DAYS in London, with my good sister Hazel. Back in Paris, Guillaume made a date with me in an eatery near his place in Les Halles. He had chosen to live in a pedestrian precinct lined with prostitutes in hip-boots. When he came home from work, he felt comforted by the sweet nothings they whispered in his ears and the pet names they gave him, like "*mon chou*" or "*mon biquet.*"

At the restaurant, he confessed that during my trip to England, he'd indulged himself a little, dipping into his black book where he kept the names and numbers of every French dominatrix he'd encountered in ten years scouring the sex-ads and trading messages with mistresses on the Minitel. He was proud of his list, which he believed to be complete. While waiting for me in Nice that summer, he'd picked up the *Provençal* at the station and stumbled on two ads from women who were new to him. In this case, he'd merely talked to them on the phone, asking for detailed descriptions of their equipment and their interiors. One was located near La Ciotat, the other in the maze of old Nice. Nothing very tempting there and certainly not the comical *midi* accent. "Hard to take them seriously with that," he complained, expecting to get my sympathy.

Occasionally, Guillaume and I would bump into each other on the Minitel. He would be embarrassed and offer some flimsy excuse like needing to clean out his "letter-boxes" or feeling a sudden urge to leave a tender message in mine.

At times like that I felt deprived: he'd never made his official dominatrix the present of a single piece of rubber gear, while I was certain he rewarded each new woman with a fitting at his dressmaker's. He had a childhood friend with a fetish for big breasts, and Guillaume had favored him with a list of phone numbers chosen for their bra sizes.

The only woman who had ever been important to Guillaume was Sylvie-Anne, the woman from Normandy he'd met seven years before via the sex-ads. For a whole year, she'd imagined she was Saint Teresa de Avila, setting down her divine revelations in a notebook.

"Sylvie-Anne is going to be getting in touch again," he warned me over a tasteless salad. "I was the one who introduced her to dressing and domination. Last year, we'd gotten so completely out of synch that I decided to break off . . . and look for true love. Today, I'm steeped in happiness, like a wave in the ocean!"

He'd just written to the operators of the site where we met to broadcast the miracle! He was full of energy that evening, and charmed me again with that brand new love for me which lit up his whole existence. He wanted to live with me. This wasn't the first time he'd said that, but tonight he seemed almost surprised to hear the words coming out of his mouth. I would be the first woman he'd ever lived with. I suggested he rent a large apartment in Saint-Germain-des-Près where I could be with him nights and at weekends. For the moment, I preferred to keep my own little hideaway.

Only days later, I chanced on the ideal place. It was just opposite the underground garage on the Place Saint-Sulpice where I kept my car: huge bedroom, living room with fireplace, and separate dining room. Guillaume found it expensive and badly laid out, but it couldn't have been more convenient for me. I said to myself he should be grateful to live so near his idol.

While the apartment was being freshened up, I dropped in for a visit, like a bride inspecting a model house. A workman was repainting the window-frames and Guillaume was rummaging through his boxes. The move had him worried. Unpacking the family silverware was a way of trying to reassure himself. At least that was how it seemed to me . . .

"There . . . my bag of marbles, in the silver sugar-dish." He took some out and held them up to the light for me. Their glittering depths seemed to have a relaxing effect on him. He opened the refrigerator. The freezer compartment was already full of convenience food and eskimo pies. He laid one of the glass balls from his childhood on each frozen cube in the ice-tray.

"If they melt and freeze again, the marbles will have sunk to the bottom and I'll know I have to throw away all my frozen food. Power cuts are rare, but you never can tell . . ."

In virginal tones, I did my best to reassure him over the choice of the apartment, stressing the dimensions of the living room, big enough for a trampoline. He took me aside and showed me two sturdy metal hooks in the palm of his hand. "Could you ask the painter to install one on each side of the bed? If it comes from you, he won't ask questions."

The worker grumpily wondered what anyone would want to hang so close to the floor.

"Religious icons to protect me from the Devil! You don't think there's something diabolical about my future husband?"

My new confidant nodded sagely, picked up his power-drill, and put a cushion under his knees.

Guillaume finished arranging his books in alphabetical order and invited me back for dinner in the evening.

Three blocks away in my apartment, I fretted all afternoon. I couldn't even read the papers. I couldn't concentrate. Sylvain dropped by, but he was *de trop*. I thought of sending for Luigi, my cleaning boy, just to watch him shine my collection of shoes, but he spent Sundays with his family. The question was: Should I take personal items to this love-nest? Around 7:00 P.M., I decided against it.

As soon as I stepped into the new apartment, I was glad I'd come empty-handed, for Guillaume's first words were: "You won't believe it, the closets are already full!" and helping me out of my raincoat: "I'll spread this on an armchair, it would get wrinkled in the closet." Defiantly, I threw the white PVC coat on the floor. It was by Thierry Mugler, and was the one present my fetishist had ever given me.

That night, we inaugurated the hooks. I used chains with leather cuffs to spread-eagle Guillaume notch by notch till his limbs were stretched as far as they would go. Then I ripped at his armpits and the tender insides of his thighs with my sharp nails. He bit his lips but managed not to make faces. In memory of the tokens of ownership he'd worn to Madame C's dinner without my knowledge, I put clothespins on his nipples and he whimpered happily.

In short, he responded to each manipulation of his body like a man-machine. I could increase his erection at will by adding clothespins; I could make him come exactly when I wished.

Deciding I wanted some satisfaction of my own, I began to guide his hands, but he was not very good at taking instructions, and the fingers he trailed over my body were about as warm and sensuous as a skeleton's bones. He used only one hand, propping up his head with the other. Halfway to a laborious orgasm, I let go of the tiller. Whenever his clumsy efforts annoyed me, I'd give a clothespin a vicious twist.

XI

Frustrated once again by Guillaume's insensitivity, I needed a change of scenery. My favorite sex magazine agreed to send me back to the land of sweet perversity, and on September 14 I was marching through the streets of London to the sound of beating drums.

This was the S&M Pride March[3], wending its way past leather-trousered bikers and dumbfounded passers-by. Happy to get away from the daily grind in her dungeon, Hazel had offered to help. Elbowing her way through the army of reporters, she took photos to illustrate my article. I noticed couples wearing hoods or scarves over their heads for fear of being recognized.

Dressed from head to foot in rubber, oblivious to the hot sun, a tall woman led the parade, striding heavily in her platform boots. Frothing at the bit, a Centurion in a short black leather skirt trotted along, harnessed to a buggy. Wearing an officer's jacket, the thin, bony driver kept reining him in to keep pace with the women's rig. This consisted of a trio of pony girls driven by a booted Indian woman on the high front seat of the carriage, while three very British ladies sat chatting in the back. Wearing high-tops and shorts, the trainer jogged alongside, keeping his eye on the harnessed girls, while supplying the passengers with cool drinks.

Mademoiselle Sentimase, a highly cultivated left-wing journalist from Paris, asked me to hold her leash, in addition to my notebook. She was carrying a big sign which read: "It's my ass but it's everybody's freedom."

The four floors of a London University building had been rented for the occasion, and the march was followed by "The Dungeon in the Sky." Two thousand people milled about the college entrance, preparing for a few hours of "study." I followed Mademoiselle Sentimase into the building for a tour of the workshops.

By the computer stand on the ground floor, there were students fighting over some gray public school short trousers and curvaceous "drag kings" (lesbians dressed like men, with goatees and moustaches) wearing skimpy T-shirts that revealed the jewels in their navels.

In a vast hall fitted out with tubular scaffolding and devoted to practical exercises, a very didactic teacher was explaining the proper distribution of the weights attached to a learner, hung from the ceiling in a straitjacket. In the next room, a bondage lesson was going on. A teacher was demonstrating the use of a "muff," a leather pouch in which both fists are tied together. Volunteers jostled each other to serve as guinea-pigs.

On the heels of Jean-Paul Gaultier, I jumped a queue of water-sports enthusiasts. The workshop was called "Wet and Wild" and the leader explained that this year there would be theory only. The university officers had not appreciated the golden showers that had soaked the carpeting at last year's colloquium. An MD specified that in the event of infection, viruses like hepatitis could get into the urine and that we should avoid the mouth and eyes. Sitting on his boyfriend's lap, a young man told the audience that he suffered from "hysterical retention" whenever his partner asked him to urinate on him. It was suggested that he listen carefully to the sound of running water, rub his skin with an ice cube, urinate alone in unusual places and positions—such as standing in his bathtub or squatting on a lawn.

A workshop run by two lesbians was just starting on the floor above. The boss-lady was wearing a fishnet body stocking, trimmed at the wrists with red leather. Her virile assistant had a dildo with black leopard spots protruding from her fly. The discussion was about "edge play," such as masturbation while driving a speeding car on a busy freeway. In many situations, it was agreed that the danger should be confined to threats, that words were often enough to frighten a person out of his or her wits.

In the rumpus room, after a Slash contest in which bare-chested men threw buckets of paint at one another, there was a session of ritualized cling-film wrapping. Several mummies already lay in their shiny cocoons when a dog-race was scheduled to start. The bodies were hastily unwrapped and replaced by cages containing the contestants. One woman was actually built like a greyhound, tall, slender and naked, with cropped hair; a plump master had her on a leash. A German Shepherd, who looked like a sheep in his synthetic fur, took orders from an uncanny Mae West look-alike. It was an obstacle race, but with only one fetishist touch: contestants had to crawl under a rubber sheet stretched out on the floor. After going through all the required contortions, each participant had to bring back to his or her Master or Mistress a pair of dirty panties, a teddy bear, and a bone, then lap up a bowl of gruel and munch some dog-biscuits.

The race was well underway when the German Shepherd fainted into his dog food. Neither the referee's whistle nor the spectators' cheers could revive him. The other dogs began to misbehave, frenziedly gnawing ears and sniffing behinds. The naked greyhound won hands down and was awarded a ribbon: Sadly, she had nothing to pin it onto.

The obstacles were quickly removed to make room for Miss Creant's Academy. A handful of pseudo-clergymen had a whale of a time on the bottoms of schoolgirls with their skirts pulled down around their thighs. A master took the girls' temperature by holding the thermometer to their reddened posteriors. Wearing a leather *bustier*, Mademoiselle Sentimase came into the classroom just as the ad lib whipping began, followed by a dark and handsome Englishman. Several submissives were looking for a woman to thrash them. One was a genuine Scotsman in a kilt, who put a cane in my hand. I took out all the ire accumulated over the past few days on his bottom, ordering him to count the strokes and thank me for each.

My body tingled with welcome release as I gave him back his cane after the sixtieth "Thank you, Ma'am." In the distance, I glimpsed the figure of the mysterious Englishman. In the relative privacy of a balcony, he was whipping Mademoiselle Sentimase. I went out for a closer look. Unsettled by the instructions she kept giving him about how to hit her, the man was beginning to lose confidence. When she saw me standing in the French doors, my fellow journalist asked me to take over. Immediately she told me to pull out all the stops and turned towards the setting sun buttocks whose purple hue was enhanced by the last rays of daylight.

I saw the couple again in the long line to the cloakroom. Bored with waiting for her clothes, Mademoiselle Sentimase, who wore nothing on top but her skimpy *bustier*, dropped to her knees, unbuckled her friend's belt, and jerked it through the trouser loops. The Englishman blushed at the outrageous proposition but methodically began striping her back. The shrill screams and thwacks of the belt caused a respectful hush to fall over the waiting line.

XII

Back in Paris, when I handed in my article on the Spanner Case and the S&M Pride March, the editor suggested I have a go at a new site on the Minitel. I returned to my keyboard with gusto and began corresponding with *Plastic*, a courteous man who aroused my curiosity. I sent for him immediately.

Squeezed into trousers that corkscrewed over his moccasins and wearing a checkered sports jacket, Plastic looked like a good-natured intellectual. He was actually a technician on network television. Discovering me encased in a black Lycra body-stocking, his eyes laughed behind his glasses.

"Why, you're exquisite! How lovely you'll look in transparency. Sit down, my dear, and let me show you my collection!" He led me to my couch quite as if it were his home.

First, he told me about his bad experience with a

woman he'd invited to his apartment after exchanging messages on the Minitel. Out of gallantry, he'd even picked her up in the Porsche he was so proud of. Hardly had he taken his fetishes out for the lady to see when she'd maced him and tied him up with adhesive tape. Leaving him bound and gagged on the living room floor, she'd made off with his wallet, his watch, and the keys to the Porsche, parked in front of the building. The next day, his head was bathed in blood when the *concierge* heard him banging on the inside of his front door. A special delivery letter had saved his life.

His traveling salesman's sample case inevitably reminded me of Guillaume's. But this treasure chest contained layers upon layers of see-though plastic. With a sharp tug, he smoothed the wrinkles out of the first garment:

"Trousers . . . a bit large for you, I'm afraid. You wear a small size 10, I expect . . ."

"A rather large 10, actually . . ."

Next, he took out a pile of deflated balloons which I realized were little panties, but which looked to me like rompers.

"Now, now, you'll see: the elastic bands keep the air out."

I reached in and took out a transparent rectangle.

"What's this ?"

"It's a cape by Courrèges. Look, I've also got a doctor's blouse with a high collar. . . . It ties up the back with little bows. Take your pick."

I took off my catsuit and held a pair of rompers in front of me, then a bra, the trousers, the cape, and a pair of floppy gloves. *Plastic* flattened each piece of clothing against my body, explaining the air had to be driven out to feel the plastic on the skin. Then he too removed his clothes. He put on a pair of drawers and a one-piece overall, whose long sleeves were trimmed with Velcro. Our vacuum-packed bodies brushed against one another with a dull rustling sound. I tried pinching his nipples to force him to the floor but my fingers slipped on the plastic: "Hard to grab me, eh?" said he, rubbing his belly against me. Then he began to lick the plastic covering my shoulders and breasts, lingering around the areolae, trying unsuccessfully to nibble them. Locked into those sweatclothes, I was intoxicated by the dampness oozing out of my pores. Finally, I pressed up against him and embraced him. But he shook himself free and tried to provoke me with a smirk:

"You could whip me, you talked about it on the phone the other day, but I wouldn't feel much through all these thicknesses."

"Then what would be the point?"

Our damp skin shone here and there through the transparent undulations. By dint of repeated rubbing, my sex was beginning to grow moist with excitation when Plastic suddenly backed away and came boisterously. I burst out laughing when I saw the creamy fluid spreading over the inside of his wrapper, as if he had a container of soy-milk between his legs. In the bathroom, I removed the successive layers and in my nudity felt as cold as an unwashed baby's dirty bottom. I felt abandoned, deprived of a mother's love, of any kind of love at all, and tears came to my eyes. I put talc all over my shivering body and found myself communing with those Japanese men who go to specialized clubs to be put into diapers; I suddenly understood their kink. When Plastic had left, I slid under my quilt and went to sleep.

The moon was waxing and Guillaume was champing at the bit: He'd gotten dressed up with me only twice in the three months since we'd met. The need for a little session to allay his demons tormented him day and night. I was gradually bringing things to the apartment: a few jars of face-cream, rubber gear, some high heeled shoes that had never touched the sidewalk. But I'd pretended not to notice the furrows of tension on his forehead. Our conversation was mostly about cultural and intellectual subjects. Everything personal, intimate, we avoided by tacit consent: Neither of us was straightforward enough to just open up. One evening, however, our two frustrations dissolved in the flames of a chandelier. Fireflies danced on the PVC top which was all I had on under my damp raincoat.

Guillaume had obeyed my orders and was wearing a garter-belt, fishnet stockings, and high heels. Clinging to his nipples were black bird-shaped clamps. I decided to talk to him first about the way I wanted him to caress me, I required a leisurely pace and great concentration on everything he did. Then I sent him to soak his hands in warm water. He made a real effort and in the end did manage to give me intense pleasure, licking first my armpits and then every little mound of flesh between the straps of the corset. Words of passion even welled up in my throat but I swallowed them. There was a nice surprise in store, though: his erection lasted until I came.

At other times, I liked to hope he'd rough me up a little, get a bit violent, the way women like to be fucked occasionally. When I got to the apartment after seeing one or two submissives during the day, I was tired of having to go on giving orders all evening, too. But no, I had to keep on speaking firmly, guiding and scolding . . . I found myself hankering after the warrior's rest.

One night as we were making love on a tiger skin in front of the fireplace, I ordered him to tie it around his shoulders. Guillaume demurred:

"You ought to know by now what excites me! With PVC or latex, I can get a hard-on, otherwise I'm likely to lose it!

When you're not around, I've got my little method, a scrap of plastic with your face in my mind does the trick! But when you're here, and you're naked, for example, to have a good erection I have to work it up in my mind with fantasies about my fetish clothes. So how do you expect me to get any satisfaction with you dressing me up in the skin of a dead animal!"

After ten years of fetishism, he was hooked on latex like an addict on his drug. I cradled him in my arms, trying to sooth his anger. And again that night, I catered to his kink. Standing well clear of the tiger skin, I put on tight PVC toreador pants and a bustier which lifted my breasts but left them naked. Yet he'd hardly begun to touch me when he started complaining about the time it took me to come. He even had the gall to compare me with Sylvie-Anne and her quick, loud orgasms. She owed him her first orgasm, he added, obviously very pleased with himself. I refrained from flaunting my Black lovers' prowesses, or reminding him how often his cock was cold and limp. Instead, I pushed him away with both hands, went into the kitchen, and came back with a pair of black rubber gloves trimmed with lace, a gift from good sister Hazel.

I pulled them on and went straight into Guillaume without any preliminaries. Immediately, I knew this wasn't his first time, it was too easy. The tiny mouth expanded eagerly as I pressed, undulating, opening up, drawing my middle finger into the abyss. As I burrowed, he moaned a little for the sake of appearances and then began to chortle as my fingers did their lively little dance.

The next day, in a shop in the Rue Saint Denis, I bought two pairs of rubber gloves. Preparatory to sprinkling the insides of the fingers with talcum powder, Guillaume laid out his collection for me: Vétiver from Crabtree and Evelyn, *talc de Venise*, Florentine Bortalco from Roberts. The reproaches of the night before were forgotten; his childish sense of fun was back. He helped me on with one pair, pulled on the other and we fucked with gloves. Once I got over the idea of a medical examination, I enjoyed the touch of the rubber. My sex was soon wet and we came together. He helped me pull the gloves off. Sitting up in bed with his legs crossed, he had a great time blowing up each finger and then twirling the glove in the air till they were right side out.

The only thing that seemed to interest Guillaume in me was my *trajes de luz*. He would sometimes bring out an old camera and take a dozen or so pix of my wardrobe. While I posed in an outfit of his choosing, I would stare straight ahead, past the lens, past his face. Snug in a bubble of near-sightedness that made the world a magic blur, I thought of complicated erotic situations to take my mind off the boredom of modeling: my cleaning boy's head trapped between my thighs, for example, or the head of one of my johns, *Le Baigneur* he called himself, who had lost every hair on his body after a terrible shock. And while I was leafing through my best moments with my most devoted submissives, Guillaume was enchanted with the excitement he could read on my face and which indeed showed up in the prints.

After each photo session, we made love. At such moments, I was in a state of inebriation and the slightest touch of a hand increased the effect. When I emerged from my own private drinking bout, I tied him to the wall-hooks at the head of the bed and explained to him in hypnotic tones how he was going to lick me and kiss me. When he'd done his very best to put the lesson into practice, I rubbed my pubis against his half-tumescent cock, spacing my spasms at will. Some of the shock-waves went up my back while others, my favorites, exploded under my skull like fireworks. When the *bouquet final* burst forth, my thighs were streaming with Guillaume's sperm and for once I had the orgasm a woman could have given me.

Outside of these rare moments, I seldom wore his fetish clothes. After a session with a submissive, or an evening in the apartment with Guillaume, I was often exasperated by having to wear the uniform of a comic book Mistress. As I serviced Guillaume's body, I had the unpleasant impression of working overtime without pay. I began to identify with women who work as cooks and waitresses and then go home to make meals for their husbands. When he wanted me to wear a certain corset, I began finding excuses: It took half an hour to lace up, or else, glancing at my watch, "it's too late this evening." Out of laziness, I mostly wore one of the many presents Hazel had given me in London: a coal-black latex skirt that zipped up the front.

Yet one gray October morning, I was amazed to find myself sufficiently smitten to want to play house: I brought Guillaume a three-tier steamer for cooking vegetables and began spending every other night at the apartment. It was still a part-time job without a contract, I said to myself cynically. Feeling overworked as a financier, Guillaume, too, was rearranging his life. He'd applied for a teaching job in a *grande école* which would leave him enough free time to serve our dinners in drag. Right now, this was out of the question, considering his work schedule. It took him two hours to make up properly, plus half an hour and four hands to lace up his corset. But if he did get his long student holidays back, we would visit the prisons of Scotland or a country like Slavonia. And of course, we'd take along a supply of gear and props in the "bag of tricks" or "survival kit" as he liked to called my travel case.

Back in my own apartment, this fantabulous vision of the future collapsed like an overdone soufflé. In spite of my entreaties, Guillaume had never cleared a single coathanger for me. At the end of the week, he would play polo with his friends and business connections, bragging to me afterwards about their many qualities and extensive real estate holdings. Those same friends, who lived in couples, often invited him to dinner . . . alone. "I've known them for ten, twenty years, I know how much they'd bore you. They're just your garden variety bourgeois."

So on those Sunday evenings, I'd leave him to his bachelor's devices and go fishing for submissives. It was the ideal time to contact men returning from a weekend in the country or an outing with the children of a divorce. But my heart wasn't in my whippings.

Towards the end of the month came a week of disasters. On Monday, Guillaume worked late and it wasn't till the witching hour that he rang to say goodnight. On Tuesday evening I had a date with a publisher who'd promised to have my novel translated. On Wednesday, it was his turn to be invited to a symposium in Poitiers which would last until the following day. We decided to have dinner on Thursday . . . but he missed his train and called from the station. He sounded out of sorts, as though somehow I were to blame.

For several days, I wasn't allowed to set foot in the apartment. When the quarantine was over, I had to listen to a daily phone lecture which betrayed not the slightest compunction, except that he was sorry he'd missed his train. I was angry now, and asked him to bring back my steamer.

He arrived one morning around eight. He'd crammed my high-heeled shoes and my face-creams inside the cooking pot. He wouldn't come in.

"I was afraid you'd ask for this steamer back," he said icily. "Well, here it is."

XIII

I WANTED TO CLEAR MY BRAIN of a love affair which no longer even seemed to correspond to Guillaume's own aspirations. Sensing that Sylvain was anxious to see my good sister Hazel again, I invited him to London the following week. My confederate went with me to the casino where I collected a sizeable sum representing a tiny percentage of what my Chinese gamblers had lost at the tables, and we hurried down to Skin II to spend it. In that Ali Baba's cavern for fetishists, two half-naked women were quarreling over the last red rubber dress, while indifferent saleswomen in violet wasp-waist tops looked on. I tried on a tunic-shaped coat of mail, a latex collar bristling with spikes, a striped sheath, a laced corset in red rubber, and a studded circus leotard in royal blue rubber, all of which the saleswoman stuffed into a big plain bag.

We moved into Nell Gwynn house, a classy but somewhat dog-eared mansion block in Chelsea. Preceded by her dog Cathy, Hazel showed up in the evening to admire my new wardrobe. Right away, she inquired about Sylvain's shoe-size.

"11, 11 1/2," was the reluctant answer.

"Then I have just the shoes for you! You'll both go to the fetish ball tonight, so Gala can show off her new finery."

An hour later, Hazel was back from her underground lair with one of her long leather coats, an embroidered corset, a pair of fishnet stockings, and high-heeled court-shoes that were too small for Sylvain. He did not, however, complain. A brunette wig of natural hair, a plumed hat, and brush-on makeup completed the masquerade. Hazel named her creation Nanette de Valois. This tall brunette with her old-fashioned gestures and walk might have been one of those women on the promenade through the Bois de Boulogne in the thirties. As her escort, I wore the rubber sheath with its zebra pattern, and gloves.

The East End club where Hazel deposited us was in a mostly Asian neighborhood. The Hell's Angel tending the cloakroom was tall and fair-haired. No sooner had we started down the steep stairs to the cellar than the tobacco-ridden, moldy air began to sting my throat. Behind the bar, two stork-legged Gwendolinas were serving beer by the pint. The lighting made their blotched and hairy skin seem even more obscene, "an Englishwoman's skin," said Nanette cattily. Groups of people sitting on the edges of their metal chairs seemed to be posing for a photo in *Vogue* while they commented on the costumes around them. Pretty girls on leashes, in skimpy gym-slips or wasp-waist corsets, were being walked about by booted masters. In the semi-darkness, mistresses in high collars, gloved and corseted, threw alarming shadows on the bare stone walls. Some were keeping a professional eye out for prey.

On the dance floor, Sylvain was in for a surprise: A few of the English men were taller than he was. They obviously took time after office hours to practice walking with six-inch heels. Soon, however, Nanette had nothing to envy them. "She" swayed happily about on her heels, very lady-like, simpering through puckered lips, sticking out her breasts, and brandishing the cigarette holder which had been Hazel's final touch, along with a round black mouche on her cheek.

Mademoiselle de Valois danced alone among the ambiguous couples, waving her arms and scraping the stone vault with her nails, exploring her femininity in motion. Though squeezed into shoes a full size too small, her feet forgot their pain. Music that Sylvain loved was carrying Nanette away. Personally, however, the more I looked around, the more the place was beginning to bore me. Except for Nanette, everything seemed vulgar and artificial.

I was about to suggest we leave when a man arrived who seemed completely out of place in his business suit. The short curly hair and bunched muscles under a red shirt reminded me of a fairground roustabout. He took three whips out of a sports bag and laid them on the ground with a lion-tamer's smile. He removed his shirt and stood with his chest to the stone wall, offering his bare back. He spread his arms so that his shoulder blades stood out. And he waited, still with that same smile on his half-turned face. The dancers drifted away, whispering among themselves.

An Asian dominatrix in black leather picked up one of the instruments. She backed away and struck the wall in slow motion, evaluating the impact, then took one step sideways. The single strand of rawhide lashed into the middle of the man's back. The woman handled the whip at a distance, like a lasso. She struck him several times in exactly the same place. But though the muscles twitched, the face was still smiling. The Asian struck harder, trying to wipe that smile off, but in the end she had to give up:

she'd hit him with everything she had. There was meager applause as she turned away.

The man tapped her on the shoulder: "Thank you, love!"

Again he laid his three whips on the concrete floor, stared defiantly at the onlookers and again turned to face the wall. A thickset woman, about five feet ten, her sturdy arms encased in latex, picked up the cat-o'nine-tails. The thongs were tied in close, thick knots. With the brutality of a galley master she gave the man such a wollop that his chest smacked against the wall. "Harder, love!"

Mesmerized, the audience counted up to thirty. With each blow, the woman uttered a savage "han!" When she put down the cat, the man turned and thanked her with a curt bow. He laid the instrument back on the ground next to the others and resumed his position.

A gaunt man, wearing a boiler suit which made him look even thinner than he was, stepped forth and examined the whips. He chose the other cat, black and stubby. The first blow fell. The roustabout's whole body rebounded against the wall, he pressed his hands to his head and twisted it in circles to ward off the pain, or perhaps to disperse it. The officiant waited, his arm raised. The audience held its breath. The roustabout took up his position again, concentrated for a moment and then nodded. Under the shock, his head bobbed around as before, but the circles were smaller. The onlookers began to count and shout like a crowd at a fair. At fifty, the man turned around, went to his punisher and shook his hand:

"Thank you!"

Slowly and carefully he pulled his red shirt over his ravaged shoulders. His smile was not quite so self-assured. He put away his whips and left as he had come. At a loss for words after what we'd seen, Nanette and I sat down for a beer. A slave with his leash hanging from his collar, crawled to my feet on all fours, looked up, and begged permission. I held out my court-shoes for him to lick. Then Nanette held out one of hers. Seeing the huge appendage looming in the darkness, the man started back in fright and crawled away under the tables as fast as he could go, towards a woman whose expression promised severe chastisement.

We retrieved our coats, grateful for the clear air. The Hell's Angel gave me a knowing smile: "Congratulations, you've won a prize!"

"Beg pardon?"

"Your cloakroom number came up in the draw!"

With his tattooed hands, he gave me a copy of Sacher-Masoch's *Venus in Furs* with a violet cover. In the taxi going home, the ink came off on my beautiful white PVC raincoat.

The next day, Hazel wanted to dress Sylvain as a cat for the Halloween parties that were about to begin, culminating in the "Rubber Ball," whose theme that year was "The Circus." Aficionados from New York, Montreal, Seville, Hamburg, or Stockholm were spending the weekend in London, going from one party to the next, warming up for the main event. But Sylvain balked when he saw the secondhand items in imitation python and synthetic fur she'd brought with her. He claimed to have an aversion for wild animals in general and housecats in particular, but Hazel pleaded the originality of the costume and finally had her way.

Balancing on high-heeled hip-boots in pastel lizardskin which matched the spotted pattern on the fun-fur leotard, Sylvain came out of Hazel's hands haloed with lacquered curls. His face was covered with white makeup, and a spiderweb made by shredding a polka-dot scarf, hung from the tip of his nose and disappeared under the wig. She'd used a black grease-pencil to extend the contours of his green eyes fanlike towards the forehead. With calculated slowness, Sylvain ran his tongue back and forth over his pink-rimmed chops.

Near Vauxhall station, under the dismal railway arches, chains were draped across the thick wooden panels of a huge double door that swung open to reveal a vaulted brick ceiling. "The Dungeon" it was called, but "Hell" would have been more accurate. As I entered the first hall, I was blasted off my feet. The sound system, apparently meant to transport the audience, literally threw me against Sylvain. We embraced to dispel a moment of panic, but an even more powerful beat drove us forward, so unbearable was the pressure on our rib-cages. Sylvain paused by a small, L-shaped cage in which a dozen dominatrixes were busy working over slaves. Some were standing, some seated on metal chairs; some were whipping, others trampling their victims. An Asian in a leather G-string put his hand through the bars and begged for my foot. I held my boot out to him. He gave it a few licks and then begged for my hand. But when I slipped my fingers through the bars, he bit them. Instinctively, my arm shot out and he took the heel of my palm on his nose. The guy loved it, and I was foolishly about to play into his hands when Sylvain dragged me into the next room. There we both gasped: this really could have been Hell!

Under flickering fire-red lights towered huge crosses: male and female slaves were tied to them with coarse ropes. Others were hanging back to back on Saint Andrew's Crosses. A fetish fashion display on a huge video screen was no doubt meant to reassure. Sylvain observed that the huge wheel on the main wall was slowly revolving and that the men tied to it were being whipped, then quickly detached to make room for fresh meat. Here and there, a beating would suddenly turn into lovemaking, when one partner untied the other. These couples would then vanish into a room at the back, hung with white sheets to suggest a grotto in the clouds.

Standing in front of the wheel, another roustabout, a Belgian with a cloak-and-dagger physique, took off his shirt to display his neck, bristling with safety pins and needles. Then he laid his knapsack on the packed earth floor (scattered beneath the crosses were many such bags containing the masters' and submissives' equipment), and took out little see-through boxes which he laid in a row. I bent to examine them. He trained a flashlight on his "sewing kit" and asked if I would like to plant some needles in his belly. With a cute chrome thimble that made it easy to pierce the flesh without pricking my thumb, I planted a star of needles. Other dominatrixes let themselves be tempted. Gallant hands held out cigarette-lighters so they could see what they were doing. Not a drop of blood fell from the Belgian's stomach, which began to look like a pincushion. A tall brunette made it more like a flower-holder by sticking a couple of big darts under his ribs. The fakir whispered something in her ear—in English, the woman was from Florida—and she coolly began to strip. Slender and lovely, her skin tanned and firm, the now-naked American stepped onto a bench, leaned forward, and spread her lips for the fakir. The Belgian started sewing up the woman's vulva while an American man supported her and kissed her on the mouth, helping her to sublimate the pain. During the operation, she hardly whimpered. When this display was over, I felt an urgent need to sit down again. Sylvain helped me into a small room lined with red rubber from floor to ceiling, and I dropped onto a circular bench beside two more garish creatures: A hugely fat woman, wearing metal-blue gear to match her nail polish, was drawing blood with her claws from a Roman wearing falsies over his raw-hide toga. He lay on his side like Nero at a feast, while a fat man licked his toes.

Curious to see how the needle games were progressing, we went back into Hell, but the winds of discord had begun to blow . . . Near a group dressed as police officers and paratroopers, one man wore a genuine SS uniform. Harried by grumbling, hostile participants who moved away when he approached or pointed accusing fingers at him, the man finally beat a retreat. In the meantime, the Belgian had let his beautiful masochist disappear with her big lips stitched, and had planted a good thirty needles inside his cheeks.

The next time we met the fakir, it was at Adrenaline Market—a vast fetish gear mart under a big circus tent. He'd already found a new victim, the celebrated G. from Amsterdam. She was strapped into a tressed leather sheath hanging at the end of a rope and the fakir was having a great time hoisting her to the top of the tent, then letting her down slowly, spinning her round and round in the swinging bag with his whip. When he saw me arrive with Sylvain, still perched on his pastel hip-boots, he brought his punching bag to rest and opened it up to make the introductions. G. brushed the tangle of fine black hair from her ecstatic face and opened her eyes long enough for a child-like smile, then withdrew behind closed lids. Kissing her remarkably pale lips, the Belgian bared her breasts so she would feel the lashes better. Then he shut her up in the leather sack again and set it in motion. From afar, he aimed at the breasts with his long bullwhip that whistled as it flew. He again became absorbed in his task and ignored us.

Night was falling when we entered a nearby club, the Whiplash. In the huge hall, dim and scruffy, elderly men were wandering about with leather suspenders on their bare chests, swilling pints of beer. Revolted by the dingy look of the place and the ugliness of the habitués, Sylvain was already pulling me towards the exit when we spied, in one candlelit corner, a lovely English rose dressed as a schoolteacher, looking very severe with her cropped hair. She was giving instructions to three old men wearing only harnesses. "Stand, sit, lie, heel!" She repeated the same words over and over again indefatigably, beating out the rhythm with her foot. The pupils obeyed as if it were an aerobics class, struggling off the floor after she'd made them bite the dust. The teacher slapped a shoulder here and there with her riding crop, belabored an elderly latecomer in the hollow of his knee when he joined the group at the last minute for a taste of discipline from a beautiful woman. Pleased to conclude our visit on this joyful note, we made a beeline for the exit.

We waited a long time for a taxi to take us back to Nell Gwynn House, fantasizing about the tall illuminated construction crane that towered over Adrenaline Market and Chelsea Bridge. From inside the rare cars still running at that late hour, people stared at us and dreamed perhaps of hurling us, locked in passionate embrace, from the top of that very crane.

On Monday night, for the Skin II Circus, thirty-five hundred people took Hammersmith Palace by storm. I wore a rubber dress trimmed with ostrich feathers and golden contact lenses, wanting to play hawk to Sylvain's cat (he'd slept through the day in his costume, hip-boots and all). A group of French dominatrixes, encased in PVC from head to toe, had joined us in a Chinese restaurant where we had dined on delicacies prepared with aphrodisiac seaweed. For dessert, our waiter, a handsome Englishman with a beard, had let Sheherazade, a beautiful Algerian, put a collar and leash on him. Kneeling by our table, he'd even accepted a few little whacks on the behind. Surprised by his radiant smile, we had asked him if he were a "practitioner." His only answer was: "I'm English!"

At the party, noses, tongues, ears, navels, nipples, even the tiniest appendages twinkled with metal. Unpiercable body parts, like shoulders, torsos, backs, or buttocks, were covered with tattoos. Many women displayed opulent breasts, pear-shaped, apple-shaped, hung with nipple-clamps, tusks, or rings. Young pastel-colored women wore as many as three pairs of painted rubber breasts on their torsos. The rhythmic writhing of these she-wolves attracted dancers who would press up against them in hopes the perspiring bodies would leave a little color on them. Next to a cute Barbie doll, a voluptuous, seductive bitch from the sixties sported a huge bosom with a frieze of blue flowers tattooed across it. The frieze was actually drawn in mentholated sugar and she let anyone who wished have a taste: many tongues volunteered. This was about the best one could hope for on that cold and rather artificial occasion, under the watchful eye of guards with fluorescent truncheons, whose task was to enforce the ban on sadomasochistic practices. It was a strictly fetishist environment, and we were reduced to admiring a kind of fashion show *à l'anglaise*. Cages were wheeled in with roaring hostesses disguised as leopards and panthers inside. In the galleries beneath the arches, English mistresses were assembled, with their regular slaves kneeling at their feet. Dressed as clowns, monkeys, or acrobats, the men bent to honor the high heels of these languorous dominatrixes, who did their domination sitting down, delivered their slaps with gloved hands. Beneath their elaborate hairdos and silver glue-on lashes, their haughty gazes shined as they examined their footwear to see if the cleaning was up to snuff . . . then collapsed giggling onto a girlfriend's shoulder.

In an emergency exit hallway, Sylvain found an abandoned whip. Uninhibited, half-naked girls were sitting on the stairs, beating every man who happened by, with riding crops or with their hands. I gave the whip to one of them who was hurting her palm on a submissive's bottom.

When we got back to our residence, Sylvain-the-cat carried me in his arms to the lift. The night-porter at Nell Gwynn House, a gentle Pakistani with a wasp waist, was delighted by our costumes. When we reached our room, I struggled in vain to get out of my feathered dress and the cat began scratching the ostrich. He licked the red marks left by the rubber on my shoulders and buttocks, tugging at the tight sheath that clung to my skin. But he stopped halfway, leaving me trapped in the rubber straitjacket. He fetched a pair of nail-scissors from the bathroom and showed me with gestures what he wanted me to do. Arms still pinned inside my sheath, I watched his pantomime in silence. Finally he helped me out of the dress and lay down beside me. I leaned over him and cut the tights around his cock which lept out at me, huge and vibrant. He tried to put it into my mouth but I pushed him away. He smiled: "Come now, little bird, do you want me to wring your neck?" and then he penetrated me. My fluids flowed onto the bed.

When the night-porter brought us our morning coffee on a tray, he burst out laughing at the sight of the ostrich fluff embedded in the carpet. At noon, when it came time to evacuate these lodgings and fly back to Paris, we noticed in the hallway a trail of feathers leading to our door.

XIV

In the meantime, Guillaume had gone to the Vincennes zoo. A French dominatrix had told him about the dashing figure I'd cut at the fetish ball with a cat-man. He wanted to know what I saw in felines. Waiting for our food in a Chinese restaurant in Belleville, he told me about his visit to the zoo.

He'd looked at all the lions and the tigers and had been particularly taken with a panther, not the black one with the flat nose and heavy movements but the spotted one, slender and elegant, the jaguar. It had stopped pacing briefly and looked him straight in the eye. He'd stood for a long time in front of the cage trying to catch its eye again, and the few seconds when he did succeed reminded him of what he felt when we made love together.

Under a semi-transparent split skirt, I was wearing a rubber garter-belt. But the first thing he asked me about was the violet stain on the white PVC. We were eating my beloved jellyfish salad, and as we chewed on the white strips he remarked: "I see you like rubber well enough to eat it, darling!" He badgered me about the cat-man. I became aware that his mechanical voice bored me.

As he was about to follow me into my apartment house, I hurried on ahead calling "good night" over my shoulder. Ruefully, he watched his favorite piece of clothing vanish up the stairs.

And yet the very next evening I was back at his place. Maybe I meant to hurt him or even to break it off. He looked at me with languorous eyes, took my hand, and said: "I need to dream a little, darling, and the dream can only come from you." Then he patted me on the back of the neck and pushed me towards the bedroom.

"Aren't you going to take your clothes off?"

"You want me to sleep here?"

"Why not? You've slept here lots of times."

"Not recently, or hadn't you noticed?"

I stripped the way you do in a doctor's office, with no attempt at being sexy. He fucked me straightforwardly, questioning me gently about the costumes I wore to the London parties. That evening he seemed to attach some importance to my pleasure—he even took time to stroke me properly—but as I lay in his arms I superimposed the cat-man's face on his. Contaminated by my visions, Guillaume clawed my back. In the erotic torpor of my mingled memories, the gladiator's corset he wore the evening we met fused with the cat-man's leotard and their youthful torsos became one. Guillaume must have been thinking hard about his rival: he left an enormous love-bite on each of my buttocks.

At the end of the week, we went to Normandy to see his mother, Irène, a cold woman in a long skirt who put us into a lodge at the bottom of the garden. On Saturday evening, we went up to the manor to eat with the family. With wool pads under our shoes, we skated ponderously over the waxed marble floors into the dining room. No kitchen odorous could be detected: the food was already cooling on an electric hot-table.

As we cleared away after dinner, Irène stood over the dish-washer, humming "*Le travail, c'est la liberté*"[4]: the only work she had ever done in her life was "home management."

We took coffee in the sitting room, where the monumental fireplace was bricked up: Irène had once found a dead field mouse caught in the springs of an armchair, which must have come in through the chimney flu. "Animals make a house dirty and so do plants," Guillaume's father chimed in. He was a retired industrialist who spent his time reading history books. Poor Guillaume had never had a guinea-pig or a white rat, or even grown a bean-sprout! I could imagine how starved for affection his childhood must have been, but with a start I realized that I fell into the wrong category for him, and that he was constantly building walls to keep me out.

In the lodge at night, the moon would beckon to us through the open window. The next evening, a white muslin scarf suddenly dropped over my eyes. Through the diaphanous material, I could make out Guillaume's trim body slipping into a shiny corset. From my bag of tricks he took a rubber leotard and dressed me in it. He laid me out on the bed, pulling at my ankles to straighten my knees. While his cock rubbed against my belly, he held my hands apart as if he were afraid I might push him away. He was alive with a possessive desire the likes of which he had never displayed before. A thick stream of saliva ran from his mouth into mine. He pinched the tip of my breast with two fingers: "You're going to have to learn to let go, darling!" I was letting go with all my might, but the pain was burning a hole in my thorax! And then an amazing thing happened. A few seconds after he'd pinched me, my cunt began to flower. It was like the delay between the thunder-clap and the lightning bolt. Each time he gave my flesh a vicious twist, my vulva grew softer. There was a pause of several minutes and in spite of my apprehension, I wanted him to hurt me again. I finally understood what Guillaume experienced deep inside when I took time to tease him with little tortures. It was relaxing to be passive. Finally, his cock replaced his finger inside me, filled me gradually, withdrew, banged in, stopped, withdrew, banged again, and then went away soft: Guillaume had come inside me.

On the train-trip home, our relations became strained again somewhere near Lisieux. Guillaume's manner was distant; he pretended to be absorbed in his technical papers. With my elbows propped on the little table, I had my fingers spread apart to do my nails, bracing my wrist against the thick novel Guillaume had with him, Albert Cohen's *Belle du seigneur.* He threw sideward glances at what I was doing. When I'd filed the nails on one hand, I held them up for inspection. Guillaume took the opportunity to bend over and blow the nail-dust from his book. I pretended not to notice. One by one, I did the nails on the other hand and then opened a bottle of Rouge Passion. Guillaume had been waiting for this stage of my manicure to explode:

"I'll be picking up 800 pages one by one if you go on treating my book like that!"

He tore the book away and jammed it between the table and his knees. I hummed as I carefully lacquered my nails.

XV

One month after Guillaume had fucked me without a condom, a pregnancy test came out positive and I went to a gynecologist. He was known to practice vacuum tube abortion in his office without any of the usual red tape. The receptionist told me a preliminary examination would be necessary.

I filled out a detailed multiple choice form and began to feel tense. As I sat in the waiting room next to a woman with too much makeup on and who just stared at a watercolor of a Bedouin on a camel, I kept repeating that none of this was real. A spicy odor suddenly wafted through an open door and a voice inquired "Mademoiselle . . . ?" The doctor was inviting me to enter his inner sanctum.

Close to my eyes, his forearm held the door open. A tanned soldier in some desert outpost, Clark Gable wore a beige shirt with the sleeves rolled up. "Bonjour, Docteur!" That had been a close call, I'd almost said "Bonjour, Mon

Colonel!" The mustache on his upper lip was thin, revealing perfect teeth. He put a paternal arm around my shoulders and showed me his domain. Behind a Chinese screen, there was a coat-rack for my clothes. All my clothes. I balanced on one foot, then the other. On one side was a high table covered with tawny leather, on the other a lacquered desk featuring a ship's compass and an African statuette. "From Benin" he specified, with a knowing smile. We were in the captain's cabin, ready to weigh anchor for a cruise, and as I unhooked my bra behind the screen, I let myself drift into a spicy dream. I hung my black silk panties in plain view, like a trophy.

"Lie down on the table and put your feet in the stirrups."

I gave a start as I touched the leather with my hand: who was going to ride whom? Swallowing my professional reflexes, I resumed my role as patient and solemnly climbed the two-step ladder. As I settled into place, I avoided leaning forward; I wanted him to see my breasts at their best. In a neutral tone, he asked me to relax my legs and I realized I was pressing my knees together above the stirrups like a horsewoman without a mount. I spread them just enough to ride a small pony but then, sizing up the man leaning over me, I opened them shamelessly. The movement of my legs created a tiny breeze that ruffled my pubic hairs and raised goose-pimples on the insides of my thighs. I felt suddenly ashamed of this brand new pleasure and covered my face with my hands in a ludicrous effort to hide. Hearing him open a drawer, I peeked through my fingers. He was pulling a rubber glove over the dark brown hairs on his forearm. "Don't be afraid, I won't eat you," he said reassuringly as he came back and grasped one of my breasts with a practitioner's hand, firm and knowledgeable.

The gloved hand joined the bare hand and the two began dancing a drummer's jig on my bosom, kneading my nipples one at a time, sliding down my ribs, massaging me all the way to the heart. A flow of lava rushed up my back and around my shoulder blades. A wave of pleasure. Hot. Weird. Lying there naked with this man kneading my flesh had unleashed a storm in my solar plexus that was spreading to my stomach.

"Nothing out of the ordinary there," he said in that same paternal tone.

"How long since your last period?" he asked.

Offended by such a clinical question, I stammered: "Two months . . . more or less . . . I'm usually very regular, uh . . . every twenty-eight days."

His hands moved downwards and quickly skirting my naval, began vigorously manipulating and sculpting my stomach.

"Am I hurting you?"

I was annoyed that he should mistake my excitement for pain.

"Oh no!"

The words cried out my pleasure when I was supposed to be there for an abortion. His gaze rose slowly from my breasts to my eyes. His hands were pressing just above the pubis. I imagined he knew what I was feeling. And that he was enjoying himself, modulating his effects with consummate virtuosity. His massage was making my sex glow. Echoing the movement of his hands, my heart began to beat inside my stomach. When the pressure ceased, it went simply wild, pulsing hollowly against my ribs, making a fearful din that only I could hear.

On the high table next to the right stirrup, the man picked up the other glove and greased the rubber. He circled the table and calmly planted himself between my legs. The hair on his forearms brushed against the skin inside my thighs while he parted the lips of my slit with his gloved fingers. His touch was cold now and a bit mechanical. The rubber slid from one side of my vulva to the other, pulling at it.

"Now I'm going to examine you, just relax, let yourself go . . . There, that's fine . . ."

Under his clinical gaze, my sex let go and my thighs fell away to the sides. Focused on my cunt, his eyes were inspecting and warming it at the same time. Gradually, the chill went out of the rubber sheath on his hand. My thoughts were bathed in torpor, I was like a smitten animal, ready to moan. A thick finger was probing me. All the way. Bending, twisting. Giving little taps. Smoothing the walls, stretching my vagina. Higher. Deeper. Wings flapping uselessly, I fell spinning into a bottomless pit. As more digits joined the middle finger, I heard my sex begin to salivate.

Gentle pulsations swam through my ass. I arched my back.

"You're very excitable, Mademoiselle. Do you have frequent sexual relations?"

I said I did.

"Your vagina is firm and flexible. The walls are perfectly elastic," he said getting back into the rhythm, pulling my slit further apart. Now his words were coming to me through a tepid fog. The spotlight on my crotch, blinding and warming me at once, was all the sun I needed. I gave up trying to glimpse the face of my benefactor, stooping between my thighs. I half-closed my eyes, letting a few faint rays of light toy with my lashes. In a sensual gesture, my arms reached out, touched his hair, and fell back weakly. His fingers then began to masturbate me vigorously. On the spicy aroma of his toilet water, I drifted away to a luxuriant tropical garden where I was almost alone to deal with an uncontrollable, ever-increasing physical desire. Creeping plants made their way inside me, filled me with their living warmth. My body arched with each new inroad, played hard-to-get, then swallowed it. Now a finger was patting my clitoris. The rest of the hand abandoned the moist sheath which contracted on emptiness. Suddenly everything stopped. The garden vanished with its plants. In place of the sensual trailers, a cold metal object was barging in.

"Now don't worry about the speculum, it's no bigger than a good-sized penis and the tip is nicely rounded."

Through the hole in the metal lace-work whose teeth were spreading me apart, he looked into mine, gaping before him. The jaws relaxed their pressure. The iron dildo clicked against the table and the fingers returned to console me.

"There, there . . . You see, it's all over."

His finger stroked the sore flesh, reviving the pleasure that had momentarily fled. I delivered myself into his hands once more. The slight pain had excited me again, as with Guillaume in Normandy. Over my knees, he peered intensely at me and I melted. I heard the zipper on his fly. His other hand was busy somewhere, in his pocket perhaps, looking for a condom. His cock replaced his finger inside my wet sex. The appendage made two or three circular movements around the vulva just to get acquainted, backed off and came in. It was a powerful fuck. My first orgasm sent me reeling. I clung to his hair to keep from sinking. There was a respite, but his battering ram was ready and waiting to attack again. He took one of my breasts in his mouth and I was drunk with the spicy odor of his neck. Timidly, I stroked his cheek. He lifted one leg then the other out of the stirrups and placed them on his shoulders. I locked my ankles around the back of his neck, and his cock began to move again. Violent waves swept through my belly and the pleasure returned stronger than ever. Bracing his arms, he battered on insanely. I had the impression we were flying together when my second orgasm traveled down my legs and swept him up in my mad dash. He came for long seconds and then removing my hands from his neck, exclaimed joyfully: "After a warm-up like that, you shouldn't even feel the suction pump!"

I opened my eyes and was dazzled by the spotlight. Realizing he had fucked me with the light on, I closed them again and didn't even notice when he turned on the pump connected to the tube he'd just put up my vulva. Guillaume's fetus slid down it as easily as the field mouse down the chimney to its death in the family house in Normandy.

XVI

ANXIOUS TO FORGET that incident, I made up games to play with my newly acquired mobile phone which I could use to give instructions from a distance to strangers willing to act out my kinkiest fantasies. It was always easy to spot the man I'd sent for, using our satellite link-up: I would ring his mobile number and he would tell me what he was wearing. The men I chose would in fact never set eyes on me. But of course I was always there, posted out of sight, to enjoy the show. The poor things generally harbored hopes of a regular relationship with a Mistress and supposed I was testing them, never suspecting that for them I would always be a woman without a face. Later, in conversations on the Minitel or the Internet, my performers were always sure they'd spotted me at the scene of our near-encounter, wearing a black PVC raincoat or a leather suit. In the wake of their disappointment, all my guinea-pigs became obsessed with the idea of my presence and spent hours wandering in public places, looking out for women with mobile phones.

In the Gare d'Austerlitz I was about to give my phone instructions to a young stockbroker. I'd been shadowing him since I'd made my first call to him from beneath the "departures" board. Now, in the vast ticketing hall, I told him he was to put away his phone when he had received his final instructions. To win my approval, he was to put on the following performance: he would throw himself at the feet of the first woman he saw with a patent leather shoulder bag and, holding out a hundred franc note, beg her on his knees to slap his face: "A hundred francs for a slap, please Ma'am!" The first woman walked around him without a glance at the money. He had to try several more until one finally did slap him. The next woman, seeing him on his knees, took pity on what she thought was a beggar and got out her purse. Having realized her mistake, she stalked off muttering about people who made fun of the homeless. Several women hurried by without a glance until finally one reacted with a swift kick in the calf. Hiding behind a newspaper rack, I laughed at his dismay when a young woman who looked like a student finally took his money, slapped him and went cheerfully on her way, tucking the money into her jeans. When I called my stockbroker on his mobile phone, he wanted to know if I was the one who had given him that vicious kick!

To punish him for his unfounded accusation, I made him put on the leash and dog collar he'd brought and go to the head of a departure platform. There, he was to wrap the leash around the post that supported a ticket punching machine. Then he was to get down on all fours, like a dog outside a supermarket. The stockbroker pocketed his phone and hastened to obey. I followed him through the passageways to the departure hall. There, I walked past like any woman he might accost and when he whimpered and asked me to untie him, I just glared.

Pretending to be waiting for someone, I took up my observation post near the departing train, glancing pointedly at my watch, impatiently toying with my empty suitcase. A woman took pity on him and kneeled to undo the leash. It didn't seem to occur to her that he could have untied himself: he had arms and obviously wasn't a paralytic. Now he carried out the second part of his instructions: he asked "the kind lady" to take him with her on the train, since his last mistress had gone on vacation without him and he was looking for a new home. The woman went away, shaking with laughter. The man soon tired of playing the clown. He took out his mobile phone and waved it over his head so I would call to congratulate or scold him. He waited for some time. Finally admitting to himself he'd been abandoned, he became aware how ridiculous he looked and stuffed his leash and collar inside his coat. I stepped up to him holding out a cigarette and asked him for a light. He glanced at me absent-mindedly and held out his lighter. I saw sweat running down his forehead and disappointment in his eyes. Satisfied, I turned away.

XVII

VINCENT CAME TO ME one afternoon. As it turned out, he was to be my last patient.

On the little screen, his name had been . . . "ANONYME."

When he removed his glasses, I was overpowered by the animal force of his gaze. The square shoulders and determined, furrowed chin reminded me of Gregory Peck and Mastroiani rolled into one. There was something trivial about the way he laid a few bills on the table. He was fifty-five, he said. He'd never paid a woman before, and had "never ever" been dominated. He was looking for more than just a game with rules, he wanted the real thing. I asked him if he'd mind taking his clothes off. He complied, keeping his gaze averted.

I took ropes and tied him to a chair, with his arms twisted across the back and his ankles tied together behind the front legs. He stared into the distance while I scolded him: he really didn't know how to surrender to a woman? Was he some lone ranger riding in the wilderness? His replies were curt and disdainful. I said humiliating things to him, about how proud he must be never to cry, about his undersized cock, about being a cowboy at heart behind that expensive tie. I called him an armchair adventurer and when he looked up at me with defiant chin and insolent eyes, I slapped him as hard as I could. He grinned evilly, spat in my face and bit my wrist. I smiled as I wiped my face, and thought to myself "Quite a character!"

I wanted to blindfold him and let him taste a different kind of fear, but he wasn't having any of that: he wanted to see. He'd been with the OAS[5] when he was young; he'd been tortured but he hadn't talked and never once had he looked away. We spent an hour staring one another down, the man's eyes flashing now and then from the pain of my pinches, while mine glowed with a will to win. In the end, he untied himself and left without a word.

The next day, a calling card came with these words written on the back:

> I cannot forget those moments of exquisite pain, that incursion into my dark side.
>
> It was neither Eldorado nor the Inferno, but to learn more would be to venture out beyond the harbor mouth onto a vague, indefinite expanse, craggy, strewn with obstacles, shrouded in mist and seemingly unlimited.
>
> Was I wise to want to look at things we can see only through closed eyes?
>
> Be that as it may, this adventure is embodied in your face now, and it's a face I like.
>
> Vincent

I liked the message . . . and the guy. At last a manly man, reluctant to submit, forged by the values of the fifties and older than anyone I'd been involved with before. A rare bird . . . I smiled to myself as I disinfected the gashes his teeth had left on my wrist.

XVIII

STREAMING ACROSS THE DRAWBRIDGE, the guests passed through the main gate. The checklist included visitors from Cologne, Hamburg, Nuremberg and Düsseldorf, admitted to this private evening either as members of "S.M.art" or for having been recommended several weeks in advance by two founder members. Gunther had arranged to have me put on the list and now, sporting a rawhide coverall, he proudly acted as my escort. Balancing on booties with high metal heels, I wore my royal blue leather circus outfit, bra, and stud-trimmed shorts.

A statuesque dominatrix in high-waist leather skirt showed me her ring. She wore hers on the left hand, while masochists of either sex wore it on the right. On a chain around the neck, the ring meant "switch." Most of the guests arrived with their material in heavy bags or converted vanity kits, though some preferred to conceal their canes and whips in billiard cue cases.

By the light of the standing chandeliers, a bare-breasted "M," a Gretchen with a scarf on her head and a fork in her mouth, was waiting for her master to serve her. On the next floor, where couples were necking in armchairs, I circled around a Black Room with a sign over the entrance: "Occupied." The curtains which enclosed the space were gently stirred by the movements of a "sling," just visible through the cloth, a kind of child's swing made of leather on which legs can be spread as far as they go.

Nearby, a German woman of generous proportions straddled a man, thrashed about like a fury on the fist he had inside her. The woman's wail formed a counterpoint with the shouts of the couple in the sling. Gunther caught my arm as I was about to lift the curtain. The clothespin on the sign indicated "occupied, you are not invited," instead of "occupied, you are invited." He suggested we visit the cellars instead, where other private rooms had been created especially for the occasion. We might be able to get into some group activity. On the narrow steps to the dungeons, I had to squeeze back against the metal railing to let a woman by wearing clogs and a dirndl skirt; a brutal Prussian officer had her in tow at the end of an old rope. There were shackles on her ankles. At the bottom of the stairs, the Prussian jerked up her skirts, shoved her against an upright steel bar, and tied her to it. The "peasant woman"'s firm, graceful thighs grew taut. In a state of beatitude, she waited for her beating. From his belt, the officer took a long whip and practiced hitting the woman in just the right area—not on the thighs but in the middle of the buttocks—until the skin was red. Then he untied her and drew her to him, kissing her passionately. The woman was ecstatic from the whipping, and swooned under the deluge of kisses. He started to whip her again, at random now, since they stood face to face, gazing into one another's eyes. At times, he would only pretend to hit her, and she would smile and wink, and then both would burst out laughing. After another passionate embrace, he struck her without warning, eliciting a moan of surprise, then kissed her again on the mouth.

Handcuffed to an iron bar, two women were standing one behind the other: they wore leather collars and bras but no panties. Their buttocks were crisscrossed with whip-marks. Both seemed excited by what was happening to them. A master with a long whip was circling around them; he ordered the hindmost woman to kiss the nape of her companion's neck. Reckoning she didn't obey quickly enough, he struck them both with a single lash of the whip.

In front of a Black Room which the sign forbade us to enter (I was told it contained a gynecological examination table from the thirties), Gunther tipped me to the code-word "Mayday." A submissive could resort to it if the games got out of hand and he or she wanted to call a truce. Nearby a very young couple stood watching the two women, chained mouth to mouth now, and seemed surprised at their obvious enjoyment. The young "voyeuse" had skin that shined like mother-of-pearl; her short hair was a natural auburn. Her boyfriend, who wore his dark hair very long, threw me a tender glance which I took as an invitation to play. Gunther knew them. The three conversed together in German for a moment. It turned out the boy had submissive tendencies while the girl felt dominant, but they'd never done anything about it. I could tell they were intimidated. This was their first visit to the Castle. They asked Gunther to let them watch a private session between us in one of the Black Rooms.

Parting a black curtain, the four of us entered a small room equipped with a charley horse. I told my escort to strip off and straddle the apparatus. The couple stood well back with arms around each other. Gunther undressed and got into position. I picked up one of the whips he'd deposited on the packed earth floor and began slashing at the protruding buttocks. Fascinated, the German couple stared. Under my lashes, he wriggled a bit at first. I called him a ham actor and scolded him for trying to upstage me in front of our friends. He counted a hundred strokes. Then I handed the "cat" to the girl. At first, she held it like an umbrella. But I smiled encouragingly, and as she got used to the feel of the instrument, her grip improved. While she was taking a few practice swings, I picked up a riding crop and hit Gunther's buttocks again, first with the tip, then with the shank, which twanged like bamboo as it bounced off the muscles. Again and again, he whispered that his pain was a gift to me, that it existed for me alone. I was moved by his offering and struck harder, stimulated by the lashings of the cat I could hear behind me now, and by the sound of a church choir far away under the cellar-vaults. By this time, I scarcely knew where I was. "Harder, Gala, harder!" Gunther cried out. From time to time I took a rest: brimming with love and respect for my partner, I would caress his swollen buttocks, licking them tenderly. My tongue would linger on the furrows dug by the whip, tasting the acid warmth. Soon, not a square inch of flesh was unmarked. Gunther spread his legs and offered me the insides of his thighs. I struck again. Gently at first, then harder and harder: "Oh yes, I love it! Gala, I love you! More!" he shouted and arched his back, inviting the lashes. My crop came down again and again, striping and reddening every bit of skin. I ordered him to stand up and raise his arms. I stepped in close and whipped him under the armpits until he finally begged for mercy. I clasped him to me and the heat of his body flowed into mine. We could still hear the lashing of the cat nearby: the young German with his long hair dangling was now jackknifed over the charley horse. I French-kissed Gunther and admired the redhead's rapid progress. Gunther came on my leather skirt.

We resurfaced at last and turned the Black Room over to other aficionados. My head was so light, I couldn't feel the ground under my feet, I was outside my body, outside my self, I was in a trance. Upstairs, the four of us dropped onto a bench. With deep emotion in his voice, the young man confessed he'd never been whipped before. His eyes shone with a naive serenity. I was smiling too, a smile of beatitude. I was so steeped in happiness that a man on his knees leaned over and whispered: "You're smiling inside yourself."

XIX

"DO YOU HAVE A FAVORITE restaurant?" Vincent asked over the phone. I was feeling lazy . . .

"I'll let you choose . . ."

He picked me up in his car in front of my building. He'd been out riding all morning and hadn't changed clothes. He took me to a noisy, provincial restaurant, ordered champagne for me and whisky for himself, "straight up." I raised my glass and asked sarcastically:

"You don't take it on the rocks, *à l'américaine*?"

"I prefer it *à la coloniale*. I was born in Algeria; I don't speak a word of English. German was my second language at school, because after the war, Germany was everybody's scapegoat. Always learn the language of your enemy . . .

The Chinese say: "Never trust a foreigner who speaks your language."

"I suppose you speak several . . ."

"A few . . ."

"I could have learned languages when I traveled professionally. Believe it or not, I was a racing driver, Formula 1, all the Grand Prix: Brazil, Australia, Japan . . . But I was too busy concentrating on the race to communicate with the natives . . . I'd like you to show me an erotic photo of yourself."

"I don't have any . . . Except perhaps a few snaps I took of myself in my teens, buried at the back of some closet."

" I'd still like to see them."

"You're a handsome man, but you look so severe!"

" I am severe!"

The loud conversation at the next table drove us back to my place. He sat on the sofa and began using the familiar *tu*.

"I played your game the other day. I stripped for you physically and morally with no hanging back and no questions asked. I let you tie me up and I put up with your little tortures, but none of it was new to me . . . except my desire for you, the person hiding behind the role you play. You're never yourself; you're a patchwork that's been pieced together over the years, a collection of complicated defense mechanisms that you've set up one by one to ward off outside attack. You wear your dominatrix gear like a suit of armor. It's a disguise. I can force you to become yourself. It's the sensitive woman behind the mask I'm in love with. Your masquerade is entertaining, but it doesn't turn me on, my dear. I want to make a deal with you. You're going to be all mine, you're going to answer my questions truthfully and completely. And you're going to obey me, because otherwise . . . you'll be the one to be beaten. Only suffering and punishment, the treatments you inflict on others, can strip away the mask you wear. Get down on your knees.

"On the parquet?"

"Yes, not on the carpet, it's too soft."

I obeyed reluctantly, trying to reassure myself: "It's just a game, like poker . . . I'll pay to see."

The parquet floor was hard. I thought of all the submissives who had gone down on their knees on that same spot. They'd done it voluntarily. Some of them had even paid a lot of money for the privilege; they'd thought about it in advance, they'd ardently wished for me to force them to obey, to witness their humiliation. The two sides of the coin. Now I was on the other side, at the feet of a stranger. I felt no love; at best I was attracted to him. The blood drained from my aching knees; my stockings were like ice. I felt faint but I kept on eyeing him scornfully. Only my arrogance kept me upright.

I adopted the familiar *tu*: "Do I turn you on like this?"

He slapped me so hard that one of my gold earrings came off and rolled across the carpet.

"You'd turn me on more if you kept on saying *vous* and if you wiped that look off your face. I told you to cut the play-acting."

He kept me on my knees for over an hour, asking me hundreds of questions about myself. He was merciless.

"What is the most humiliating thing that could happen to you?"

I hardly dared think for fear he would hear my thoughts.

"To be led on a leash on all fours like a dog."

"In a public park?"

"Or in my apartment?" I was surprised by my humble tone.

"Are you trying to kid me? You mean you'd feel just as humiliated in here as you would in public?"

I affected a casual tone:

"Oh, no . . . In public . . ."

"Want me to beat you with my belt?"

"Oh, please! No marks!"

"Then go get the right whip for the punishment you deserve!"

He wanted me to act like a geisha and dress to please him. I put on one costume after another, waiting for his approval.

I thought a rubber dress might turn him on.

"You don't look sexy enough in that! I like leather or plastic; don't forget you're dressing for me!"

I served him tea, more and more unnerved by the ringing telephone he wouldn't let me answer. He found me inattentive and brought me back to earth with what I call my "*cajolinette,*" a leather paddle the length of a riding crop and the shape of a fly-swatter, which has the advantage of leaving no bruises.

I felt relieved when he finally left, but I also felt good. In a state of total receptiveness, I sat down to write a difficult article and finished it in record time.

That same evening, walking up the rue de l'Odéon, I paused by the young man's graffiti: "DREAM OR REALITY." The first word was almost completely rubbed out. Guillaume opened the door in rubber shorts. He hardly seemed surprised to see me. He was arranging his fetish gear in see-through plastic boxes and listening to Pavarotti. I put on my *trajes de luz* without his having to ask. Whistling contentedly, he watched me out of the corner of his eye. I gave him the orgasm I'd been holding back all afternoon, that gushing gift of my person that Vincent had unleashed. That evening, my lover had a durable erection and he finally came, shouting: "I want you, Gala, oh Gala!"

XX

"SOME DAY I'LL TIE YOU UP," Vincent had threatened as we were making love. And one night, he did tie my hands behind my back. I complained loudly when his 175 pounds caused the knots and my fists to dig into my kidneys.
I knew why Vincent wanted me tied up. He was jealous of all the things he fancied I was doing with other men behind his back, while he was having dinner with his wife and kids, for example. In a shop on the Rue Jacob, he found a book of sailor's knots and in a camping store bought yards and yards of tough, gold-colored climbing rope. We leafed through the book together. He mastered a number of complicated knots. He wanted me all to himself, he was convinced he would not have full possession of me until he'd tied me up and made me his toy.

One evening I came home to find a fax wishing me a fond goodnight: "I'm going to tie you up and I know how. You'll serve my dinner in spite of your bondage."

In my bed, I made all sorts of conjectures: hopping with my ankles tied, picking up plates with my hands behind my back, eating through a straw . . . before I finally went to sleep.

My apprehension increased as the appointed day drew near.

He made me to turn off the electricity in my apartment and take the material out of the backpack he'd brought with him. I set lighted candles around the room. He helped me extract the stepladder from the broom-closet, climbed to the lamp above the table, removed the light-bulb, and detached the shade. The lamp hung from a big hook in the ceiling, which the master craftsman had installed that time I'd felt an urge to equip my dungeon. This evening, my center light was dismembered and replaced by climbing ropes. Standing on the ladder, Vincent fastened them to the ceiling and then, with the dexterity of a sushi-roller, fed them through a big snap-hook. Soon a skein of ropes hung down.

"Off with the clothes, my dear. You must be naked to serve me. I want a marionette in her birthday suit!" I did as I was told. The squeaking of the ropes sent shivers down my spine as he tugged right and left, testing his suspension system. Still curious to explore the other side of the coin, I resigned myself to being his prisoner. He strapped leather cuffs around my wrists and fastened them to a pair of hanging ropes with two shackles. He did the same with my ankles. He pulled on the ropes attached to me until they were taut: his system worked like a block and tackle with the overhead clasp-hook as a pulley. My arms rose; I lost my balance and started falling forward: The ropes caught and held me. He hoisted me onto the tips of my toes.

I tried to recover my center of gravity. I began to feel

dizzy. He came up to me and kissed my erect nipples, sucking them one after the other. Between two kisses, he told me to spread my legs. I was slow to obey and he became a seafarer again, hauling on the sheets, gradually spreading my ankles. "That's beautiful . . . Are you all right like that?" he asked. I reassured him with a smile. He tied a fifth rope around my waist and I felt even more firmly attached to the ceiling. He got down on his knees and licked my navel, then my under-belly. I was afraid he was going to tickle me and I started to wiggle. "Don't be frightened, but don't move around too much or you'll spoil everything." Anxious not to ruin his pleasure—or mine, beginning to ooze beneath my goose-flesh—I stopped moving altogether and closed my eyes. I was floating in space.

He slipped a finger into my cunt and began gently masturbating me. He licked my buttocks, stroked the inside of my labia until he had ascertained I could be moist in that position. "Now you may serve dinner, my dear."

I went to work. I was afraid of getting the ropes tangled as I moved but I soon realized that if I avoided rotating full circle, my bonds would stay in place around me and not get tangled. I was his puppet. He let out slack so I could reach the fridge and while I was fetching the smoked salmon, he uncorked the champagne. To get to the toaster, I had to walk backwards. When the toast was done, I sat down opposite him. He planked his invisible sails to constrict my body even more. I had to keep my legs together and my back straight, as if I were indeed a Punch-and-Judy puppet or a *commedia dell'arte* player. I gained a new awareness of my appearance and my movements. I raised my elbow cautiously for each mouthful, and the rope went up and down with my fork. "What a pretty marionette you make," he complimented me, "my dream has come true." His face glowed with a satisfied smile and we ate our salmon in silence. Serving the cheese and fruit, I tripped over the ropes at my ankles. The puppet master let out some slack and lovingly set me on my feet, like a mother helping her child learn to walk. "There, my love . . . now, now . . ."

When the meal was over, he took snapshots of me, operating the ropes with one hand, raising my arms a fraction of an inch, to find a graceful pose. I felt like showing off: I arched my back, stretched my legs and stood on tiptoe for posterity. While the camera wound the film back, he let down the suspensions and assured me the ropes were long enough for me to reach the sofa. He had worked it all out. I backed away from him and the tackle followed. He took his clothes off. I sat down with my legs apart, in suspension, my buttocks poised on the edge of the sofa. He knelt before me and fingered my sex. I was so excited that I flowed into the mouth that pressed against my cunt as if my whole body had been waiting for that moment to let go. In fact, that was when I realized what my submissives meant when they talked about letting go, and I realized that there were moments when it was fun to be "used" this way. My desire came in waves and I was obliged to submit to it from within, paralyzed as I was by the tension of the ropes that tied my body to the ceiling. He came into me then and touched off a gushing fountain in my sex. We laughed together for a while and then I watched him lower the rigging of my tender torments. In spite of the weariness weighing down my legs, I helped him coil the sheets like a dutiful deckhand.

XXI

ONE MORNING, as I stowed away my fetish gear from the night before on the closet shelf which Guillaume had finally allotted me, my eye was drawn to a shiny pile on the floor next to the row of shoes. I brought the package out into the light. It was a PVC catsuit wound around an SS visor cap and a torn woman's corset. I was overcome with jealousy.

I sent for one of my old "patients," a real masochist. And though it seemed to me I was going easy on him, I managed to break my best crop over his back.

The sales clerk in the riding department at Hermès looked down his horseman's nose at me:

"This is a *cravache d'appui*, Madame, it is meant to frighten the horse into galloping faster . . . You must have hit him very hard . . ."

"Just a few love-taps . . ."

"The shaft will have to be changed and the lashes tressed

again . . . We can deliver it in three weeks. In the future, madame, to show your mount you are in command, I suggest you merely frighten him . . ."

The clerk was right, I'd lost control of the situation.

The phone rang in Guillaume's apartment in the middle of the night. Half-awakened by the click of the answering machine, I drifted into a nightmare: Sylvie-Anne, wearing an SS uniform, burst into the apartment and locked herself in the bedroom with Guillaume. When I saw my lover again, he lay on his mattress, carved up like a stewing rabbit. I bent down to comfort him and was sad to see there were pieces missing.

I called up Vincent and asked to see him right away: I didn't want to go into a slump. I told him how I felt about Guillaume, how I was afraid of being weighed against his old mistress from Normandy, who had just popped up again. My passive posture, with my head in my hands, incited him to pinch my behind and one of my breasts. He scolded me for the flicker of terror in my eyes, the pardon-me-for-breathing look. I knelt on the parquet floor and begged for his protection: My pathos was sincere.

Between Saturday night and Sunday morning, the phone in Guillaume's apartment rang several times. My stomach hurt, the way it had the day Guillaume had brought back the steamer. At dawn, I got my period. That afternoon, I went home to cuddle Rocard and brush him. (The cat was not allowed into Guillaume's apartment on account of the hairs that clung to his dark suits.) On my way back to my lover, I stopped by the pastry shop, and made up a tray for tea-time. We picnicked on the living room carpet. The last cake-crumbs had vanished down our throats and we were heading for bed when the doorbell rang.

Saint Teresa was a blonde. Guillaume stood in the doorway, hiding her face from me. She was talking softly but nonstop and a mile a minute, like a priest. He tried to push her out onto the landing but she clung to his trousers. He pushed some more and she clung even harder. With Sylvie-Anne hanging from his coat-tails, he struggled out of the apartment and slammed the door behind him. A quarter of an hour went by before he returned. We said nothing for a while, then he tried to justify the visit:

"I'm sorry, she just happened to be in the neighborhood . . ."

The next night, Sylvie-Anne's presence had become so overpowering that we slept on opposite sides of the bed.

Returning home the next day, I found a folded note on my door with a lipstick imprint on it. Some words were scribbled on the outside: "Carried in his mouth by Guillaume, in drag and on a leash." My hands trembled as I unfolded the letter.

Dear Sylvie-Anne:

I feel a deep sense of submission. You command and I obey. This situation is terribly exciting. My corset, my stockings, my collar, my leather straps, my chain, are all tokens of my submission to you. The pain from my nipple-clamps takes me away from the daily routine to a world where I can forget about myself and think about you. I feel drawn towards ever more submission, ever greater dependency. You order me to masturbate and I come, I have a direct awareness of the pleasure I derive from such a situation. The excitement is more than just sexual. The fact that my feeling of submission and obedience lasts after ejaculation shows the depth and durability of that feeling.

I love you,
Guillaume

Were those Guillaume's words? The letter read like a dictation.

I picked up the phone and spoke to the author in person, who claimed he couldn't remember what he'd written in that letter. He was currently trying to keep away from his old mistress after having "stupidly" gone to see her while I was away in Germany. Sylvie-Anne, however, had persuaded herself they were united by Destiny. He came to spend the night at my place, stroking Rocard as a sign of atonement.

The next day he called me up at noon. He sounded worried and told me not to go out: Sylvie-Anne was prowling around the neighborhood with a loaded pistol in her handbag, intending to kill her rival. With time off for good behavior and considering it would be a crime of passion, she didn't figure on serving more than two or three years. "A spotless record," Guillaume reminded me, implicitly comparing Sylvie-Anne's eminent career in the civil service with mine in the art of domination.

I was furious with Guillaume, I called him a dishrag, I called him a spineless amoeba, I called him a faggot. Like a she-lion trapped in a cage I paced the living room floor. I sent for Sylvain and burst into tears in his arms. At the end of the day, I called up Guillaume and asked him to bring me my things. That very evening, he brought back my rubber gear, handing them to me with a wry pout. He also gave me a bottle of olive oil from the mill at La Bastide Blanche, in memory of our summer vacation. Before I went to sleep, I took a long wistful look at the bottle, and the next morning emptied it into the sink.

XXII

I WAS GETTING INTO fur fetishism, cuddled up night after night with Rocard. I spent Christmas alone with my cat. The few friends I still saw thought they could read heartbreak in my eyes, but I wasn't thinking about Guillaume anymore, it was love I missed. I would stand staring at the rubber dresses hanging in the bedroom closet and my glands would begin to salivate again.

Vincent no longer demanded a marionette or a geisha; he helped me out of my depression with small attentions, flowers, new perfumes, and lots of magazines. He took me to a houseboat restaurant on the Seine for dinner, and hoarsely confessed he'd fallen in love with me while enduring the torture of divorce proceedings, begun before we'd met.

I had a little accident driving on the riverside highway, and felt suddenly helpless. I called up Vincent, who arrived like Zorro, filled out the insurance form, and took the Volvo to a friend's garage.

A few days later, I went down to my car park, hoping a drive around the city would help me decompress. I noticed that the black rubber shock-absorbers on the front bumper had gone soft and were hanging down on either side of the radiator grill like roasted marshmallows.

Using my hands, I tried to describe the bizarre shape to Vincent: he looked perplexed. It turned out the garage mechanic had changed the things because he'd noticed they were worn.

One evening, a month after my break-up with Guillaume, I turned on my Minitel the way you open an oyster before you remember yesterday's stomachache. And discovered I just couldn't get into those question and answer games, they suddenly seemed so meaningless. On the other hand, I didn't feel the least embarrassment when *Belle domino* ran across *Anonyme*, but the jealous scene that followed cured me forever of the *messageries roses*. Vincent was beginning to spy on me. One day I caught him going through my appointment book. The bags of trash he so graciously carried downstairs on his way out never reached the garbage cupboard under the stairs: he took them home to search for condoms, letters from submissives, or any other proof that I was still "doing" the Minitel. I took to feeding Rocard on fresh vegetables: his liquid excrement filled the trash-bags . . .

The phone rang day and night, making me jump every time, but the caller never spoke. On certain evenings, Vincent would fill my answering machine with monologues so long I ended up playing them at fast forward. Whenever I did agree to meet with him, he'd badger me about how I spent my days, refusing to believe I went out only to see old friends.

"Who else is going to put up with my glum face and sad eyes?"

"I love that sadness in your eyes!" he claimed, drawing me close by the scruff of the neck.

He might call at any hour to say he'd just spotted me on the Minitel, accusing me of using such disguises as *Femme d'esprit, Maîtresse*, or *Poppea*. His fits of anger terrified me. One day, I mentioned the anonymous phone calls I'd been receiving, without actually accusing him. I then learned he'd gone to see Guillaume's mistress, Sylvie-Anne, to "shake her up" a little; though I hadn't said anything to him, he was certain that wildcat was still harassing me.

I began to feel frightened.

In my bookcase, he found an invitation signed "Cringingly yours."

"Oh come on, it's just a card from a little gay photographer who's always adored me!"

But my efforts to reassure him merely made him angrier.

Determined to catch me out, he made me take him to the opening. It was an exhibition sponsored by Madame C. in her studio near the Place de la Bastille.

"If this photographer is a six-foot he-man, I'll never trust you again."

At the cocktail party, Vincent had to admit his scapegoat was on the effeminate side, was in fact practically a dwarf in his rubber trousers, shirt, and cape!

The next night, Vincent dreamed I was fucking a naked boy in a rubber cape. He acquired a deep aversion for the velvety feel of latex.

One evening, he insisted on sleeping with me but couldn't get it up. Half-awake, I heard a sharp crack coming from the bathroom, then another . . . It was 4:00 A.M. by the alarm clock, and moonlight filtered through the venetian blinds. Vincent came tiptoeing back into the bedroom and cautiously opened the door to the closet. My voice sounded far away:

"What are you doing?"

"I'm breaking all your riding crops and throwing them

down the toilet. You've been in this domination game long enough."

I saw him at the foot of my bed, stark naked, arms dangling, staring at me through demented eyes. I thought I was looking at the Cyclops. Struggling to control my racing heartbeat, I pretended to be half asleep, and murmured:

"Maybe you'd better go home."

I sighed and buried my head in the pillow again, but he turned on the ceiling lamp and grabbed me roughly.

"Come on, get up!"

"What is it? A war? An air-raid?"

He dragged me out of bed and into the living room. His hands crushed my wrists as he pulled me along.

"You're hurting me!"

"What about you? You don't think you're hurting me? The high and mighty dominatrix would no doubt like to see me groveling at her feet like all those men she sees on the sly! If you really didn't look into your Minitel mailbox any more, your pseudonym would have self-destructed after thirty days, you pervert!"

My head hit the low table and I bit my lip. I tasted blood in my throat, but he rattled on: "No one will ever love you the way I do, do you hear me? No one! I'll save you from your past, I'll trash your rubber gear the way I did your canes and your crops!"

When he dragged me into the kitchen, I started to scream and he gagged me with a dish towel. I lay naked and trembling on the tiles, grunting behind the gag, my ears buzzing . . . I could feel convulsions coming on, and thought they might just save the rubber collection I'd talced so lovingly over the years . . . When I came to, dazzled by the cold light and drenched with sweat and urine, he was kneeling on the tiles, pillowing my head in his arms.

"Rest, my dear. Tomorrow, we'll put all your gear into a

big trash bag and we'll go somewhere together and throw it on a garbage dump. And after that sacrifice, life will be wonderful together, you'll see!"

My heart was beating irregularly, and I had a terrible headache. There was just one thought in my frozen brain: This ecstatic man cradling my head against his chest had to get out of my home and never come back.

"There are no men like me any more," he went on, "you've never met a real man before, you've been hanging around with queers all your life. I've contacted some of your submissives now by pretending to be you on the Minitel. I added a dot between Belle and Domino. Your old johns never noticed a thing and they just loved reminiscing about the good old days, with detailed rundowns of what you used to do together. I even ran into the sports columnist who interviewed me for my last race, can you imagine? I could just see him, dressed in drag to your orders and kneeling on your parquet floor with that stupid face of his!"

"Get out, please!"

My teeth were chattering. He carried me onto the bed and tucked me in as if I were a corpse, joining my hands across my breasts.

"If you need anything at all, call me at once, my dear. I want to marry you and I will marry you. I'll call you in the morning. Sleep well!"

Purging my stomach of the gall that sickened me, I saw that the pieces of broken crop had disappeared from the toilet bowl. Maybe Vincent had developed a fetish for broken riding whips.

My answering machine was soon saturated, for he gave out my number, assorted with attractive prices, to different *messageries roses* under the names of *Domina, Femme vicieuse, Lucrèce,* or *Diane chasseresse*. The machine recorded propositions from all sorts from fetishists, from men wanting to be initiated, from couples where one partner wanted to see the other dominated by a woman, from masochists, from devotees of bondage, spankings, or judo holds, from lovers of confinement, humiliations, water-sports or scatology, from gays to be feminized or old babies to be diapered. I called a few sites and managed to curtail his activities on that front. But there were too few personnel to deal with all of Vincent's many female personalities. I had my phone redirected to his sports consultancy office, and for several days the secretaries took calls from slaves in search of a mistress. He began to lose his temper, but couldn't reach my answering machine, since my line automatically fed back into his switchboard. The love letters he slid under my door, in which he constantly confused the masculine and feminine genders, piled up in a folder which I had chosen the color of madness: yellow. I dreamed of having him locked up in the mental hospital at Cadillac (Gironde), the height of snobbism for a former racing driver.

Now that his office personnel had been enlisted, various male voices began threatening me over the phone: "You'll soon find out who you're dealing with!" or else "Your neighbors are fed up with all those comings and goings in the hallway! We're going to call the police!" Listening to this last message, I recognized the voice of a former press officer whom he still employed to chauffeur his car while he read *l'Équipe* on the back seat.

One evening, Luigi was finishing up the housework and commiserating with my pitiful plight. I was late for the theater and was urging him to put away the chain he wore around his waist when the doorbell rang. Through the peephole, I caught a glimpse of the Cyclops, ramming his head against the door.

"Open up! I know you've got a john in there! I heard chains and high-heels on the tiles! Open up or I'll break it down!"

I dived for the phone and called the local *commissariat de police*. As soon as they arrived, I went out on the landing and shut the door behind me, locking Luigi inside. Vincent had sunken eye-sockets, hollow cheeks, and a scrawny neck. The officers were young and friendly and turned out to be staunch defenders of harassed womanhood. I answered their questions while Vincent ranted about the chains he'd heard rattling in my apartment. I recounted a number of recent events, such as a telegram sent in my name to the IRS inquiring about a mythical tax adjustment, and my mailbox being robbed. That very morning, some spiteful person had shut off the building's water supply.

When they asked for his ID, Vincent spluttered: I was a professional dominatrix who sold her body on the Minitel. Right now, there was a chained submissive in my apartment!

I showed one of the officers my theater invitation and he allowed me to leave. I waited on the corner until the coast was clear, then ran back to free Luigi. He had never lost confidence: "I knew you wouldn't have left me locked in here all night, Madame! But believe me, it would have been a wonderful experience!"

That evening, I attended a memorial in music for a young actress. It seemed to me the performers were also acting out the death of my peace of mind.

The days that followed were like a horror movie. Vincent spoke very softly to my answering machine, saying he was going to pick me up in his car and take me to the country. At the end of the tape, he muttered that he was going to break down my door, take away all my rubber gear, and put an end to my activities. I gathered my *trajes de luz* into two big trash bags and stashed them in the trunk of my car. The rubber on the bumpers was even softer now; it trailed on the ground. I suddenly grasped the extent of

Vincent's hatred of rubber: it affected even the spare parts he'd ordered for me.

The next day, the car was stolen. I didn't report it: who would have wanted to steal a car with such unwieldy mustaches?

Sylvain had a hunch and did the research for me.

The Volvo had burned up on a side road, not far from a garbage dump. Vincent's body, hardly recognizable, had been found inside, next to the charred corpse of a woman whose only mark of identification was a Saint Teresa medal.

Hazel took advantage of the opportunity to buy a new hat and come to Paris. We went to Anonyme's funeral with Sylvain. Vincent's family stared at us and whispered among themselves.

After the burial, I slipped away from my friends and went to the empty garage. I shut my eyes in an effort to see my Volvo again. On the concrete floor lay two fat tongues of black rubber. I picked up one of them and stood crying over what was left of my car. I also shed a few tears in memory of Vincent who had, after all, once been a well-known racing-driver.

NOTES

Sessions

1. A toasted Swedish roll.
2. A metal throwing-star. Can be worn as a pendent round the neck.
3. A short stick that can be hidden in the hollow of the hand. A jiu-jitsu expert can use it to deliver devastating blows to sensitive nerve-centers.
4. Two sticks linked with a short rope or chain.
5. Ninteenth century author of sadistic tales for children.

Memoirs of a Left Bank Dominatrix

1. Long before Internet became generally available, the French national phone company made home terminals available to subscribers, which were quickly put to use by swingers of every kind, via the famous *messageries roses.*
2. A rag for ironing.
3. The S&M Pride March was originally a response to the Spanner Case: in 1990, the Birmingham police broke into a private home where homosexuals regularly organized evenings of S&M games. No complaints had been received from either neighbors or participants, and no medical attention had ever been required as a result of these evenings among friends. Two days before the affair was to be examined by the High Court in 1991, the First S&M Pride March was held in London as a protest. Liberal papers like *The Guardian* and *The Independent* came out in favor of the right to dispose of one's own body. In 1997, the European Court of Human Rights upheld the English verdict of guilty, no doubt because of the media confusion with the notorious Dutroux pedophilia and murder case in Belgium.
4. "Work is freedom." This popular thirties song ironically prefigured the inscription over the entrance to Nazi concentration camps: "Arbeit macht frei".
5. Organisation Armée Secrète. (1960-1962). Far right underground militia created by dissident French generals fighting what they saw as De Gaulle's defeatist approach to the Algerian War.